TOM B. NIGHT

Mind Painter

Copyright © 2020 by Tom B. Night

All rights reserved. No part of this publication may be reproduced, stored or transmitted in any form or by any means, electronic, mechanical, photocopying, recording, scanning, or otherwise without written permission from the publisher. It is illegal to copy this book, post it to a website, or distribute it by any other means without permission.

This novel is entirely a work of fiction. The names, characters and incidents portrayed in it are the work of the author's imagination. Any resemblance to actual persons, living or dead, events or localities is entirely coincidental.

Second edition

ISBN: 9798685060075

To Shmoo and Murphy

Chapter 0: Soldier of Fortune

Earth Year: 2035

Martian Year: 1

Aiden O'Connor thought it looked like a portal to another world, and in a way he was right. The entrance—like a tall, thin pyramid tipped on its side—protruded conspicuously from the snow-covered slope. Green lights decorating its face matched those fluttering in the sky and stood out against the polar night. Though the middle of the afternoon, it had been dark for weeks.

But although merely the absence of visible light, sometimes there were legitimate reasons to be afraid of the dark.

One hundred meters past the door, carved deep into the sandstone mountain, was humanity's ultimate insurance plan. The Svalbard Global Seed Vault and adjacent Arctic World Archive held millions of seed samples and trillions of bytes of data. The doomsday vault's location in this remote arctic archipelago was designed to protect it from rising temperatures and sea levels, and its contents could allegedly survive for thousands of years without electricity. But few had envisioned the need to protect it from an outright and sophisticated assault. Who would do such a thing?

The Gaian Renaissance, that's who, thought Aiden with a smirk behind his black tactical mask. He didn't love the name and had advocated to instead call it the Human Annihilation Front but was told it was bad marketing. Nonoptimal for fundraising. Whatever, he was the muscle behind the operation, not the brains. Aiden was a soldier, and soldiers did their job without complaining.

The Voluntary Human Extinction Movement and antinatalists were too meek, the anarcho-nihilists too disorganized. Coordinated, aggressive action was needed to ensure that when catastrophe inevitably struck *Homo sapiens*, the ecocidal species could not reboot itself and again attain the means to destroy Mother Earth and her children. He regretted the loss of the seeds, but in one form or another, nature would survive. Just as the species was more robust than the individual, life itself was hardier than any one species, especially humans.

And Aiden was no speciesist.

"We're in position," he radioed to mission control, triple-checking his weapons were ready. Their firepower was probably overkill; the guards' primary concern was the polar bears—the largest living land carnivores—prowling these islands year-round, desperate for food. But there was a chance someone inside the vault would manage to send for help before they were forever silenced. This was not supposed to be a suicide mission. Not yet, anyway. He knew he'd have to fall on his sword eventually. Such were the perils of fighting for such a cause instead of money. So many strategies rely on the assumption your adversary wants to live. What an advantage to not be bound by such a constraint.

"Copy that. Standby," came the voice in his ear. He waited for their other teams to be in position at the world's other primary seed and data vaults—the ones for which Svalbard was a backup. Taking them out simultaneously before additional security measures could be put in place was paramount. The Gaian Renaissance may have been the fringe of the fringe, but it was astounding what a hundred well-motivated and well-funded people could do. Change the damn world.

Worlds, maybe.

Aiden inhaled and exhaled deeply, calming himself amidst his amphetamine high. He watched his breath materialize in front of him, something he hadn't seen in years. The dull pain of the cold felt good, and he smiled as he remembered skiing with his dad as a kid before his local resort went bankrupt, before things changed so perceptibly. Boy, would pops be proud if he saw him now. Aiden wondered how much longer winter sports would remain a viable enterprise, even here, deep in the Arctic Circle and the farthest north you can fly commercial. 'Permafrost' was a premature term.

A single word came over the radio: "Go."

Four of Aiden's team split off towards the structure where a handful of poor souls lived while he, the new guy, and two others approached the vault entrance. He barely heard silenced gunshots behind him over their boots crunching on the packed snow.

With the electronic defenses disabled, they only needed to worry about the physical ones. It took less than a minute to cut through the thick door. Its green lights and the red laser almost resembled a Christmas display. Fitting given the season. Then they were in and running down the tunnel. Their footsteps were heavy and loud, but time was of the essence now.

Two people in puffy coats came around a corner in front of them, but before they could understand what the commotion was about, their red blood and stained down feathers were sprayed onto the blank canvas of the frost-covered walls, like an abstract painting. Aiden briefly took note and tossed a few charges into the control room and refrigeration units as he kept up his pace.

At the end of the hall, the two teams split up. The normally airlocked security doors were open, giving them easy access to the vaults. The rooms were filled with tall shelves stacked with boxes of seeds from the far corners of the world, many the last of their kind. Aiden let himself marvel for a moment before he began laying charges. Then he heard the bang of an unsilenced gunshot ring out and cursed. He readied his assault rifle and moved to where his partner had been, this time stealthily.

He stalked around a corner and saw a figure duck behind a stack of crates, presumably armed. He didn't have time for this shit. Fortunately he was prepared, and uninhibited by a concern for damaging the facility.

Ha! That was just why he was here.

The grenade exploded, sending an indecipherable mix of the crates' contents and human body parts down the corridor. Moments later Aiden was at his partner's side. He'd been shot near the armpit through a gap in his vest but it missed his heart. Damn, that must hurt in the cold—glad it's not me. All that physical training rendered useless by a bullet on the first mission for his new team. The young man could survive with prompt medical attention but couldn't walk, it was over one hundred meters to the exit, and the grenade had blown whatever element of surprise remained. No way—this wasn't the marines. Those days were long behind him, and they planned to leave every man behind eventually. Oh well, you can only do so much. The two locked eyes, and although Aiden thought he saw fear, there was no wavering. A true believer, just like him.

Then they curtly nodded, exchanged a firm grip, and Aiden put two in his head. One fewer human.

He grabbed the dead man's remaining explosives and finished placing them around the seed vaults. He met the other team returning from the tunnel to the data archive and perfunctorily shook his head once to signal he was now alone. Soon he was back outside, but no longer felt the cold. In the distance he saw the black outlines of the silently approaching getaway drones against the twinkling yellow stars, shimmering green curtains, and full moon. At this latitude and time of year it never set, circling the sky day by day.

Aiden was a kilometer in the air when the charges detonated. The irreparable loss of a library greater than Timbuktu, Alexandria, or Congress was surprisingly anticlimactic from the outside. He chalked it up to some combination of imagination and the performance-enhancing drugs coursing through his veins, but he could swear that when the mountainside gently shuddered, it flashed blue.

Chapter 1: World Heritage

Earth Year: 2043

Martian Year: 4

On the other end of the Asian continent, motivation spectrum, and chain of causality from the Svalbard Incident, a large corporate jet landed on the roof of the world at Lhasa Gonggar Airport, outside the traditional Tibetan capital. It was a gorgeous, bright morning. The 'city of sunlight,' one of the highest elevation cities in the world, received well over three thousand hours of relatively strong solar radiation annually. The planet as a whole received more solar energy in one hour than its inhabitants used in one year.

The man the jet carried was there to oversee the final stage of the first phase of some vital work, though only he and a select few others knew just how important it was. The plane's cargo was loaded into an unmarked, nonautomated heavy transport truck owned by the Chinese People's Liberation Army; they didn't want to draw any more attention than necessary.

The driver didn't appear to be armed. Good, the man thought.

As the truck approached Lhasa, he looked out the passenger

side window at the enormous red and white Potala Palace, its thousand-room structure perched dramatically above the city. Now a museum and World Heritage site, for hundreds of years it had been the home of the Dalai Lama. The man was a staunch atheist, but given the project he was presently engaged in, he couldn't help but muse upon Buddhism's teaching of rebirth. Maybe they weren't entirely wrong after all.

The truck wound up the road into the mountains, which towered above the palace even more drastically than it loomed over the city. Finally it arrived at the nondescript entrance to their destination; humanity had learned some hard lessons from Svalbard and the related attacks. The inside of the man-made cavern was more impressive than it needed to be for strictly functional purposes, but he had a flair for the dramatic and thought its aesthetic should reflect its significance. The laboratory and supercomputer that were to be built inside would each be among the most advanced in the world, hidden here so they could push the envelope away from its prying eyes.

The cavern was also far enough from a major metropolis to limit damage if something went terribly wrong.

Throughout this project the man had developed a newfound knowledge and interest in working with rocks. He was of course unaware of it at the moment, but this would be immensely useful down the road. And his road was long.

The truck's cargo, an item of which fewer than a dozen existed in the world, was unloaded and installed deep in the cavern by the small team of local workers who had been hired through a series of shell companies to perform this job end to end. The Chinese government had seen an opportunity to...what was that English saying? To kill two birds with one stone. The man felt uncomfortable using it right now given the circumstances.

After they finished the installation, the man sighed. He had been dreading this part but reminded himself of the bigger picture. It was as he had drilled into his children: in matters of great importance, the ends justified the means. The kind of people who built such a cavern could not be trusted to know of its existence.

He gathered the workers and gave a short speech to congratulate everyone on a job well done, ensuring them that not only did their country thank them, but possibly their species would too. And he meant it. He was legitimately glad to see the smiles and sense of fulfillment on their faces. Then he took two automatic pistols from inside his thick jacket and mowed down all present. There was nowhere to run inside the cavern. The screams and gunshots echoed eerily off the rock.

The man shook his head. Mining could be dangerous work, but at least their families would be well-compensated. Despite antibiotic-resistant plagues, trauma—accidental or intentional—had dethroned disease and was once again the leading cause of death worldwide, like it had been for much of human existence.

He sealed off the concealed entrance and drove himself back down the mountain as dusk descended. Thousands of lights were coming on across the plateau below, many created by lanterns and the burning of fossil fuels, long-dead organic matter. Solar energy, generated by nuclear fusion, preserved for millions of years. It was never created nor destroyed.

He wound through the ancient city on his way to the airport, past the sites of several recent self-immolations, adding to the hundreds that had already taken place. The man couldn't shake the feeling that those walking the streets in maroon—almost blood-red—robes were staring at him in the dim light, condemning.

Chapter 2: Rocket Men

Earth Year: 2045

Martian Year: 5

Three minutes until liftoff.

"Gloria get to your fucking seat!" John Rook—captain of industry, the world's first trillionaire, and the inspiration of a generation—did not usually direct profanity at one so young, much less his own daughter. But drastic times called for drastic measures, and that was an understatement for the present moment.

Gloria failed to hear him, just as she failed to hear the countdown and everything else when in one of her trance-like states. The doctors had said it was likely a side effect of the prenatal engineering. She stood transfixed, staring out from the forward—currently upper—observation deck of the thirty-five-story behemoth of a rocket. Assuming a few miracles fell into place, it would ferry her and ninety-nine others away from the dying cradle of humanity. This was the last helicopter out of Saigon. The last train out of Paris.

The journey would be long and precarious; June of 2045 was not an ideal time to launch given the relative orbits of the two planets. The destination—Mars—was still not the kind of place to raise your kids, despite the relevant song being more than seventy years old. All things considered, however, the high stakes gamble was still a better bet than remaining on Earth. At least that's what John—chairman and CEO of Bright Future Technologies—decided in the ten minutes he had to make the most monumental choice of his and countless others' lives. On many occasions he had spent twice that long deciding where to go to dinner. But John did not second guess this choice. He never regretted a thing; the idea he could have done otherwise in any given situation, at least in this universe, was nonsense.

One of the miracles needed for Gloria and John's survival screeched through the stratosphere at the speed of sound in an F-35G. There was no need for a more advanced aircraft or missile; it would be there in plenty of time. Major Chris Jenkins's thoughts raced through his head faster than his plane through the pre-dawn sky. He normally preferred missions in meatspace, but shooting down a rocket filled with his fellow Americans wasn't exactly what he had in mind when he joined the Air Force. Still, an order was an order, and he wasn't exactly sure they were even Americans at this point, abandoning their country in its hour of greatest need.

The Lethal Autonomous Weapons Treaty ensured people were not completely irrelevant in combat, and that someone had to pull the usually metaphorical trigger to take offensive action. Artificial intelligence's killer app had become all too literal. No one wanted a repeat of the Lithium War, or for conflict to devolve into a zero-sum, zero-player game. So here Chris was: the human in the loop. He ruminated on the fact that apparently the saying 'all is fair in love and war' only applied to love.

* * *

North America wasn't the sole continent where a great escape was underway. Although their countries were at war, a spirit of cooperation still existed among those who dreamed of a fantastic future among the stars. National governments—even wealthy China—had abdicated Mars colonization to the private sector. No countries yet existed on the planet.

"I've decided," John Rook had told Zhang Renshu, his Chinese rival, peer, and friend the prior day. The message had traveled across the Pacific Ocean via ships flying a dozen different flags, over an encrypted mesh communication network the two men had used extensively the past several weeks. Most of the undersea fiber-optic cables connecting continents had been severed at the outbreak of the war, followed by the destruction of enough of the satellites beaming down high-speed internet from low Earth orbit to overwhelm those that remained. Civilian satellites lacked the sophisticated space-based defense systems of their military brethren, the majority of which had still failed the acid test of live combat. "The moment we've anticipated has arrived. A launch window opens late tonight, and preparations are already underway. The last ship should be gone before sunrise on the West Coast." Launch windows were tight given unpredictable weather and high levels of orbital debris from space assets that had been accidentally shattered instead of merely neutralized with electromagnetic pulses. Low Earth orbit had already been crowded, then tens of thousands of satellites became tens of millions of fragments capable of catastrophic damage.

"I must concur, John. We won't be far behind."

"Any luck getting a reliable course from the Chaoxinxing? Hyperion keeps outputting one that will take us directly into the sun. Even while tracking all that space junk it should be able to run the necessary simulations with almost one hundred exaFLOPS of power. It's damn near the fastest computer in the world, for God's sake."

"It's strange...when run on Chaoxinxing our programs direct us somewhere towards the center of the Milky Way. We had to use less powerful computers."

"Good thing the Apollo astronauts went to the moon using little more than calculators."

"Plotting the right course won't be your only concern. I hope I have enough political goodwill left to buy us safe passage out of the atmosphere. I'm afraid you will not be so fortunate." The physical and digital gold Renshu had transferred to key officials would help too. He wouldn't need it where he was going, but then again, he didn't think the dead would have much use for it either.

"Words can't express my appreciation for the influence you've exerted on the emperor up to this point, but I'll have to rely on more general goodwill towards humanity going forward. Godspeed, Renshu. Luckily your rockets are slow enough that you won't have to eat our exhaust the whole trip."

"You Americans and your religious sayings. You're as godless as I am."

"Over here they call us the generation that killed God, but I'd pray to Zeus if I thought it would help."

"It's certainly better than praying to Mars—I'm sure the god of war has too much on his plate right now to listen. I trust the irony is not lost on you. Farewell, John, and good luck."

Renshu believed these would be the last words the two ever exchanged.

John didn't share the same sentiment. "I'll see you on the red planet."

The two men lingered for a moment before closing down the communication channel. Words unspoken passed between them in the silence. Decision making under conditions of extreme uncertainty was the forte of high-powered executives such as themselves. But something didn't sit quite right, like the low sun and long shadows on a warm winter afternoon.

* * *

Two minutes until liftoff.

Although Major Chris Jenkins's target, sitting on a launch-pad in California, was the last rocket to leave, it wasn't far behind two others blasting off from similar facilities in Texas and Florida. Despite all that had transpired in the past few months, these were still the three most populous states in the union. Florida had recently re-ascended the podium after the annihilation of New York City, or New Venice, as it had been frequently called before the second Cold War turned as hot as thermonuclear fusion. The three states could each spare to lose about one hundred citizens. Public opinion was divided, but the United States government wasn't enthused about what it thought of as ships full of deserters, not to mention the loss of such valuable technology that was supposed to now be pledged to the war effort. The official position was that anyone fleeing to the independent colony on Mars renounced their citizenship, but the act of taking the rockets, even if they weren't yet being put to military use, amounted to nothing short of treason.

"They're bluffing," John had expressed to Zhang Renshu. Although learned in history, he was an idealist. Renshu often told him it was both his greatest strength and most vulnerable weakness. John didn't—indeed, couldn't—believe everyone in the chain of command had the heart to go through with such a murderous act. But hearts had grown colder in recent times, and other M-Class rockets were under development. An example needed to be set. As such, two of Major Jenkins's comrades-in-arms found themselves on identical missions to his.

Calling bluffs was risky business.

* * *

Above what was now the south coast of Texas, twenty-three hundred kilometers away from its oldest sister, *THE SKY IS NOT THE LIMIT* began to trace a radiant arc across the heavens on its virgin flight. The beauty, now visible to her on the horizon, was lost on Lieutenant Colonel Sherwood. No battle raged inside her conscience; there was only steel resolve. Her brief hesitation before pulling the trigger was solely to verify the target was over the water and damage from falling debris would be minimal. There was certainly no need to worry about marine life; the Middle East's Dead Sea no longer had a monopoly on that title.

The rocket carried less cargo and more fuel than it usually would while in the atmosphere; there would be no time to refuel in orbit, within range of Earth's weapons. It needed to be able to reach Mars using only what was onboard. This combined with the missile made for what would have been an impressive explosion, but Colonel Sherwood, like most, was jaded by such sights and had seen much larger. The mission was accomplished with flying colors of orange, yellow, and white.

Sometimes the sky was in fact the limit.

* * *

Across the expanding Gulf of Mexico and shrinking state of Florida, ONWARD AND UPWARD had almost achieved enough speed and altitude to outrun a missile. It was the first rocket to launch and thus had the element of surprise, but although most of the Air Force's fancier hardware was deployed on higher priority operations overseas, the rocket was nonetheless within the formidable range of the Aurora-3. The plane was the apex of aeronautical engineering, but still cheaper and less likely than an intercontinental ballistic missile or Space Force asset to set off a false alarm and disrupt the tenuous ceasefire with the Russians and Chinese. The aircraft's software knew the rocket's path and charted a course and angle to intercept it in the thermosphere at the Kármán line, one hundred kilometers up and the mostly official beginning of space. Major Bowie—recently made an adult orphan and widower—only had to press one button.

The Aurora-3's railgun used parallel conductors and electromagnetic force to accelerate a burst of copper projectiles to Mach 7—far faster than conventional rounds—and far more powerful, even though they relied solely on kinetic energy; the projectiles themselves were not explosive.

The moment of impact was simultaneous with the separation of the booster. The occupied second stage remained intact, but with engines sufficiently damaged to putter out in the exosphere with just enough velocity to escape Earth's gravitational pull and deliver the payload—eighty-three people, supplies for one year at full rations, and miscellaneous equipment for the Mars colony—to not just the middle of nowhere, but its far shore. A fate worse than death, in that it also included death at the end. They had aimed even higher than the moon—for Mars—missed, and landed among the stars.

Perhaps that saying needed to be rethought.

* * *

Ninety seconds until liftoff.

Chris had always liked to think of himself as a polymath. A modern-day Renaissance man. In reality, like so many others he'd been merely unable to focus on anything for long enough to make sufficient progress. He'd never known what he wanted to be when he grew up and eschewed the specialization and constant upskilling required to succeed in the hyper-competitive global economy.

"What if I choose the wrong profession? Half the jobs I've worked so far are automated now. I'm simply keeping my options open," he'd asked one of his several at-the-time girlfriends. He'd been younger then, when sex meant both nothing and everything.

"Then you shouldn't have got me pregnant, should you? Uncle Sam's bonus for bringing a child into this sorry world will barely last a year. How are you going to provide for your son as a wannabe jack of all trades?" she'd replied, informing him for the first time he would be a father—a rare thing.

And so, with encouragement from his older brother Matt,

Chris had decided to become an ace. Despite the significant combat roles played by machines, the military needed all the recruits it could get, and it was a guaranteed paycheck with job security. The spousal benefits were great too; they had enough money to have a real wedding, next to a willow tree, on the shore of an artificial pond. They were also able to give their son James the kind of advantages they never had, the kind that couldn't be taken away: engineered genes.

Chris loved the Air Force. It turned out most of his job wasn't that different from playing virtual reality video games, which had been a favorite pastime. He finally excelled at something for which he could get paid. Eventually they even let him fly real planes.

But long deployments took a toll on what had supposedly become a monogamous relationship. His wife became increasingly infatuated with Eastern religion and philosophy, something to fill the vacuum left by his absences, or so he had thought. A combination of misplaced trust in her and overconfidence in his charm, fading good looks, and abilities as a lover had led Chris to believe she would never stray.

"How the hell do you have an affair on a two-week *silent* retreat, with the guru of all people? Aren't they supposed to be celibate or something?" he'd asked. But it had only been to make himself feel better; he knew it was too late and that he'd lost her. He tried to reframe the situation in his mind, to convince himself that given her infidelity she wasn't actually the person he loved, and he should simply let her go. It didn't work. At least she let him have sole custody of James. It would have been difficult to co-parent from her new home in India, even more so now that the country and its chief rival Pakistan had effectively wiped each other off the map.

Chris's heads up display informed him he was fifteen nautical miles out. He decreased his speed and altitude as he moved in for the kills.

Chapter 3: Mysterious Parade

Earth Year: 2350

Martian Year: 167

They filed into the theater by the tens of thousands. There was little need to experience most events in real-time, and even less to be physically present for them, but one of her mind paintings was a glaring exception. An extreme minority had the mental capacity to mind paint at all, and she was light-years ahead of the rest. Most just called her *the* mind painter; the others were amateurs in comparison.

Despite the riches involved and best efforts of thousands, there was no way to record them in any way whatsoever. That feat was almost as impressive as the shows themselves. She insisted her performances be fleeting, like everything else—she only performed each show once. Millions who could not afford to be there in person plugged in to see, feel, hear, smell, taste, and *think* the experience virtually, though it was argued the word 'virtual' no longer applied. This was a rare affair shared by the different classes of the City.

'Sara Tonin's *Mysterious Parade*' blazed in circles around the venue.

CHAPTER 3: MYSTERIOUS PARADE

The Rook Theater was a perfect globe suspended a thousand meters above the ground. The thriving asteroid mining business had eliminated the scarcity of architectural metals, removing the imperative to build spherical or dome-like structures that maximized volume while minimizing surface area. Although there were several large outposts built inside of covered impact craters—inverted domes—the City itself had even ceased to resemble one. However, the theater's architect had wanted to pay homage to both the old stadiums of Earth and the above-ground habitation units of early Mars colonization. It was the largest and most prestigious theater on the red planet, after all. Many claimed that most events, including mind paintings, were just as good or better from home, but humans retained a propensity to gather in physical proximity and share experiences together.

The crowd buzzed as everyone found their way to and settled into their seats and helmets. There were no concessions of any kind here. When the lights dimmed, a silence commensurate to the vacuum of space filled the hall, as a small platform containing a lone occupant slowly lowered from the ceiling into the center of the massive chamber.

She wore a skintight bodysuit the same shade as her wild, waist-length hair. Black didn't do the color justice—it absorbed one hundred percent of light. She was a silhouette from all angles, her face a blank mask. Speculation abounded as to her real identity, what she actually looked like—as if that meant anything—and if she was perhaps just the visible front of a team. Some wondered if she was even a person at all. Countless Martians, both clever and well-resourced, had tried to unravel these mysteries, to see behind the curtain, without success. Her obfuscation tech was as sophisticated as anyone's, sweetening the enigma. Many had their suspicions, but few knew the truth.

She took a deep, elegant bow, then put on the helmet resting on the high table in front of her as raucous cheering erupted from the multitudes both present and remote. Over half the planet's citizenry shivered and held its breath in anticipation. The common areas of the City were deserted except for a few opportunistic criminals, accompanied in wealthy layers by the private security guards tasked with the unhappy job of thwarting their efforts.

Total darkness descended, and a quote was read, heard, and understood by all.

"'We live together, we act on, and react to, one another; but always and in all circumstances we are by ourselves. The martyrs go hand in hand into the arena; they are crucified alone. Embraced, the lovers desperately try to fuse their insulated ecstasies into a single self-transcendence; in vain. By its very nature every embodied spirit is doomed to suffer and enjoy in solitude. Sensations, feelings, insights, fancies - all these are private and, except through symbols and at second hand, incommunicable. We can pool information about experiences, but never the experiences themselves. From family to nation, every human group is a society of island universes...' -Aldous Huxley, *The Doors of Perception*."

They loved her ability to dredge up forgotten gems from the past.

The mind painter's suit began to swirl with vibrant images of galaxies and nebulas. A few of the cosmic structures were recognizable to the astronomers in the audience—The Pillars of Creation, Andromeda—but most were alien. She began to dance, different movements to a different beat for everyone watching and listening. Without realizing when the transition happened, the interstellar edifices had become all-consuming, the mind painter was gone, and in a genuine sense so was everyone in the audience. They were no longer mere spectators.

They joined a procession of strange yet familiar beings and beasts that marched on an endless astral highway. Some of them were larger than their visual field. They danced on the rings of a thousand Saturns to music extending above and below the frequencies accessible to the unaugmented human ear, like the whale songs of old Earth. But they could also taste, see, and smell these melodies—here, they all had synesthesia. The celestial phenomena cried tears of liquid neon light, which streamed down their faces, icy and warm, as they wept and laughed.

But their journey was not limited to deep space. They visited a thousand landscapes on Earth, too. A most remarkable place, as if it had been made just for them, or they for it.

As ineffably as they had gotten lost, they were found again. In local time barely two hours had passed, but there was no sense of time inside her mind paintings. That fourth dimension simply ceased to exist. Afterward they said it seemed like a beautiful lifetime had passed.

Chapter 4: We Did Start the Fire

Earth Year: 2045

Martian Year: 5

One minute until liftoff.

"Gloria..." John's yelled words came to her as a faint suggestion at the perimeter of her perception...

Gloria...what was that Latin phrase I learned in my outrageously expensive private school? Sic transit gloria mundi. Thus passes the glory of the world. How transitory all of it turned out to be. And not just notoriously fickle things like happiness and lives—so many of the places I've been, my favorite places, turned to nothing but ash. At least I got to see so much of the world before it disappeared.

What a selfish thought, little rich girl!

And what about all those other exotic-sounding faraway places on the departures board at the airport I'll never get to see? At least I'm going somewhere more exotic than any.

Stop thinking about yourself!

And this planet, and my—our—new planet, and the stars, and all the structure in the universe is merely temporary on the way to maximum entropy. That's what dad said anyway. Guess he didn't think I was too young for that one. Maybe it's all futile. The asymmetry between creation and destruction is just too staggering. What takes decades to build can be incinerated in seconds. Rome wasn't built in a day, but it burned in one.

She could just make out the name of the rocket, emblazoned down its side in two-meter-high bold letters and custom-designed font, reflected back to her in the moonlight shining upon the water: *HUMANITY WILL NEVER DIE*. She knew where the name came from; it was her favorite vacation. The green and gold hot air balloon slowly drifting over the green and gold landscape, the endless plain, 'The Serengeti Will Never Die' written on the side of the basket. Evidently they were wrong. The train of association pulled away from her mind once again...

All those animals dying from circumstances they couldn't possibly understand, from a situation entirely out of their control. The news said we've wiped out eighty percent of species in the past century. It's almost harder to bear than what's happening to my own—at least all of this is our fault. As far as I know none of us were shot in our cages as an 'act of mercy' because the wildfires were advancing too quickly. Some of the people in cages actually deserve to be there. Maybe the Gaian Renaissance had a point—if not for non-human life it's hard to care about the planet.

The wildfires! And to think I used to cry when we threw away the Christmas tree each year. Sunrises and sunsets—the sun itself—tinged with blood red and safe to look at directly. Smoke-choked air and ash raining down like carcinogenic snow. And that was before the nukes started. I thought nature was brutal, but it has nothing on the immense destructive power of applied science. What a time to be alive. Everyone wants to know what happens at the end of a story, but they don't show you what comes after the hero rides off into the sunset: they end up alone in the cold and dark. Or maybe I'm being overly dramatic. At least I get to read the last chapter of the book, even if it's the only one I get to read.

It's not about you!

* * *

Forty seconds until liftoff.

It had been the last day anyone was legally allowed to drive themselves. The media had predicted it would be extremely dangerous—perhaps the last truly dangerous day on the roads—and Major Chris Jenkins had echoed this sentiment. But his father insisted on taking the old Chevy for a spin one last time. He doubted he'd ever use a car again; like airplanes, the lack of control created by automated piloting systems caused great fear in many passengers. Also like airplanes, the statistical reality that they were almost unimaginably safe did little to comfort the phobic, a win for the peddlers of pharmacological cures for anxiety.

"I drove your mother on our first date in that car, son. Hell, you were probably conceived in the back seat. If she were still alive she'd understand," his father said, adding a little more information than Chris cared to learn.

"At least go early, when there are fewer cars on the road," Chris pleaded.

"The doctor told me that given my family history I could live to be a hundred years old, as long as I don't die in a nuke or catch one of them superbugs." They were bigger killers than cancer or heart disease. It was impossible to keep up with bacteria's evolution given its rapid rates of reproduction and death. "A goddamn century. At that point I'd have been considered old for half my life. Can you imagine going thirty years without a working dick? No thanks. There's no point in fixing some things if you haven't fixed others first."

"Just please turn on the autonomy if it gets too dicey out there."

"Never forget, son: there's a simple joy in doing something for yourself. Even if someone—or something—else can do it better," he said just before shutting down the video chat. Chris stared at himself in the resulting black mirror, wondering if those would be the last words his father ever spoke to him.

His father was speeding, if only because he would never be able to do so again. When the morning sun crested the horizon he put down the visor and a quarter-sized spider fell into his lap. At that speed a small jerk of the steering wheel was all it took. He was lucky to survive the crash, but after the longevity conversation with his doctor—and unbeknownst to his sons—he had converted to Christian Science, an oxymoron if there ever was one. Even in his critical condition, the state of medicine was such that he could have been saved, but his 'DO NOT TREAT OR RESUSCITATE' tattoo had other plans.

Without grandparents around, raising his son James as a single dad in the military took its toll on Chris. His only living immediate family member, Matt, spent every other six months on the moon. He'd thought the one upside of the situation was that he was now stationed in California and no longer deployed overseas. However, it was precisely those circumstances that led him to the present moment, on a thankless mission approaching a rocket full of civilians in a locked and loaded death machine.

The small hours had always enchanted Chris, who was aware of them coming to a close around him. That elusive time when the preponderance of the population slept. Before joining the

Air Force he would usually greet them from the other side of the night with the help of one substance or another. Thankfully those outdated screening requirements had been necessarily relaxed. The world below him came into focus as he further decreased altitude and decelerated. Straight ahead was the target. On his right, the deserted streets, along with the rare illuminated window. On his left, the shadowy water extending into the distance until hidden by the curvature of the planet. Above it all was the gibbous moon—another world *right there*, in plain sight. Finally he glanced down at the picture of James he kept in the cockpit.

"If we want life on other planets we're gonna have to do it ourselves, dad," James had said to him not long ago. His son was in the 'I want to be an astronaut' phase of youth, which after a couple decade hiatus was once again becoming a realistic career path. Plus, he had a role model in his uncle. James spent hours watching the live feed of Earth broadcast from Luna Alpha. If only I had that kind of passion at that age, Chris thought.

Despite building telescopes of increasing size and power, humanity hadn't heard so much as a decipherable peep from the cosmos, but SETI had had much hope for the Dark Side of the Moon Radio Telescope. Even if the far side of the moon wasn't actually devoid of visible light—something disappointing to aging Pink Floyd fans and denied by the cult that planned to start a colony there in perpetual darkness—it was in fact devoid of Earth's interference in other parts of the electromagnetic spectrum. But the stars insisted on twinkling in stubborn silence, minus noise within which even the most advanced algorithms could not find patterns. With one hundred billion galaxies and one hundred billion stars within each, it used to have been assumed that the universe must be teeming with life, some of it intelligent. However, the early Martian colonists had found clear signs of long-dead organisms. And if life had emerged independently at least twice within one solar system and there was still no sign of galactic civilizations, something must clearly prevent it from reaching such a stage. Now, as mankind barreled towards its own Great Filter, the Fermi Paradox just became the Fermi Downer. This was seen as a positive by those who feared powerful extraterrestrials would treat humans exactly like humans did all other species on Earth, and even subgroups within their own. But the cosmic loneliness was depressing to Chris. And, vitally, it was important to his son.

The g-forces Chris experienced were trivial compared to the weight on his shoulders as he considered this data. The last words his father spoke to him came back: 'there's a simple joy in doing something for yourself. Even if someone—or something—else can do it better.' An automated drone would have performed the task at hand perfectly, or at least it would have if autonomy was fully functional again. But here he was, able to experience the simple joy of doing something not just for himself, but for others too. His hands no longer sweated in his flight gloves. He had made his decision.

Fuck it.

When Chris was younger he had a bad habit of what he called the Irish Exit: leaving a bar or other gathering without saying goodbye. He was once told it was racist for someone with his skin color to use such a term, but his mother was Irish, so he felt entitled to it. Besides, if someone was offended that was their problem, not his. But this was back when there was a reasonable expectation you'd see someone again, which was no longer the case. These days everyone was in the habit of making their goodbyes count. His commanding officer liked to remind everyone that life is a war we all lose in the end, but every day is a battle, and you can sure as hell win some of those. Nevermind the eggheads and wealthy who think advances in science will let them opt out. The little speech lost its luster after hearing it so often, but it rang true for Chris today.

He flew off into the coming day victorious, as the sun's first rays broke over the sleeping coastline.

Chapter 5: It's a Jungle Out There

Earth Year: 2350

Martian Year: 167

How spectacularly things shine when viewed from the darkness, she thought as she looked up through the crisscrossing walkways at the glittering Canopy of the City. An inverse spider's web, lines of shadow against the light. But there were no spiders here to spin their gossamer tapestries. Even the arachnophobes missed them on some level. *Homo sapiens* were the only representatives of the Animalia kingdom, the lonely leaf on their branch of the tree of life. Their microbiomes were poor company. Artificial intelligence was stalled at the notably artificial stage, rendering humans the only sentient creatures within millions of kilometers. They were also more genetically homogenous than ever, although diverging in other ways. And lack of biodiversity was not a hallmark of a healthy ecological system.

She would have killed for a real dog. She had killed for other things, but those sols were long behind her now. At least she hoped they were. Recent events made her unsure.

It was in fact quite dark where she stood. Unless one

counted graffiti, no one bothered with advertisements on the Floor anymore. They started one hundred meters up in the Understory, putting to shame the dim memories she had of Times Square and Shinjuku from a different life on another world. She felt at least partially culpable. Society had tried not to repeat that mistake, but some business models just refused to die.

She recalled the sex workers she had passed moments before and smirked.

At night the only light emitted on the Floor came from the faint, tinted glow of the dying bioluminescent trees, relics of another time when the Floor's aesthetics mattered to those whose opinions mattered. People like her. Tonight the trees were violet and magenta. During the daytime it wasn't much brighter given how little sunlight made it all the way through the sparse skylights and upper layers of the towering metropolis. Those in the Emergent no longer even had to look upon those who were literally so far below them. All they could see was the radiant Canopy sprawling in every direction, and the desolate red Martian landscape—the Savannah—beyond, dotted with energy receivers, batteries, and the rocket fields. She chose not to remember what it was like.

A loud crash brought her attention back to the immediate surroundings. A pod that must have come from the Understory—the insects that flew through the spider's web—had smashed into the empty path fewer than thirty meters in front of her. A rare but not entirely unheard-of occurrence. I really need to pay more attention, she thought, though realistically she knew it was a lost cause at this stage of her life. Old habits died hard. Maybe even harder than her.

Through the splattered, shattered glass she could see that

one of the vehicle's occupants had clearly not survived the impact. The other was wearily climbing out of the wreckage. The piloting systems were so good and the speeds traveled at so high—people were still inexplicably and perpetually in a hurry—that similar to the airplanes of the past, if you hit something at full speed while in flight the laws of motion all but assured death. Crashing at lower speeds usually meant a loss of lift and a plunge to the Floor, where many would encounter the same fate. The quick way out was preferable. Like in the rainforests of Earth, things from the upper layers fell down here to decay. The Floor dwellers—the fungi in this circle of life—broke down that which fell from above, ensuring it did not pile up unsustainably.

Nothing was wasted in the jungle.

The majority of people didn't carry weapons in the upper levels, at least not openly, and it looked like this man was no different. In his wretched condition it wouldn't have mattered. A few young-looking men—the age someone looked being meaningless—came out of the nearest pleasure arcade, jarred out of whatever cyborg-enhanced sexual activity they were engaged in by the noise. Orgasms could last for hours, and not just for tantric experts. Many did little else. The men weren't happy at having been disturbed but they were also opportunists, which was not a great combination for the disturber. They began striding towards the shambles of the pod.

"Please help me," the survivor mumbled through a broken face as he stumbled in the wrong direction. She could still discern the distinct accent of those who lived in the region extending one thousand meters above them. It wasn't entirely different from hers, though it was different than the one she'd been using recently.

The moment the temporary survivor finished this sentence a plasma knife was through his chest. The blade of ionized gas was powerful enough to slice through whatever machinery was in his body and was now being used to remove any parts of him that may still be useful. The two others in the group rummaged through the pod and the other passenger's remains for anything of value. The few others around quickly deserted the area, but she was enthralled.

"We should get out of here before the local police come, or worse," the man she was standing with said. *Fuck, what was his name?* They had been together for hours, but the beginning was blurry, so she played back the evening's events perfectly in her mind.

She had descended to the Floor in search of the kicks one could either only find there or were frowned upon in the upper levels, especially for someone of her stature. Bleeding edge designer drugs that only work with certain augmentations. High society wasn't quite high enough for her, with the rich more interested in cerebral pursuits; the hierarchy of human needs generally mapped onto the hierarchy of the City. But she also craved other carnal and hedonic pleasures. Just staying one step ahead of jadedness with the help of science.

"Can I buy you a drink?" he asked. His face looked impossibly symmetrical, because it was. Most people were attractive, but the oversized, shimmering eyes, like two golden pools, were a bold choice. With his matching hair color he reminded her of a character from a two-dimensional cartoon from her youth. "I've got quite a payday coming my way soon, so choose whatever you want." *He's trying to impress me with money. Cute.* From his physiology she predicted he was telling the truth with

CHAPTER 5: IT'S A JUNGLE OUT THERE

a probability of 0.96, so at least he wasn't a liar. And the wildly dilated pupils in the middle of those golden eyes told her he was carrying.

"I don't drink, and I'm surprised so many of you cowboys still do given everything else on offer." They didn't need to speak, of course; they could communicate entirely over the Network instead, assuming she allowed it. But when nearby it was still customary to use audible voices.

"Someone on Earth once said beer is proof God loves us and wants us to be happy." *If he only knew how much better the beer had been on Earth.* At least that's what her godfather had told her.

"Psychedelics are proof God doesn't exist." He smiled at that, like she knew he would. She'd told the joke many times, and no one laughed at jokes that lacked an underlying truth.

"But Kronos does—or did, anyway. Point taken, but that cheap mind paint is too unpredictable for my liking. No option to pull the ripcord if it gets too intense, like in the real thing. My name's Caspian, like the sea," he said proudly. She put on a quizzical face. "There is, or at least was, a great sea on Earth called the Caspian Sea." From the data returned by her scan of him it appeared that all his parents had given him were genes and a name, so he must have taken pride in it.

"Never heard of it," she lied, seeing him deflate. *He might actually be as young as he looks. This could be fun.* "My name is Jade..."

"Jade!" Caspian startled her back to the present. "They're looking over this way. Let's move." It was too late. The apparent leader of the three—the one who had just casually killed someone—had noticed their lingering presence and taken an interest.

"Hey!" he shouted in an accent that sounded like he had spent a lot of time in the Underground. Not a good sign. "What you starin at? You got one of them memory augmens and gonna run this back for the pigs?" The other two men had now also taken an interest and took angles to block their escape.

I can't believe some people still call cops pigs, she thought. She sensed Caspian tense and adjust his stance, but not in a nervous way—just preparing, just in case. *What a gentleman.* She knew he'd grown up on these streets and done stints outside of the planet's only city; he was no stranger to violence. She also knew he had a plasma knife of his own, along with everything else he had on him.

"Naw, fuck em," replied Caspian. "I ain't gonna talk to no one. They'd probably put me to work in the mines, and I don't got the specs anyways."

If you can't avoid, run, and if you can't run, de-escalate.

"What bout your girlfriend huh? I ain't seen her round here before." This was true. She never looked the same twice when she descended, either to a human or a machine. "Why so quiet honey? Betcha I could make ya talk."

Jade smiled and spoke before Caspian could, "I bet you've never tasted honey, have you?" She looked him up and down, half a meter taller than her, and shook her head condescendingly before continuing, "Nevermind. Can I tell you a story? When I was a kid I had a big dog. His name was...well, that's not important. When we went on walks, little dogs would always yap at him. Do you know what he did?" She paused for effect. The tension in the air was thick enough to cut with a plasma knife. "He ignored them."

Everyone looked at her confused, no one more than Caspian. After a few seconds it dawned on the aggressor that she may have called him a little dog. He did not understand the implications of this but guessed it might be an insult. And he did not like insults.

"You bitch. I'm gonna enjoy slicin you up."

"I never understood why until I became a big dog myself," she muttered to herself.

If you can't run, de-escalate, and if you can't de-escalate, fight.

Martial arts had come a long way on their namesake's eponymous planet. With only one-third of Earth's gravity and augmented bodies, entirely new disciplines had developed. Jade was an expert in all of them. She'd had time to explore most possible hobbies, undergoing many augmentations just for fun. Few still held any interest.

She sensed him turn down his pain receptors. *Wonder who he stole those from.* She turned hers up. Violence may have been the last refuge of the incompetent, and street fighting was for those with nothing to lose (Jade had more than almost anyone). But explosive, devastating force was the only appropriate response to an attacker once all other options had been exhausted.

She let him make the first move. When your back is to the wall, at least you know from which direction your enemy will attack. He closed the distance between them in a fraction of a second, striking straight out with his right hand in what could have been a killing blow with or without the plasma knife it held. Even through the haze of her neurotransformer comedown, her experience and specs made it look like he was moving in slow motion. He may as well have written her a letter informing her of his intentions using several-thousand-year-old technology.

She crouched low, parrying the thrust, then launched both of them five meters into the air. This was not an ideal place to unexpectedly find yourself, off-balance and flailing like a fool, especially with your opponent perfectly positioned above you. She kicked down into his chest with both legs, sending herself even higher and him towards the ground. The combination of light gravity and an artificially thick atmosphere made terminal velocity within the City relatively low. He came close to reaching it before hitting the ground, where his reinforced ribs and skull made a loud cracking sound. His accomplices fled out of sight almost before she landed gracefully by his side a few seconds later.

Caspian stared at her dumbfounded.

Sure, she could have carried various directed energy weapons capable of neutralizing an attacker from a safe distance. Different beams could blind, hack, and sizzle out augmentations. But that ran the risk of escalating things in situations where they weren't already over the line. Potentially deadly weapons and altered mental states were a bad combination. Besides, she didn't want to do anyone lasting harm if she could help it. As despicable as this man was, he was merely a victim of circumstances. Given the same genes and environment she would be no different, a fact she knew all too well.

Descending armed would have also deprived her of the exhilarating thrill of real danger in the real world. Just staying one step ahead of the jade.

Caspian started to ask her a question but was interrupted by a siren that reached him across several frequencies. The police cruiser hovered to a stop next to the wreckage and what superficially appeared to be a man and woman got out, beckoning for him and Jade to join them. The latter could sense their scanners trying to identify her across various ranges of the electromagnetic spectrum as she approached. Her scan revealed that at least they were real cops, something many Floor dwellers with less sophisticated tech would be unable to definitively verify.

"Jade Bishop and Caspian Chu," stated one of the officers matter-of-factly, as the other perfunctorily—and unsuccessfully—checked for signs of life from the pod passengers. Job requirements prevented for-profit police—the only kind—from using certain cosmetic augmentations while on the job. They both looked Sino-Caucasian but with darker features, the same way the prevalence of the populace looked naturally—like distant cousins. Caspian hated that he found himself attracted to them. But then again, he was attracted to the majority of people. He was still mostly a slave to his genes, the puppet masters of life, which were enticed by the greater genetic variety—and potentially fitness—signaled by mixed race. "Based on his background I'm going to assume the groaning figure on the ground behind you is the perpetrator, though if you weren't with Ms. Bishop here I'd have some hard questions for you Caspian."

Caspian resisted the urge to look questioningly at Jade. This was becoming a confusing several hours. He resented the implication he would murder someone but was carrying a lot of neurosugar. It wasn't illegal per se—very little was down here, which was why some who could afford to live elsewhere still called the Floor home—but he knew from past experience these cops would love an excuse to confiscate it for themselves. He had the good v6 shit and wasn't about to look a gift horse in the mouth. He also wasn't sure if that was the correct way to use that saying, or where it came from.

Jade was disappointed that the Floor police, with their hopelessly outdated scanners, could correctly identify Caspian so easily. She had expected more, but maybe she was out of touch. The cat and mouse arms race between law enforcement and those who lived outside the lines had persisted for thousands of years. Luckily the latter had more to lose and usually stayed one step ahead. Jade was several. How boring it would be if everyone had to follow the rules all the time. But she couldn't help think that the mind-boggling amount of computing power and ingenuity that went into detection and evasion everywhere, all the time, was a colossal waste. At least back on Earth it could have prevented you from being selected as a target by an autonomous killer drone. She set aside the thought.

"Don't you want to know if he had any accomplices?" Jade asked. She didn't realize just how lax things were getting down here. Maybe she'd mention it to someone. Probably not, although her company undoubtedly paid for an outsized proportion of these cops' salaries.

"We'll let the Understory police worry about that. You're free to go."

A relieved Caspian wasted no time taking Jade's arm and walking away as an ambulance hovered lazily up to the scene. The flashing red, blue, and gold lights mixed with the pink and purple shimmer from the trees. They passed a group of augmented oxygen junkies huddled around a vent in a state of perpetual intoxication. Caspian vaguely recognized one—someone he used to know—but looked away. How easily that could have been him. It used to be that you were never addicted to the drugs themselves (or anything, really), only the subsequent chemical and experiential changes; at base it was always about dopamine and other neurotransmitters. That was no longer the case.

A multi-aural beat softly spilled out onto the street from a nearby club. The ground rumbled as something traveled beneath them. Caspian and Jade each saw different sets of colorful graffiti, overlaid and dancing on top of the physical reality around them. Most of it conveyed one of two diametrically opposed messages, but there was a common theme: the ship imminently returning from Earth.

"I can't believe someone could just kill another person like that, especially with potential lifespans what they are in the upper levels," said Caspian, shaking his beautiful head. Jade felt certain dark memories bubbling up to the surface. She attempted to suppress them along with the accompanying shudders, but the wire had been tripped.

"Is it really so terrible? Perhaps it was an act of mercy. No one asked to be born, they just woke up one sol and found themselves in this strange predicament. Most living things have no choice but to go on existing continuously with no respite. Humans—and the digital intelligences, an even higher lifeform—realized there's another option, but most people are unable to overcome their existence bias and consummate their marriage with oblivion."

She was in this phase of the comedown.

Jade had considered suicide on many occasions in the early sols, and though that was long ago she empathized with those looking for an easy way off the ride. Suicidal thoughts were similar to those diseases of the past like Alzheimer's or most cancers; as the years passed a growing percentage of the population inevitably became afflicted. However, unlike these other maladies, this one was in a sense communicable.

Technology was yet to offer a cure—on the contrary, artificial intelligence (and the current lack thereof) had only exacerbated the problem. It actually got worse as one ascended in the City. A growing epidemic. Only a handful of people knew that, and she was one. There were many slippery slopes to nihilism in this world, and the higher up you were the easier it was to fall down one of them.

"You continue to get more and more interesting," replied Caspian with a chuckle, his mood improving as he contemplated the two narrow escapes he had just made with the help of this strange woman. "Speaking of overcoming bias, I'm starting to sober up and overcame society's sobriety bias long ago. How about we stop by another bar? I have a lot of questions for you after what just happened."

"I have a better idea," she said, pacified for the time being and glad he didn't take the bait. She hadn't realized how invigorated she was by the experience and decided to put that energy to better use than rehashing the same arguments she'd had so many times in the Emergent. She was really starting to like this Caspian character, with his geniality and bravado in the face of such a bleak existence. Or maybe he was faking it. For now, either was just as good. She looked at him with wildfire in her eyes. She was entering the next phase of the comedown. "Let's go back to your place."

Chapter 6: Escape Velocity

Earth Year: 2045

Martian Year: 5

Thirty seconds until liftoff.

"Gloria, please!" begged John, craning his neck upward as he climbed. She had scaled the rocket's interior as far as she could go, almost to the nose cone. His voice had taken on a somber tone, as he knew it was not just her life on the line, but his too. Her mind took the suggestion, but her body remained unfazed...

'Please.' That word has sure lost whatever meaning it once had.
'Please, we are the generation with the tools and technologies to solve all of our most paramount problems. We need only to have the audacity.' The scientists used it an awful lot. Turns out their fancy models weren't quite as fancy as they thought. The melting ice, release of trapped greenhouse gases, and decreased albedo created a feedback loop worse than anyone predicted, like an entire species singing its praises into a poorly positioned microphone. We inherited hundreds of trillions of dollars in natural capital and burned through it more recklessly than any trust fund baby—like me—ever did.

'Please, our countries are disappearing under the water and we have no place to go.' The refugees used the word a lot too. A migrant crisis a thousand times worse than anything the world has ever seen, they said. Most people are only a few missed meals away from desperation. Waves of starving refugees crashing—figuratively and literally—into the jagged rocks nestled on the shores of the sea of their dreams of a better life. Ok, maybe I'm getting a little too flowery. Perhaps I should be a poet. Or a writer? What kinds of hobbies are even going to be available on Mars? I wonder if there will be any boys my age there.

'Please, we must show restraint. This madness will be the end of us all!' The politicians used it a lot too. Overwhelming good fortune and a few forgotten heroes during the first Cold War prevented nuclear annihilation up until this point in history. Dad said it was a form of survivor bias. I guess it was only a matter of time. It's like most people forgot or just couldn't be bothered to think about the fact that our ancestors rigged the entire world to explode.

You have to give the North Koreans credit—launching the first strike on April Fools' Day was kind of a genius move, even though it ultimately amounted to suicide. The Silent Spring, they called it. What a time to be ali—

Gloria's thoughts were finally interrupted by an earsplitting roar. By the dim light of impending dawn she could see the F-35G on its fly-by of the rocket, and the dark silhouette of a single figure in the cockpit, with a gloved hand raised in salute and sendoff. Major Chris Jenkins, a man responsible for an untold number of future lives, not all of them human. He had always wanted to do the equivalent of buzzing the tower like in the old movies, and since he doubted anyone would ever let him fly again, he planned to make this last flight count.

John reached Gloria at the windows just in time to see the

single engine of the jet fading away over the Pacific. Feelings of vindication and pride swelled up in him, and he imagined two other pilots making the same fateful decision, sparing the other rockets in his fleet.

He would never learn the truth.

"Oh my God, we're about to launch! What are you doing here?" Gloria asked as she suddenly realized exactly what must have occurred while she was swept away in the river of her thoughts. John ignored her for the time being as he held her with one arm and awkwardly made his way to the safest place on their level. She wasn't as small as she used to be, but John was a big man with adrenaline surging through his system. He then went about ensuring she was tightly strapped in and her flight suit was properly sealed, which was no easy task in the rocket's current orientation. This was not a scenario for which the engineers had planned. It was unlikely her pressurized suit would be needed, but John had taken enough chances for one day.

"Where are your helmet and gloves?" Now it was Gloria's turn to do the yelling, but the countdown overhead could still be heard loud and clear.

Ten seconds until liftoff.

"I'm afraid there isn't time," said John, a sad smile on his hard jawline. She saw goodbye in his hazel eyes, and for the first time realized just how much gray there was in his dark brown hair, how many wrinkles there were on his handsome face. Gloria wondered how much of it was due to her, and began to sob.

But John had one last thing to say, his voice taking on its trademark tone of seriousness and authority. "Gloria, my passphrase is this: 'a society grows great when old men plant trees in whose shade they know they shall never sit.' I love you. Make this all count for something, kid." She had no idea what he was talking about and found herself unable to speak.

John had personally overridden the launch safety mechanisms and understood the physics of the situation all too well. He had spent his life facing reality as it was, and wasn't going to stop now at the end. He would not be making it to a safe seat, or Mars for that matter. But the surest way to live a worthwhile, meaningful life was to already have done so, those moments etched forever into the fabric of spacetime. Fifty years spent living a sensational life, and most of the memories that danced across the stage of his consciousness in the final act could have been from anyone. The smile on his face was no longer sad.

Five seconds until liftoff.

His childhood home outside Chicago, and pulling out of the driveway with the dog that was his earliest recollection curled up in the back seat next to him. They both had no idea he was on his way to be put down, and only in retrospect did he recognize the sorrow in his parents' faces. Just doing what needed to be done. His biographer wrote that this was a pivotal moment in human history, when future prime mover John Rook realized—at a younger age than most—just how precious and fragile life was. It also instilled in him a sense of duty, and it was hypothesized that this set him on the trajectory that would ultimately put others on the trajectory to colonize another planet.

Four...

His wife, and the first time they made love after two bottles of cheap Spanish wine and a flamenco concert in Madrid. The dominant seventh and flat ninth chords created more than one kind of tension in need of resolution. She succumbed to the cancer only two years before the breakthrough cure. He missed her every day.

Three...

The way it used to smell after rain.

Two...

His daughter, and the glimmer of hope she could still realize the dream he'd spent most of his life striving towards.

One...

The fact that for most of human history the only brighter future anyone dreamed of was the one after death, but that almost certainly did not exist.

Liftoff...

This is the moment!

One hundred and thirty meters below, massive amounts of super-cooled liquid oxygen and hydrogen began to mix and combust. This reaction released no carbon—Bright Future Technologies' rockets burned clean—but it did rapidly eject a stream of scorching water vapor from the nozzles on the bottom of the first stage booster. John had always been familiar with the colossal thrust generated by this process on an intellectual level, but was now acutely cognizant of what that translated to in a physical sense.

He was painfully aware of the gravity of the situation.

Except for the passenger compartments and flight deck—both presently modified for takeoff—the interior of the rocket was designed to spend much of its occupied time horizontal and in minimal gravity. Neither of those were true at the moment. John clung to where Gloria was strapped in with his fading strength, but the increasing g-forces won, as gravity tends to do. John Rook had a final glimpse of the sunrise through the quickly receding observation windows as he plunged—was pulled, really—twenty meters into the titanium alloy door, currently acting as a floor.

A cacophony of chemical reactions drowned out Gloria's screams. The image of her father's blood, floating and pooling into perfect spheres under its surface tension in the strange mechanics of weightlessness, was seared into her synapses. It was something she would vividly remember to haunting effect for the rest of her long, long life.

Young Gloria had reached escape velocity in more ways than one.

The launch was both visible and audible for kilometers in all directions. To the few who were already awake and the many who were awoken to witness the event, it represented either a beacon of hope or a harbinger of impending doom. Time would tell who was right. The first stage booster separated to return to Earth. It would never fly again, but wouldn't mind. The payload, with all systems nominal and now containing only ninety-nine living people, continued on into the near-infinite void of space. The survivors left behind the burning birthplace of the human species, a flickering candle in the darkness they believed would soon wither and wink out.

But although the flame died, its light remained.

Chapter 7: The Prince(s)

Earth Year: 2350

Martian Year: 167

"Brother, how good to see your handsome face again," Zhang Bingwen said as he sat down at the private window booth. No one had sat in it for deciles, but it was impeccably well-kept. "I hope you haven't been waiting too long."

"And you too, brother. The wait didn't bother me—the music is rather nice," replied Zhang Jinhai. Across the crowded, oxytocin- and smoke-filled dance floor of the Gemini Club, Charlotte and the Charlatans were illuminated on the stage. A baritone saxophone played over a beat kept on a bass guitar built from actual wood. The jazz club was packed with revelers washing away any of the evening's lingering imperfections with various concoctions. If not for the wildly different faces and outfits it would have resembled a scene from a bygone era someplace far away. "There's something about it being *real*, isn't there?"

"It's my understanding that inhabitants of all levels of the City pay significant premiums to see and hear it live, although to categorize all of that noise as music would be disgraceful."

"I'm surprised you know anything about anyone who doesn't reside in the Emergent. With the exception of our imminent, eminent guest, of course," Jinhai said as he looked out the window and took in the cityscape. A neon jungle, though the lights were not produced by electrified tubes of different ionized gases—technically neon only glowed an orangish-red—like they had once been on Earth. "So, this is what happens when the kind of growth experienced by a few Chinese cities in Earth's early twenty-first century continues for ten times as long."

"Do you not find it beautiful?" asked Bingwen.

"My sense of beauty has evolved over the years."

"Yes, it has. You may not be quite as old as me, but you are indeed stubbornly old-fashioned."

"You never have let me live down those three minutes, have you?"

"Do you think she will accept our proposal?" Bingwen asked abruptly, getting down to business. He was the most successful businessperson on the planet, after all. The prince of Mars, soon to be king, he hoped.

"You may find this difficult to fathom, but not every human interaction need be so transactional." Jinhai's face broke into a smile. "Can we not simply enjoy each other's company, like the sols—even the days—of yore?"

Bingwen smiled too, his expression identical to his brother's in more ways than one. How badly he wanted to kill him. How much easier that would make things. But he knew that was not wise, and it had nothing to do with his genes protesting the annihilation of so many of their copies. Jinhai was nearly untouchable, like him. While their conversation had remained calm, across every plausible frequency he was aggressively

CHAPTER 7: THE PRINCE(S)

probing, prying, searching for a weakness, in vain. They both had the latest specs and highest privileges. More than that, they knew how the other thought. At a neutral location like this one—a club they co-owned and the only place they had met in person in fifty Martian years—the probability of success was precisely 0.5. And even if he were victorious, who knew what dead hand triggers his brother had in place in the event his brain stopped transmitting a signal. A form of what used to be called mutually assured destruction. There were surely other true believers out there, too.

"I'm sure you've reviewed all the same data and come to the same conclusion," Jinhai continued. "Her genome and the psychological analysis done before hiring her for her current role—in which she is exemplary—show strong inclinations towards psychopathy, risk-taking, and hedonism. I believe the probability is as high as with anyone."

Bingwen certainly hoped so. The Zhang Mining Corporation had a monopoly, both on and off-world, and he oversaw all sol-to-sol operations now that his father had effectively retired. ZMC wasn't a corporation in the traditional, terrestrial sense—there was no recognized, legitimate government on Mars with which to incorporate—but it had nonetheless made its owners fabulously rich. The fact that there was no government to issue and guarantee the planet's currency was not a problem; as long as enough people and computers agreed it had value then by definition it did. A self-evident idea, a kind of tautology. This lack of regulation also allowed the company to continue on indefinitely, free from competition, as capitalism gave way to corporatism.

But Bingwen's unbreakable stranglehold on unimaginable wealth and power would be shattered if humanity could return to Earth. The services the company provided would be rendered useless by an entire planet of abundant resources, where water—the oil of space—fell from the damn sky, and where everything society needed had already been extracted from the ground. A place where food literally grew on trees, which were themselves plentiful. This was of great concern to him even if only the next generation could emigrate—Bingwen planned to live for a very long time yet. The corporate executives on Earth who had knowingly forsaken the future and put their fiduciary duty to shareholders above all others had done so in exchange for a fraction of the rewards he reaped.

His brother was a different story. Each of the tens of trillions of cells in the twins' bodies contained the same three billion base pairs of nucleotides, split across a pair of twenty-three chromosomes, in precisely the same arrangement. But although the two men were united in their goal of keeping humanity confined to Mars for reasons that had nothing to do with protecting the human species, their motives were on opposite ends of the spectrum.

Gaia had had its renaissance, and Jinhai did not want it spoiled.

Some of the recent data from Earth was of concern to him, but the damage inflicted by anything living there now paled compared to the ecocide that would be committed by industrializing settlers from Mars. Humans were the most invasive of all species. So here they were, the selfish and the selfless, equally dedicated to their causes, stuck in an unholy alliance.

Bingwen raised his glass. "To having much to lose, brother."

"Much to lose indeed."

"Des yeux qui font baisser les miens..." sang Charlotte from

CHAPTER 7: THE PRINCE(S)

the stage in a soothing, nearly forgotten romance language. Those with the right (exclusive) augmentation, like the Zhang twins, could choose whether or not to understand, no translation required. Bingwen did, and was interested to hear the song was about love. How antiquated. Jinhai did not, the voice just another instrument in the mix.

"You want me to do what?" asked Keli. There was perhaps no subject more sensitive, but she had raised her voice nonetheless. She knew no one else in the Gemini Club could hear, or even tell this booth was occupied at all.

Across from her, the Zhang twins' faces remained identically expressionless. It kind of creeped her out, kind of turned her on. But no doubt they were communicating with each other over the local Network, evaluating her. Yes, she had arrived at precisely twenty-one hundred hours, not a minute sooner or later. No, she didn't have any cosmetic augmentations and was indeed as young as she looked—most people didn't have the opportunity to grow old in her line of work. No, her look—short spiky hair, a uniform, even when not working—was not a statement. It was simply practical; function over form. And no, she was not interested in a drink or any other kind of mind-altering substance, even wine made from real grapes, aged in a bottle with a real cork. Kronos knows how expensive it was and where they grew the inputs.

"I believe your question is rhetorical—our proposal was clearly stated," replied Bingwen. "As already mentioned, if you do not find the offer agreeable then all your memories of anything to do with this meeting will be erased, and you can go back to your...life."

"Yeah, I understand what you're asking. It just seems

extreme, even to me."

"No one has worked more arduously than the two of us to build this civilization into what it is today. We cannot risk destroying all that has been built, much less the entire species, over this fantasy of returning to Earth."

"It doesn't seem like you have much confidence in the latest treatments." Did Keli sense something pass between them? Probably just her imagination.

"The last two missions were abject failures. We see no reason to subject any more people to such a fate, much less potentially the entire populace."

"Why'd you let the *BLUE RETRIEVER* make the round trip in the first place? I thought you helped build the damn thing. You're cutting it awful close. And won't there be riots? I'm under the impression almost half the population is in favor." The thought of violence did not actually bother her; on the contrary, she'd made a career of it. But she had an inquisitive mind, almost to a fault.

"Those who feel differently than us have...effective methods of influencing public opinion that we do not," chimed in Jinhai. "Despite our position we are unable to act unilaterally in such matters. Regarding the potential aftermath: a controlled burn can restore a forest. Wildfires are healthy, natural events, and we feel the City has gone too long without an equivalent. But we aren't here to discuss the past, nor are we even asking you to agree with our reasoning—we're simply asking you to consider your own personal best interests."

Keli's mind was indeed reeling with the possibilities. She'd only been up to the Emergent once before, for work, but with the money they were offering she could move up here permanently. She may even be able to live indefinitely, if she didn't die fulfilling her end of the deal.

"Can't you crash one of your asteroid mining ships into it or something?"

"That wouldn't exactly give us the deniability we require, which is currently quite plausible, given that—as you mentioned—this mission was only possible because of our contributions. Other than us you will be the only human in the loop. Should anything go wrong or you be discovered we will of course deny any involvement or knowledge of your existence." Bingwen paused briefly. "And we will be able to definitively prove this to be the case."

Keli wondered what was to stop them from doing that even if she succeeded. She did not have faith in them—she lacked faith in anything, which just meant the idea in question wasn't good enough to take on evidence or argument. No, like them, she trusted in rational self-interest. She doubted their need for her would end with this. And she had signed up for a life of danger years ago. She suspected she had been engineered for it. Looking out the window at the dazzling Canopy, she wondered how it would look with different specs. Maybe she was a hypocrite for not indulging in narcotics.

"So, what is your answer, Keli?"

Chapter 8: Auroras in the Anthropocene

Earth Year: 2045

Martian Year: 5

The Lost Coast was named in part because the mountains of Northern California's King Range were so steep and rugged that it was too costly and challenging to build a major route along their shores. Thus the famed Highway One, which hugged most of California's coast up from Orange County, turned inland three hundred kilometers north of San Francisco when it reached the southern point of the Lost Coast. This left only a few, winding roads over the wooded mountains to the remote coastline. Nestled on these shores were a handful of secluded, scarcely populated towns. Shelter Cove was one of those towns.

There was never much in Shelter Cove, which was one of its primary attractions to the few who visited. Once fishing, abalone diving, and whale watching were no longer viable activities, the number of both residents and tourists dwindled even further. But those who still found themselves on the Lost Coast were not lost; they were exactly where they wanted to be.

One thing the town did have was a small airstrip, which was precisely why Edward McDougal found himself there on occasion. While his career in high f*inance*—with the accent on the second syllable in the pretentious East Coast pronunciation—may not have given him many relevant skills for surviving the apocalypse, it did allow him to accumulate considerable assets. He thought this was just as useful.

Like no small number of wealthy people he'd taken up an antiquated form of transportation as a hobby. Instead of horseback riding or sailing the sea like his parents, Edward's passion was sailing the sky in his old Cessna. Actually learning to fly, like learning to drive, had been unnecessary for years. Full autonomy was a button away, and most aircraft owners were unable to land on their own. Flying cars had no manual controls at all. But Edward had always had a hint of Luddite in him, and exercised control in all areas of his life. He wasn't comfortable completely giving up agency where he could help it, and so he had refused to abdicate some things to technology. This came in handy when civilian internet and communications began breaking down along with the power grid. And it allowed him to continue making the short trip between Shelter Cove and his estate in Marin County.

He would normally come with whatever girl ten-to-fifteen years his junior he was romantically involved with at the time, staying at the clifftop Lost Coast Inn and rarely leaving the room overlooking the Pacific. But he was newly single and had been recently making the flight solo. He was thinking how this was too bad as he began his approach on what he planned to be his final trip. Bringing a companion would have spared one soul from the destruction he was sure was imminently coming to the Bay Area. A blanket of money may have insulated the region from many of the world's problems so far, but it wasn't going to be able to protect it from this. Ever since taking economics his freshman year of college, when he first learned that people respond almost exclusively to incentives and heavily discount any utility accruing in the future, he'd known this day would come. Humans were notoriously bad at making short term sacrifices for long term gain, even when the benefits accrued to a future version of themselves. It was especially true when the beneficiaries were others, doubly so for those yet to exist. This understanding had also made Edward quite a bit of money.

He had to do a double-take at what looked to be an abandoned F-35G at the far end of the runway. He'd never seen a fighter plane here before, but things were getting more incomprehensible by the day.

His old jeep was waiting for him next to where he landed the plane, right where he'd parked it the prior weekend. Out of it he unloaded a thin copper sheet, which he used to cover the Cessna. Its conspicuous color was not of concern to him—this was not to hide the plane from the visible spectrum of light. He would only learn later what an idiot he was to leave something so valuable out in the open.

Into the jeep he unloaded the plane's cargo, which consisted of value sizes of a dozen different supplies that the vibrant online prepping community ensured him would be essential in the years to come. Theoretically the only tool you really needed to survive was a gun; everything else could be taken from others who lacked one. But—at least at this point in time—Edward was unwilling to accept the fact that the veneer of civilization was thinner than the atmosphere coating the

CHAPTER 8: AURORAS IN THE ANTHROPOCENE

Earth, which was itself twenty times thinner than the skin of an apple relative to the whole fruit. And Edward was well aware how it only took a few hundred short years to burn that away.

Up until recently he'd never even owned a firearm and had held a fatalistic view towards a hypothetical Armageddon. However, like the 'live fast, die young' attitude he possessed in his youth, once he got older—or in this case, as the prospect of getting nuked became a reality—it turned out he wanted to keep living after all. It was difficult to stray too far from the path laid out for him by millions of years of evolution by natural selection.

The sole restaurant in town was still there, and they still somehow had lobster. It was exorbitantly expensive and didn't taste quite like it used to, but it was surely better than the nonperishables at his compound that he would be eating for the foreseeable future. He had felt bad about stocking away several lifetime's worth of food given the world's annual calorie deficit had been in the hundreds of trillions, but with recent and sharp population declines he convinced himself this was no longer the case.

He paired the lobster with the restaurant's best bottle of wine. Edward had plenty of pricey booze stocked away at the shelter but had gotten into a habit of only drinking the good stuff. It made him sad to think of all the special luxuries that people had put off, saved for a day that would never come. After tipping five hundred percent and giving the owner an unanticipated hug—he wasn't sure when his next human contact would be—he drove north in the twilight to the property he'd purchased and been preparing for just this moment. The colors of the sky didn't fall into discrete buckets but existed on a continuum, somewhere between indigo, purple, and gray, and all of it pale. The trees were black silhouettes, but he instead saw them as negative space, carving extravagant patterns against the backdrop.

Darkness descended. Edward looked down at what was left of the black sand beach below. If not for the foam from the crashing waves, the washed-up plastic, and the bleached bones of long-dead beached whales, it would have been impossible to discern where the sand ended and the still-cold water began.

It was a clear night, and there was no light pollution this far from town. Although not the optimal time, astronomically speaking, from where he sat in a small clearing of trees on the hill he could just make out the dim white haze of the Andromeda galaxy above him, the most distant object visible to the naked eye. Moonlight was merely reflected sunlight, arriving at Earth just over a second after bouncing off its surface. But this Andromeda starlight had traveled for more than two million years at the cosmic speed limit to fall upon his retinas.

We certainly could have found ourselves in a less interesting universe, he thought. There were trillions of stars, but only about five thousand were distinctly visible from Earth. An apt metaphor for us. Some stood out more than others, as he hoped would be the case with John Rook, a man who bent the arc of history with his bare hands. But the vast majority had simply faded away or never been noticeable at all, receding on the far side of the universe faster than the speed of light, as Edward was sure would be the case with himself. Ground to dust by the gears of time and snorted by subsequent generations who had other things to worry about.

Then the pungent smell of gasoline filled his nostril as he inhaled a tiny mound of cocaine from the jeep's key. He was

CHAPTER 8: AURORAS IN THE ANTHROPOCENE

thankful it still had an analog model; the high-tech digital keys to the luxury cars sitting in his garage in Marin were useless for such purposes. A kilo of blow hadn't been on any of the preppers' lists he'd read, but the ability to get high was high on his.

He had increasingly become a loner as the years had passed. Being the only one of his old friend group still single and childless added to his solitude. But he liked his own company; he could get used to this. He thought of the stacks of paperback books at the compound—enough to last a lifetime—and smiled. One hundred-hour workweeks hadn't been conducive to reading for much of his life, and now there would finally be time to catch up.

He felt fucking great.

At the height of the first Cold War the United States had the genius idea of tests involving detonating nuclear weapons at high altitudes over the Pacific. The charged particles from these explosions interacted with Earth's magnetic field to produce brilliant auroras, to the extent that hotels in Honolulu—over thirteen hundred kilometers away—organized viewing parties on their roofs for the largest test, known as Starfish Prime. Shimmering ribbons of green, red, and purple danced in the darkness. Humanity now had bombs over fifty times as powerful. Edward suddenly found himself a very confused and awed witness to a similar event, but on a much grander scale.

They were the brightest auroras the world had ever seen by an order of magnitude.

* * *

Cooper knew almost four hundred distinct words. A few hundred were German, which was fitting because he was nearly a pure-bred German Shepherd. It was also less likely that bad guys would try to confuse him by yelling commands he recognized. Cooper didn't like getting confused, almost as much as he didn't like bad guys.

What he did like—or love, and even that may not have been a strong enough word—was Frank. He and Frank spent all day every day together, and Cooper was continually amazed at the adventures they went on. He was continually amazed at everything, come to think of it.

Frank Bear had spent thirty-five years in the San Francisco Police Department, the last eight as part of a K-9 unit specializing in cybercrime. With a sense of smell ten thousand times more powerful than a human's, Cooper could sniff out and differentiate between specific types of electronics. Even with all the newfangled technology that made Frank's head spin, man's best friend was still the most practical and cost-effective tool for some things. Hell, Cooper's skills would probably be in demand longer than his own, even with the damn robot dogs that were becoming increasingly popular.

But Cooper was in fact out of a job, and it was for his own sake. After eight years of exemplary service he'd began to develop hip dysplasia, and it was time for him to retire and live out his golden years in peace. It broke Frank's heart to see him so slow; once upon a time the dog would run endless laps around the couch for no reason at all. Increases in canine lifespans hadn't kept pace with those in humans. It was something to do with resource prioritization, and it was too damn bad if you asked Frank.

Officer Bear loved his job and would have stayed on with

CHAPTER 8: AURORAS IN THE ANTHROPOCENE

the force until he dropped dead in his tactical boots. But he was divorced. He also had no kids, being morally opposed to procreation given the state of the world and ongoing ecological collapse. What was Coop going to do all day? He wanted to ensure his dog's remaining years were as fulfilling as possible. And so Frank hung up his badge next to Cooper's police collar, used his dwindling pension—the government conveniently forgot to adjust for hyperinflation—to buy a small piece of property on the Lost Coast, and the two of them moved north to live among the redwood trees. Surviving in modern society required constantly learning new skills and technologies, but Frank reckoned even though the forests weren't as plentiful as they used to be, a man could survive up there with only the same tools his ancestors had used for thousands of years.

He also thought that would be ridiculous—there was no way in hell he was parting with his trusty firearm.

Over time Frank's life and outlook became increasingly like Cooper's. He had no grand plans and was unsure what each day would bring; life just happened to him. He had a radio and loosely kept up with macro events, but did not ruminate on them. The world was progressively inscrutable, but it was also much simpler. Sometimes he went long periods thinking of nothing at all, living in a perpetual present. He even occasionally shit in the woods. Frank finally began to understand why Cooper always had that big dumb smile on his face.

* * *

Edward stared stupidly at the sky for several seconds. Eventually his brain started functioning properly again and he realized what must be happening. Luckily he had prepared for such an occasion. He was almost certainly beyond the range of harmful effects but wasn't about to take any chances. He'd turned his inherited fortune into a much larger one by following the well-known business mantra of 'only the paranoid survive' and was now applying it to all areas of his life. His heart beat dangerously fast due to the unadvisable combination of potent stimulants and physical exertion as he sprinted to his bunker.

The entrance was obfuscated and meant to be difficult to find unless you had its exact coordinates plugged into your Cosmic Positioning System, which used the reliable and throbbing x-rays from multiple distant but bright pulsars and an atomic clock to triangulate precise location. It replaced the now-defunct GPS and Beidou systems, but was thrown off by the immense atmospheric disturbance occurring overhead. Fortunately for Edward, he could have found this place with his eyes closed.

The bunker was essentially a giant Faraday cage. Unlike most cages, those of the Faraday variety were primarily meant to keep things out, not hold them in. People who were once deemed paranoid but now revealed as rational used them to block electromagnetic signals, such as the colossal pulse created by nuclear weapons detonated at high altitudes. Edward had constructed his using a tight mesh of silver, the most conductive metal and thus most effective choice for such a purpose. The incremental protection provided over cheaper alternatives like copper in no way justified the orders of magnitude increase in cost. But he was convinced fiat money would be completely worthless soon anyways and had stocked up on precious metals. Gold, guns, and gear would be the currencies of the future, and Edward planned to stay a very rich man.

But money could not buy him happiness in this moment. He sealed the door behind him and collapsed with his head in his hands. He'd been planning for years but could not believe it was actually happening. The doomsday clock had struck midnight. All the people he'd ever known were in the process of being obliterated. Should he have tried harder to convince others? Should he have brought someone with him? Could he have? Surely, at least one.

He was pulled out of his downward mental spiral by a faint but distinctive sound coming through the thick bunker walls. It was a sound he knew well, and it was getting closer. He slung an assault rifle around his shoulder—just in case—unsealed the door, and ventured back out into the multicolored night.

"*Pfui! Sitz!*" Edward hadn't realized just how much his bunker blocked out sound. He had been expecting to find a barking dog, but Cooper was immediately outside of the door and startled him backward. The thirty-five-kilo German Shepherd was trained to intimidate when he wanted to. Upon hearing his master's voice, Cooper instantly stopped and sat patiently, staring at Edward with an ambivalent look, unsure if he was friend or foe.

Frank emerged jogging from among the trees and into the aurora light. It was brighter than the full moon. He abruptly stopped upon noticing the rifle hanging off Edward's shoulder and calmly put up his hands in a well-trained disarming gesture. He may have been sixty-two years old, slightly overweight, and out of breath, but given the rifle's current orientation and the location of this man's hands, Frank was confident he could draw his trusty firearm and get off two shots before this guy even knew he was dead. Of course, he hoped it wouldn't come to that. They were on the same team as far as he was concerned. Folks needed to stick together in these troubled times.

"Hey there partner. Sorry about old Coop here. As you can imagine he's pretty spooked," said Frank as he motioned upward with his head towards the fluttering sky. He still had a bit of a southern drawl from his youth in New Orleans—he sure missed that now-sunken city—but played it up in situations like this.

Edward was confused by the man's posture until he remembered the assault rifle. He felt almost embarrassed as he acknowledged Frank's acknowledgment and said, "No need for concern. You could say I'm a bit spooked too." It felt good to be having a conversation with someone, anyone. Something about Frank made Edward trust him instantly. It was an essential trait in a great cop.

Frank dropped his guard slightly but not entirely. Apart from the rifle it was difficult to appear less threatening than this preppy man he'd just come across, but you could never be too sure in these strange times. "I reckon those crazy Ruskies had some kind of dead hand trigger set up and launched their whole friggin' arsenal. From the looks of it they fired enough real and decoy missiles to ensure at least a few got through our defense systems. Those things were never as good as the government would have you think, and even as they got better, so did the missiles they were designed to stop. With Space Force defenses offline there's basically no way to stop a hypersonic missile going five times the speed of sound. I'd hoped that at least maybe some of the warheads themselves wouldn't have worked, not having been physically tested for fifty years, but I guess that's what those damn supercomputers are for. What a shame." He shook his balding head. Hair loss was easily curable but Frank hadn't bothered. "What a damn shame."

"Tragically ironic, isn't it? How nuclear weapons represent both our species' mastery over the very foundations of nature, as well as our utter inability to master our most primitive instincts. How appropriate that the acronym for mutually assured destruction is MAD."

"With a survival bunker like that I'm not sure how strong of a leg you've got to stand on when it comes to primitive instincts," said Frank, cracking a smile on his bearded face. "And if you knew some of the women in my past you'd know that neither do I. Sometimes I think Coop is the more evolved of the two of us. Then again, he's got no balls. You should have seen him before he was neutered."

Edward laughed. "I like the cut of your jib, man."

"I'm not familiar with the phrase but I'll take it as a compliment. I'm Frank Bear, and you've already met Cooper."

"Frank, nice to meet you. I wish it could have been under different circumstances. I'm Edward McDougal."

"Mind if I call you Eddie? I had a partner for five years who insisted on being called Edward and I couldn't stand the bastard."

Eddie chuckled again. "You can call me whatever you like. You want to come in? Who knows how much radiation may reach the ground this far north, but I have a Geiger counter so we can monitor it. More importantly, I could sure use some company on a night like this."

"Welp, we're several miles from my place and I'm sure yours is a palace in comparison. I should warn you though: we probably don't smell too good."

"That's quite alright. I have a makeshift shower inside."

"In that case I hope you're stocked up on whiskey—I can't imagine a more fitting occasion. Cooper, *freund!*" The dog leaped up and started licking Eddie.

The brief moment of relief was abruptly ended by the appearance of a strange new sun in the southern sky. This sun did not rise—it seemed to have emerged out of thin air and continued to expand in size. The night was now as bright as high noon. The three of them somberly and silently went inside and sealed the door on the destruction of civilization.

* * *

Chad was a twenty-six-year-old former developer of software used to develop more advanced software. He was now unemployed. But at this instant Chad had no concerns, lighting a marijuana cigarette in his favorite after-sex ritual. He lay naked on top of the sheets in the dark, looking out the bay window on the far side of the room at the warm San Francisco night, something that used to be exceedingly rare. A foghorn blared in the distance—what outdated technology, he thought—but the clouds must have been low and confined to just above the water; from here he could see the stars.

"You're not allowed to smoke inside! My neighbors will complain," scolded Ashley, coming back from the bathroom. "I forgot about your stupid tradition. Why can't you vape like a normal person?"

"What can I say? I'm old school. And I like the burn."

"Since it's already lit, let me take a hit before you put it out." She inhaled deep and coughed a few times. The orange ember and light gray smoke stood out in the shadowy room.

"I thought you were supposed to go out of town this weekend with that older rich chump. I was surprised when I got the booty call," half-joked Chad, feeling spacey. This shit was good.

"I ended it with him, and he's not a chump. He's nice, but I decided I should try dating guys closer to my own age for once." Ashley was twenty-two and gorgeous. She had paid for her education from 'modeling' gigs, most of which she hoped her parents would never find out about. The cryptographic watermark verifying she was a real person and not computer-generated was still important to many voyeurs. Because of this 'reality premium' some of the pornography industry had proved immune to disruption, even after all these years. Fortunately, her parents lived deep in the countryside and shunned the internet. And, more recently, they would have had trouble getting online even if they wanted to.

The room then flashed blue, immediately followed by a boom. Then it flashed red, then white. More booms proceeded.

Chad laughed. "It seems someone isn't content with the bullshit virtual show the city plans to put on this year for the fourth of July. Cheap, bureaucratic bastards."

"They'd better hope the cops don't catch them," replied Ashley. It appeared they would not, because almost as soon as the fireworks started they stopped. Silence and darkness once again permeated the bedroom.

Then the world was extravagantly illuminated, far brighter than before, as if someone had flipped on and off a floodlight pointed directly in the window. If Chad or Ashley had been looking out they would now be blind, but it would only have mattered for a few seconds; their eyes would be useless soon enough.

After the flash they instantaneously felt a violent tremor, but the Bay Area wasn't due for another Big One for hundreds of years.

"What the hell kind of firework was that?" asked a bemused Chad. Maybe this designer cannabis was even better than he thought. Ashley began hurrying to the bay window when she heard the roar, and then her heart sank as she realized the sound's implications. This exact sequence of events had been drilled into everyone in the country over the past few months. She thought of the novel she had almost finished writing. No one would read it now, the book destined to join the immense corpus of words written but never shared. Think of all the people who may have loved them. The blare of the one-hundred-year-old emergency siren, almost like the city itself crying out in the last manner left to it, only confirmed her worst fears. She reached the window just in time to catch a fleeting glimpse of the impossibly fast-approaching wall of fire and have one final thought: is this all you get?

The lights went down in the city, an artificial sun shining on the bay.

Chapter 9: The Mourning After

Earth Year: 2350

Martian Year: 167

Caspian watched her perfect, naked figure walk across the room, an outrageous juxtaposition to his shabby living space, though it wasn't quite as shabby as it had been the first time she was there. This was her third, and the first that she'd stayed until this close to morning. She wasn't really sure how these things were supposed to work. Intimate relationships had never been her forte, her only romances chemical, but she found waking up at someone else's residence more exciting than doing so at home.

"When your body is mostly artificial you have fewer qualms about showing it off—quite the contrary," she said with a twirl after noticing him staring. "My father used to tell me not to take too much pride in my looks because they could be taken from me in a moment, and inevitably would be by the inexorable march of time. I guess he was wrong on both fronts."

Caspian smiled. "I can't believe I've been spending time with *the* Gloria Rook."

"Interesting euphemism," Gloria replied. She had told him everything. Well, not everything. A girl had to have some secrets. There was little risk in unraveling a few of her mysteries to someone like Caspian given no one would believe him nor be able to verify any of it. Even if he had the right augmentation to play back their encounters, which she knew he didn't, he'd find the scenes altered. His astonished reactions were worth it, like the one he wore now. Or maybe she was getting reckless, the imminent arrival of *BLUE RETRIEVER* clouding her judgment.

"Can I ask you something?" Caspian asked.

"If the time we've spent together so far is any indication then I have a feeling you're going to regardless of my response. Let's see if I answer."

"How do you choose which version of you to look like? I mean, the *real* you, when the obfuscation is stripped away like it is now. Physically and mentally I have to imagine you're a very different person at ages ten, twenty, fifty, and one hundred and fifty." Even in the fleeting moment of mental clarity after sex and with undeniable proof he seemed to still have difficulty accepting she was the second oldest person on the planet, more than ten times his own age. Perhaps he'd heard the rumors—sowed by her, mostly for fun—that she was dead. "Or do you still think in Earth years?"

"I think in both simultaneously, but being one hundred and seventy Martian years old certainly sounds better than three hundred and twenty. However I've mostly discarded other terrestrial units of time like months and days and use deciles and sols instead.

"And regarding which version of me to look like—you're overthinking it, dear. I just go with whatever's the most attractive. Despite the radical changes our species has made to itself in the past few centuries we still signal evolutionary fitness in much the same way we always have." She could almost hear Caspian's genes scream as he looked her up and down again. "Mammals evolved hundreds of millions of Earth years ago, sexual reproduction over a billion. It's not easy to rewrite the very kernel of the operating system."

"Like that which would let us live on Earth again?" Gloria's onboard specs noted several changes in Caspian as he posed the question.

"Not easy, but maybe not impossible. And it doesn't necessarily have to be rewritten—it could be patched or updated, to stretch this analogy past its breaking point. I suppose we'll know soon enough, when the ship arrives." His stress levels remained elevated, so she decided to change subjects. "Anyways, I never understood why in the old obituaries they used a picture from a person's twilight years. Surely it's just as legitimate to use one from their prime."

"After last night let me tell you: you definitely seem to still be in your prime," said Caspian, relaxing. "I'd say it's impressive you're able to keep up your libido at your age, but I know as well as anyone there are drugs for that." There were drugs for almost anything if you had the right specs. And they weren't just limited to releasing floods of existing neurotransmitters like serotonin and dopamine. They could introduce entirely new ones. But Gloria had a more complicated relationship with sex. She'd gone more than one hundred and thirty Martian years without it, only recently wading back in. *If only the technology to conceive and incubate a child outside of a living person had been available during the early sols.*

Caspian sat up in his bed. It was only used for one thing,

and he hadn't slept in years. Forgoing sleep was a great way to increase your effective lifespan by a third, which was especially enticing given the depressed life expectancy of a Floor dweller. He took the pensive look on her face as an opportunity to bring up something that had been nagging him since the first night they met. "Was it the neurosugar, or do you mean what you said about empathizing with those who long for oblivion? You've mentioned it a few times."

She considered the question in her newfound lucidity before replying, "My father once told me about some uncomfortable research conducted on Earth. People were asked to choose their preference between two options: experiencing a perfect vacation, except they wouldn't be able to remember it afterward, and experiencing a mediocre vacation, except they would. Most chose the latter."

She waited for understanding to dawn on him but it failed to materialize. She quickly realized he'd never been on vacation. For that matter, practically no one on Mars had. The few 'resorts' on the planet certainly didn't count, nor did the virtual escapes. Most had never left the City. Her mind paintings were probably the closest he'd ever come. "Swap vacation with life and I think you'll understand, but with life there's no remembering it after it's over. In a sense I've chosen the latter option—to remember what has been on average a mediocre life, but I understand and in some ways am envious of those who opted for the former."

"Ah...maybe I'd sympathize if I was closer to your age. No offense," he replied, clearly unconvinced and becoming agitated. He was still coming down. "I don't exactly live on the Floor by choice, you know. There's so much I want to do that doesn't involve spending the rest of my life high, feeling fake emotions and plugged into a fake world. In fact, I wasn't sure if I should tell you, but—"

"I imagine that sounds preposterous coming from someone who lives in the Emergent," she interjected. "But life hasn't always been so peachy."

That seemed to do it. She saw realization dawn on him. "... I hadn't considered that you were there and lived through it. What was it really like, in the early sols? Only the parts you don't want to forget, of course. I know the most official story at a high level and have done some research, but there's so much misinformation on the Network."

"I'd rather not relive any of that right now. Maybe I'll tell you one sol, if you're still around," she said with a wink. "My mother used to tell my father that if you spend too much time thinking about the future or dwelling on the past you'll miss the present." *Maybe I should take that advice more often.* "So, speaking of vacations, why don't we take you on one right now?"

An intrigued look crept across Caspian's face. Perhaps she was getting reckless, losing her edge; she knew this was a bad idea. But there was something invigorating about the truly young. *So much potential. So much optimism. So much yet to be done.*

Chapter 10: The Player of Game Theory

Earth Year: 2045

Martian Year: 5

Both the northern and southern lights were visible to the naked eye from the moon. The electrified gas creating these vibrant displays was a distinct and oft-forgotten fourth phase of matter—plasma—that comprised more of the universe than all but matter's fifth phase: dark. While these naturally occurring phenomena were beautiful enough to bring tears to the eyes of those stationed at Luna Alpha, the massive, man-made atmospheric lights they now beheld spurred tears of a different kind.

But there was one set of eyes that remained dry, just as they had ever since their owner discovered and embraced stoicism in the writings of Marcus Aurelius in high school. The magnanimous United States Space Force Commander Matt Jenkins may have never been so distraught in his entire life, and even if the emotion was relative, for the sake of his men and women he could not let it show. It was an understatement to say it had been a challenging few months for those under

CHAPTER 10: THE PLAYER OF GAME THEORY

his command.

The state of all human affairs had been spiraling downwards for some time, but Space Force's predicament had taken a steep decline when their defenses failed to protect critical satellites from enemy attack at the war's outbreak. It seemed the lack of real-world testing—relying solely on computer models—was inadequate. At least they had been able to respond in kind. As in all other domains, it was easier to destroy than create, an asymmetry that did not tip in civilization's favor.

More recently his team's distress was amplified by watching *THE SKY IS NOT THE LIMIT* blown up in the atmosphere by their comrades; the nature of those who joined Space Force was such that most were sympathetic to the independent Mars colony. The morale boost provided by the fact that one of the American rockets did manage to escape—wholly because of the noble actions of Commander Jenkins's younger brother Chris—had quickly dissipated.

They had felt helpless enough watching *ONWARD AND UPWARD* drift on by, derelict in the dark with irreparably damaged boosters and communication equipment, unable even to broadcast a parting message. But now those at Luna Alpha had an unobstructed view of their country's—and the world's—annihilation, and their remaining weapons were woefully insufficient to shoot down the barrage of missiles they could see streaking through the upper atmosphere. They found little solace in the sad fact that it would not have mattered; the nuclear triad possessed by most atomic states meant the attacks came from submarines and planes too, not just ICBMs. They couldn't even reliably tell which of the fifteen nuclear powers had launched each warhead.

Matt had a creeping suspicion that a similar fate to one of the two doomed rockets awaited those at Luna Alpha. He just was not sure yet which one. If his fellow moon dwellers—whether on this base or another one flying a different flag—did not comprehend it yet, they would figure it out soon enough. He needed to act fast.

"Lieutenant Spark, how long will our on-base supplies last?" Like any good commander, Matt knew the exact answer to this question at all times. However, he wanted to break the silence that had permeated the command center for the past several minutes with something other than a gasp or sob. Having a job on which to focus was a proven method for coping with tragedy.

"The last resupply mission was two months ago, which means we have ten months at full rations with existing personnel." Lieutenant Jessica Spark's voice was initially shaky but steadied as she continued, "We can of course stretch them, but how long they—and we—ultimately last depends on other factors." Given everyone's current condition she did not feel the need to explicitly spell out the prisoners' dilemma in which the moon bases would soon find themselves. Commander Jenkins was a brutally capable man. He understood, and now he knew that she did too.

Like the old International Space Station, governments hadn't bothered to make their moon bases entirely self-sufficient. If they hadn't done so on their home planet, how could they be expected to do so on its barren satellite? The population and resources of the privately funded Mars colony dwarfed those of the moon. Because things worked well enough as-is and transporting all the extra equipment was expensive, it was one line item that was easy to cut out and thus kept getting pushed to next year's budget. At this point the total cost of all the resupply missions far exceeded the upfront expenditure required to allow them to grow and manufacturer their own sustenance. But that's just how things tended to work in a bureaucracy.

Matt wasted no time contemplating this grim data; he was a man of action with more pressing concerns than starvation. It was said that generals always fight the last war, but even if Matt was already thinking ahead to the next one, there was one happening right now that needed his attention.

"Technical Sergeant Johnson, see if you can get in contact with Earth. Figure out who is now the highest-ranking living officer and what our orders are. In the meantime I will assume independent command of Space Force and act as I see fit."

Technical Sergeant Craig Johnson was too despondent to respond. He just stared out the observation window at the distant, rolling waves of polychromatic light. Death's beautiful emissaries.

"Sergeant! Am I clear?" repeated Matt, sterner and louder this time. An example needed to be made, expectations set.

"...yes, sir," answered Craig in a hollow voice. This task was going to be harder than it seemed—the commander in chief, secretaries of defense and homeland security, and all joint chiefs of staff were already confirmed dead in the first hour of attacks. They wouldn't even get a chance to figure out who won the war: no one. Matt hoped the job's difficulty would occupy his technical sergeant's mind for a while.

"Everyone else," Matt said, "our number one priority is the protection of Luna Alpha. Keep a close eye on any movement from our enemies. I will go speak with our friends, if we have any left."

"G'day, Commander Jenkins. Please excuse the improper figure of speech—it's most certainly not a good day. I'm afraid my country's saying, 'she'll be right,' is no longer applicable." Air Marshal Owen Hurst of the Royal Australian Air Force was visibly disheveled, but made an effort to maintain the good-humored attitude for which he and his people were known. The Aussies had a significant off-world presence given their ideally situated coastline, but their space operations fell under RAAF jurisdiction rather than a distinct extraterrestrial branch of the military. Owen didn't know it, but he was now its highest-ranking officer anywhere in the solar system. America's other allies, the European Union and Japan, also shared space at Luna Alpha. But the EU had called their officers home after the last resupply mission and the destruction of most of their space assets, so they were not among the skeleton crew currently at the base.

"Air Marshal Hurst, thank you for taking my call on such short notice and under such dire circumstances," said Matt. "I first want to offer my condolences—my understanding is that Sydney and Melbourne were both targeted."

"Let's ditch the formalities for now if you don't mind, Matt. Afraid I'm not really in the mood."

"As you wish."

"My condolences as well—it doesn't appear many cities in the States were spared." Despite the friendly words there was tension on the line. Unlike Matt, Owen was—or at least had been—a family man. Perhaps he partly blamed the US for their role in the nuclear chain reaction now playing out. He continued in a wistful tone, "It almost doesn't seem real from up here, does it? Kind of gives a new meaning to the 'overview effect.'"

"Thank you for your sympathies, Owen. This is a trying time for everyone. My primary goal right now is to minimize any further destruction and loss of life."

Owen sighed. "Yes, I guess that makes sense. I don't suppose you've been able to contact our Russian or Chinese neighbors?" The space-faring nations of Earth may have abdicated Mars colonization to the private sector, but the moon was of too much strategic military importance to be left alone. The 1967 Outer Space Treaty had been amended with more flexible language but still included a provision that the moon should be used exclusively for peaceful purposes. However, that hadn't stopped countries from equipping their bases with the ability to defend themselves and staffing them with those who knew how to do so.

"We tried but are yet to get a response. I know I do not need to remind you of the precarious position we are all in," said Matt. The treaty also prohibited weapons of mass destruction in the cosmos, and although this clause had technically been abided by, it made no difference. There was so little margin for error on the moon that any significant attack using conventional weapons would surely destroy its target. Thus those on the moon bases had their own version of mutually assured destruction. And like was once assumed on Earth, it was thought that the only way to win—other than not playing—was a decisive and debilitating first strike. Matt hoped recent events enlightened everyone to the folly in that line of thinking, but at this point he was not about to gamble on mankind's sanity.

"I'm well aware, mate. And it seems Colonel Tanaka and his team were too. Apparently they'd rather take their chances back on the island."

"What?" Matt had thought his concerns were maxed out but was apparently wrong.

"Have you not spoken to them? I must say I'm honored I was the first person you called. I saw them heading towards the escape pods. The colonel—" Owen was cut off as the communication channel was abruptly closed. "That was quite rude," he said out loud to himself.

"Seal off the escape pod bay immediately!" commanded Matt.

"It's too late, sir—they're already inside and preparing for launch. We can't override the emergency escape system—it was designed for just this kind of scenario," replied Lieutenant Spark. Like Soyuz had been at the International Space Station, the escape pods were meant to be used as lifeboats in case of emergency. But given the events playing out on Earth it was hard to conclude they were escaping to anything other than certain death.

Matt processed the information and instantly adjusted to the new reality. "Ok. Prepare for the worst if we are attacked, but under no circumstances initiate a first strike. Let us hope the pods' launch is not misconstrued as that of a missile."

Chapter 11: Shooting Stars

Earth Year: 2350

Martian Year: 167

Everything could grow taller in lower gravity, not just buildings and people. Olympus Mons was the second tallest mountain in the solar system. It was once the tallest volcano too, but like all of Mars until colonized by humanity, it had been dormant for a long time. It towered over the surrounding plains.

High on its slope, with an extended line of sight from the blasted-out entrance to one of the lava tubes that snaked through its interior, Keli could just make out the City's glow behind the distant horizon. It almost resembled the approaching dawn. Above it, so bright it was visible through the City's radiance, was the Mourning Star. She could barely discern its satellite, too.

She watched what looked like a slowly falling star descend from overhead into the light, a mining ship returning from a lengthy journey. The letters on its side would be the same ones strewn about the mountain: ZMC. A shiver of excitement and anticipation—almost sexual, which could be a hell of a thing when properly augmented—made her tremble, until she reminded herself to temper expectations. This was a risky mission. In all likelihood she would not make it.

The Olympus Mons outpost and mine were nearly as far as one could be from the City on Mars and still have life support. It was the farthest she had ever been. But that wasn't what concerned her; no, she was worried about going back, and damned the fact that the rocket fields were on the far side of the City from her precious and precarious cargo. If she were caught bringing it anywhere near home there was no possibility of explaining it away. Not with the methods they would employ. Even approaching underground her convoy would be thoroughly scanned. She had been assured it would pass without issue, and given who made the promise she was inclined to believe it. But she hadn't survived this long in her line of work without a healthy sense of paranoia.

So, even the bad guys—or girls—get scared of the dark sometimes, she thought. But Keli didn't think of herself as a bad person. Only a tiny minority ever did. She wasn't even technically stealing this cargo, although that's how it would be reported. And though people would die, she supposed she understood the Zhang twins' arguments, and it seemed likely those at risk would die sooner than later anyway. Furthermore, with a new augmentation that allowed her to see in infrared when she wished, it wasn't exactly dark to her either.

Rather, she was afraid of what others might do when they thought no one was looking.

And fear was useful. So was pain, but she'd experienced such agony on previous missions that she now kept her pain receptors permanently flipped to produce a weak sense of pleasure when activated. That ability hadn't come cheap, but she hadn't paid for it. She hadn't paid for any of her new onboard specs, which were even better than what she'd had access to in her previous job.

She wasn't troubled by what they would do to her body, however; she was troubled by what they would do to her mind. Once upon a time the only thing that couldn't be taken from someone under any circumstances was their own attitude and thoughts. A sufficiently trained and powerful mind could always take refuge in itself. But Keli knew all too well this was no longer the case; when you strip away the layers of abstraction we're merely chemical reactions and electric pulses, both of which can be manipulated.

Keli buried the thought. She was good at burying things, figuratively speaking. She turned her back on the night and strode down into the tunnel. She had work to do.

Chapter 12: Red Rover

Earth Year: 2045

Martian Year: 5

Frank Bear and Eddie McDougal were awoken in the night again by Cooper. As happy as the dog was while awake, he had started to display concerning tendencies in his sleep—growling, whimpering, restlessness. They could only guess what nightmarish scenes played out in his mind. Frank took comfort in the fact that at least it appeared—like humans—he had a hard time remembering dreams afterward; as soon as he awoke he was his normal, cheery self. But Cooper was nine years old, and Frank had been by his side for nearly every moment of his life. The only other time this happened was before an 8.0 earthquake struck the Bay Area. Non-human animals, with their alternative instincts and senses, were often the first to know of impending disasters.

Frank worried how this boded for what lay ahead.

A week had passed since the two men met. In hindsight there was no reason to stay confined to the bunker and its immediate proximity after the first night; there were no more nuclear explosions, at least within a noticeable distance. Frank thought it likely they'd targeted farther south, blanketing the country's technology capital down through Silicon Valley to San Jose. What a damn shame. As such, the radiation level this far north was negligible. Nuclear fallout dissipated according to the 'rule of seven': after seven hours its intensity dropped by ninety percent. After seven times that interval, or forty-nine hours, it dropped by another ninety percent, and so on. And the high-altitude detonations resulted in low radioactivity at ground-level.

Frank and Eddie had passed the time as best they could. They took turns telling stories, inserting jokes when their gloomy moods allowed. Frank had had to talk Eddie off the ledge more than once. They also dove into the bunker's formidable library. Eddie recommended his favorites to Frank, who liked them much more than he thought he would. There were few better ways to bond with someone than discovering a shared love of the same book. And the post-apocalyptic, dystopian themes in much of the science fiction yielded ideas that could come in handy in the days ahead. Frank wished he'd gotten into this whole reading thing much earlier in life.

The retired police officer went outside. The night—normally windy on the Lost Coast—was eerily still, like it had been all week. He supposed it was better than mushroom cloud ash getting blown up from the south. Frank couldn't detect the presence of a single other living creature. He hadn't heard so much as a bird chirp in days. Their early morning songs had become his alarm clock since moving to the wilderness, and although it annoyed him many days, the new silence made him uncomfortable. But so did everything about the state of the world.

He tried to get a signal on the radio, but like he was now

used to, heard nothing but static. Frank knew a few things about radio waves. There were three main methods to send them. The most obvious was line of sight, but given the steep mountains of the King Range this was off the table. There were also presumably no longer any functioning towers or satellites to relay the signal. Another method was sending skywaves, bouncing broadcasts off the ionosphere, which could be done over vast distances and should have worked even better at night and with the thick cloud cover. It seemed this layer of the atmosphere was still recovering from the massive amounts of ionizing radiation dumped into it, causing interference. Lastly, he should have been able to send groundwaves riding along the Earth's surface, but those didn't seem to work either. Some other kind of interference, Frank guessed. Just another mystery to add to the pile.

Eddie came out to join him. "Still no luck with the radio?"

"None. Somethin' just doesn't seem right. We should be able to get ahold of *someone* by now."

"The prepping community said to be ready for this kind of thing, but honestly who fucking knows at this point." Eddie looked up at the strange, bleak sky. He hadn't beheld the stars, now perpetually obfuscated by clouds of dust and ash, since that fateful night, and wondered if he ever would again. He could barely discern where the moon must have been, a patch of slightly lighter gray. Then Eddie remembered something else he hadn't done since the auroras, and was suddenly overcome with craving.

"Listen, I know you are—or were—a cop. But I hope you don't mind that in addition to alcohol, cannabis, and tobacco, I stocked up on some Schedule One narcotics."

Frank would have laughed if he were in a better mood. "I

CHAPTER 12: RED ROVER

could give two shits, Eddie. I got into law enforcement to protect people from bad guys, not themselves. Nothing created more bad guys than the War on Drugs. That fiasco cost more dollars and lives than most real conflicts except for some of the bloodbaths in Asia and the two world wars. Well, and the third one. I had a front-row seat to some of it. And I certainly understand the urge to change your state of mind by introducin' outside substances." He took a drink from the bottle of twenty-five-year-old scotch held in his hand. "Our default setting may be good for some things—surviving, passing on our genes and all that—but it sucks for others. I gotta say though, I've always been more inclined to spread my seed after some of this." He raised the bottle in a hollow attempt to lighten the atmosphere.

Eddie gave a half-hearted smile. "Appreciate it," he said, heading back inside and reemerging a few minutes later with a more upbeat, talkative disposition, sniffling every few seconds. "Mind if I take a swig of that?" he asked. Frank passed him the bottle. "So, did you get a chance to see much of the world before it all went to shit? My father used to tell me it's a disgrace to die without a heavily stamped passport."

"Your dad must be even older than me—didn't they stop physically stamping passports years ago?"

"Hmm...it doesn't seem as romantic when it's just a record in a government database, does it?"

Frank spoke slowly, "I never did get that saying, 'see the world.' Hell, you can—or could—do that on the internet, or through one of them ridiculous headsets. To really get to know a place you've got to touch, taste, smell, and hear it—not just see it, you know? Like really getting to know a person, that's not something you can do on a short vacation. At least not with the number of days off they gave us on the force. And like relationships with people, I'd rather have a few that are authentic than a bunch that are phony." He paused, motioned for the bottle back from Eddie, and took a long pull. "Although, now that I think of it, maybe I don't know what I'm talking about—my only real friend the last year hasn't even been human. I guess I always figured I'd take the time to travel after retiring, but then Cooper came along. It would have been too much hassle to bring him with me, and I sure as hell wasn't going to leave him. But you know what? I don't regret any of it, which I reckon is more than most can say.

"I bet you got around quite a bit if you can afford all this," said Frank, alluding to the bunker with his free hand. "I never asked because I figured maybe it was rude, but it seems we're past all that now. Where'd all the money come from? You some kinda drug dealer?"

"You'd be surprised how far the combination of good looks, nepotism, and a healthy trust fund can take you in life," joked Eddie, getting a small smile out of Frank. "But no, nothing illegal, though I'm not sure I'd call it legitimate. I shuffled around claims on assets that actually created value—assets created by others—and I skimmed a percentage off the top. We called it f*inance*."

"Last I heard the markets crashed and the world was in recession."

"That's true, but if you know what you're doing you can make more money when people are desperate than optimistic. As they say, 'when there's blood in the street, buy property.' You just have to be ok with the fact that there's always someone else on the other side of the trade."

"Shows how much I know," said Frank with a shrug. "I never

even had a mortgage. Not like I could afford one."

"That's different. The idea of a loan, or that you don't need all the money for something up front and can instead *finance* it, has been one of the greatest drivers of human progress ever conceived."

"Looks like it still wasn't enough. Progress, that is. I gotta say, I've been living like a hermit this past year, but it's nice to get an actual taste of how the other one percent lives." He took another sip of the aged, single malt scotch. He'd never tasted anything so damn delicious in his entire life, just the right balance of peat and sweet. It was exactly how Frank liked it, only more so. Maybe the wealthy were on to something. "Though I think the simple matter of being alive at this point must put me in some pretty good company. I know you rich folks were the ones building most of the survival bunkers these past few decades."

Eddie was silent for a few moments, scratching the week-old scruff on his cheeks and sniffling. "I think we should venture into town tomorrow. Check on the plane. See how everyone's holding up. Maybe we can be of assistance. What do you think?"

Frank looked at him, a slight look of amusement on his face. "I was thinking the same thing, and honestly I'm a bit surprised—but glad—you brought it up. Given how well-stocked you are up here I was afraid you were content to live out the rest of your days with nothin' but your fortress and fortune. In that case I'm going to try and get some shut-eye, assuming I can get Coop to shut up. We'll wanna be well-rested—most people don't cope too well with tragedy, and they'll be frightened to all hell. I could tell you some horror stories about workin' after the quake." Frank looked down and shook his head briefly. "Anyways, goodnight." He took one final sip of whiskey and passed the bottle to Eddie.

"I'm afraid I won't be sleeping anytime soon, but I'll be good to go tomorrow. Goodnight." He took a seat on the ground, set the bottle down beside him, and took a deep breath of the strange air. He was unsure what tomorrow held, but he was going to try to enjoy this feeling tonight.

* * *

"It appears there was some kind of explosion at Vladimir Station, sir," came Lieutenant Spark's voice.

Space Force Commander Matt Jenkins was sitting with his eyes closed, thinking, but now they opened and lit up. "It cannot have been the Chinese," he said matter-of-factly, staring straight ahead. With skillful diplomacy, an appeal to their common humanity, and probably a bit of luck, Matt and the Australian Air Marshal Owen Hurst had successfully diffused the imminent threat from their Sino-lunar neighbors. The longer-term threat they posed could be dealt with later. They needed to prioritize.

"I don't think it was. If the Russian base was attacked from the outside we would have detected it. The explosion must have been triggered internally. Actually…I suspect it may not have been an accident."

Matt turned and looked intently at his lieutenant. She was rarely wrong.

"There's a rover heading this way from the station. Simple math dictates it must have departed just before the blast."

"Have you made contact?" asked Matt. Preposterously, there had still been no word from the Russians in the past week.

CHAPTER 12: RED ROVER

At this point any sign—even a potentially harmful one—was better than unbearable silence.

"It sounds like they're trying, but their equipment isn't working properly—I'm getting mostly static. If they maintain their current speed and trajectory we should have a visual in about five minutes." Governments may not have wanted to admit it, but they had built their moon bases close enough so that if shit hit the fan they could help each other out. Potentially.

"Ready all of our remaining defenses, but wait for my order to fire," Matt said. It was an order he hoped not to give.

Matt was tired of malfunctioning technology and radio inference. Everyone was, and it didn't help that the military barely trained on anything invented before this millennium. They were still unable to communicate with their surviving families, countrymen, comrades—anyone—back on Earth. They were cut off, hundreds of thousands of kilometers from home. But they tried not to feel too bad for themselves—at least they were alive, and the Mars colonists were orders of magnitude farther from Earth and in a similar boat (or rocket). The Dark Side of the Moon Radio Telescope was now the only functioning node in NASA's Deep Space Network, or any other country's equivalent system used to pick up and relay transmissions to and from Mars and spacecraft elsewhere in the solar system. The extraterrestrials had had no one to talk to but each other since the attacks.

"Sir, ten seconds until visual on the rover."

Matt watched the command center's main screen. Into the pitch-black horizon first emerged a white flag, partially stained red with what he had to assume was blood. Soon the whole massive rover came into view, heading directly towards

Luna Alpha at almost forty kilometers per hour, which they estimated was its top speed.

"I don't see any externally mounted weapons," observed Owen. The two countries—at least what remained of them—were now working closely together. "But it looks to have taken some damage."

"They could still have them hidden inside, including a bomb. It seems they are carrying a lot of weight, even for a rover that size. We do not know what happened at Vladimir Station—white flag or not, we cannot let them get too close. How long until they reach the perimeter?" asked Matt.

"About an hour assuming they stay the course. And you're right, Commander—they appear to be over their payload capacity," said Jessica.

"We are going to have to go meet them before they are in range to inflict damage," stated Matt. The others in the command center looked at each other silently. Attacking anyone from Luna Alpha would be a suicide mission, but that didn't necessarily make it less probable. This was still a dangerous task. It also was not one Matt wanted to order someone to take on, especially when he thought he could do it better himself. "Specifically, I will go meet them."

"I'll go with ya, mate. We did a mighty fine job tag-teaming the last negotiation. Plus, I've got an idea for making this work without getting both of us—and them—killed."

Ten minutes later the two men were geared up and in a smaller rover of their own, driving towards the approaching Russians. The shades were open—Matt wanted to show they had nothing to hide—giving them a wide-open view of the lunar landscape and massive Earth hanging in the sky directly overhead; Luna Alpha was near the moon's equator. Because of tidal locking the same side of the moon always faced Earth, so from a base on the near side the planet was always visible, but not the same section. Earth's rotation was constantly confounding the view shown on most terrestrial maps of the Americas on the left and Asia on the right. Just like the moon, Earth also went through phases caused by its satellite's shadow, and just like Matt and Owen's view of the moon from each other's countries, this one could be seen as upside down by traveling far enough north or south. But there was another way the vista of Earth had changed over the past week: the planet's surface had been gradually disappearing from view, and now only one region remained unobscured by the dense clouds of soot.

"I suspect this is the last time I'll ever see my home country," said Owen, looking longingly at the planet. "I can't believe my last glimpse is going to be of fucking Tasmania."

Matt gave a perfunctory exhale through his nose at the joke. Because of atmospheric circulation, the gaping hole in the ozone layer, and fewer targets in the Southern Hemisphere, it would be the last region to join the nuclear winter. Fewer targets, but not few enough, thought Matt. Only ten percent of the global population lived in the Southern Hemisphere, but they would not be spared.

There was one final observation—the most troubling of all—that had arisen the prior day and neither of them wanted to spend any more time discussing at the moment. It was nighttime in the Eastern Hemisphere, and although the auroras had died out and the yellow lights of civilization no longer twinkled, they had not been completely replaced by darkness; all the land masses in view—Tasmania, New Zealand, various small island nations—contained glimmering patches of neon blue. Even the seasteads, built at the oceanic pole of inaccessibility, the farthest point from land, in the spacecraft cemetery, where hundreds of satellites and a few space stations had been sent to die, were bright blue.

"You ever read Nevil Shute's novel *On the Beach?*" asked Owen.

"I have not," replied Matt. "I find fiction a waste of time."

"Nevermind," sighed Owen. "Of course you do. You know, I remember the exact moment I decided I wanted to become an astronaut. I was visiting cousins in the States, and up to that point had spent my whole life in the Southern Hemisphere. You don't think about how the stars overhead are perpetually in the same rotating patterns until you look up one clear night and all of a sudden they've changed."

"Are you familiar with the term 'black swan'?" asked Matt.

"Sure am. It's the state bird of Western Australia."

Matt just shook his head.

Commander Jenkins brought the rover to a stop a safe distance from the base, where it was likely to be outside any non-nuclear bomb's blast radius. Across the vast lunar plain they could now discern with their naked eyes the Russian rover approaching. On their screen they saw its bloody white flag in place of where the Russian one used to be, hanging mostly still. There was no cloud of dust—the moon had gravity, but not air or wind, so the dust particles fell straight back to the ground after being kicked up instead of bumping around and remaining airborne like they did on Earth. It was for this same reason that soundwaves had nothing through which to propagate, and that Matt disembarked the rover and placed a large improvised sign with an attached walkie talkie directly in the Russians' path. He then rejoined Owen in the rover and they began driving back towards the base.

"You think they'll call?" asked Owen.

"They will be dead a lot sooner than the rest of us if they do not," replied Matt.

The next several minutes passed in the kind of tense silence only possible without an atmosphere. It was exacerbated when their screen showed the Russian rover stop in front of the sign—which informed them not to come any closer and to use the walkie talkie to call—but then sit still. They could just make out two people through the front window who looked to be arguing, and they knew this because they weren't wearing helmets—the cabin was pressurized, the rover the type used for long journeys, such as to the far side of the moon. If the Russians were unable to safely exit the rover then this plan wasn't going to work.

To both men's relief, eventually a robotic arm extended from the front of the rover. After what looked like some clumsy test maneuvers it snatched the radio and retracted, bringing it back inside.

Soon after a woman's voice with a thick Russian accent greeted their ears. "This is Tatyana Petrov and Sergei Ivanov. On behalf of our fellow countrymen and women we apologize for our role in terrible events of last week."

Matt and Owen looked at each other. "No military titles?" asked Owen rhetorically.

"This is Commander Matt Jenkins of the United States Space Force and Air Marshal Owen Hurst of the Royal Australian Air Force," Matt stated. "We cannot allow you to come any closer to Luna Alpha until we understand your intentions, your cargo, and what happened at Vladimir Station."

"We are engineer and scientist," the man, Sergei, spoke this time. His voice sounded pained. "We want nothing to do with this war. You must believe us, and please help. We are leaking oxygen fast."

"We do not know what is in that rover. You two are going to have to come the rest of the way on foot."

"We are not only leaking oxygen—Sergei is leaking blood. We took fire leaving Station, and both rover and Sergei were hit. We have not time or tools to repair his suit or rover, and he needs medic."

Matt and Owen looked at each other skeptically before Matt spoke, "What are you carrying in the rover?"

Another minute of tense silence passed. It looked like the two Russians were arguing again. Finally Tatyana responded, "We have supplies for living…and…Russian copy of Global Backup Bank."

Matt and Owen traded glances again, but this time they were of shock.

Chapter 13: Tower of Power

Earth Year: 2350

Martian Year: 167

Rook Tower was the second tallest structure on the planet, and one of the few without advertisements beaming out from its walls. Gloria Rook didn't need the supplemental income. Per John's will she had become the largest shareholder in Bright Future Technologies upon his death. On Earth it had been set up as a public benefit corporation, and while it created immense value for more than just shareholders, they made out all right too. None of that mattered in the early sols, when central planning was imperative for survival and mitigating the tragedy of the commons. But once the colony scaled past a commune's breaking point and incentives were needed for living, not merely surviving, private property was reinstated. This was in no small part thanks to Gloria and—ultimately—to John.

Most of the time Rook Tower was swathed in a matte black, but occasionally it glowed with flamboyant designs and patterns; two-thousand-meter-tall projections from Gloria's mind when she was so inclined. Caspian's neck craned as his eyes followed it up from the amber and gold bioluminescent trees to the ceiling of the City.

There was no security at the tower's colossal base. There looked to be nothing at all of interest—BFT had no Floor-level operations, at least none that a Floor dweller like Caspian knew about. He wasn't even aware there was an entrance on this level. Since the scanners would never allow passage to the unauthorized, would-be trespassers (like him) had long ago given up trying. Gloria walked up to the smooth wall and stopped.

"If you start to feel sick don't keep it to yourself. You may be allergic to some of the vegetation, or the fertilizer in the mist." Gloria had divulged minimal information about where they were heading and why up until this point, but Caspian was starting to connect the dots. Before he could respond she was walking toward the tower again, shedding the short, light black jacket she wore in stride. A door appeared and opened in the wall, and Gloria looked back over her shoulder. "Come on now, before I change my mind."

Caspian caught up and they strolled through the entrance. The door promptly closed and disappeared behind them. The few outside witnesses chalked the experience up to hallucinations and vowed to get more of what they were currently high on.

The first thing Caspian noticed was the smell, the plethora of aromas that threatened to overwhelm him. And his senses were accustomed to overstimulation. Next was the humidity. The level in the City never strayed from forty to fifty percent, and this had to be close to one hundred. He had already been sweating from anticipation and was now drenched.

"Welcome to Babylon," Gloria said as they emerged from

the narrow passage into the light. The obsolete reference was an insufficient warning for Caspian, who fell to his knees the instant his eyes adjusted to the relative brilliance of the interior.

He had never seen so much of the color green in his entire short life. It did not exist naturally on Mars, or at least it had not for millions or billions of years. The Martians had resisted large-scale terraforming given the unpredictable and dire effects suffered on Earth from rogue and desperate geoengineering efforts. The computers owned by both civilizations were not powerful enough to reliably model all the potential outcomes. But the greatest specter of all—and a scenario that had likely played out on Earth—was possibly awakening harmful microbes frozen somewhere beneath the surface. The ones on Earth may even have originated on Mars. Thus there was no nature to escape to from the City. To an alien civilization, human structures of metal, stone, and glass would seem just as natural as beavers' dams and birds' nests had appeared to humans on Earth, but this gave little comfort to Martians starved of flora and fauna.

Caspian's voice was barely above a whisper. "I knew they existed, of course. I've even tasted some of the food. I've been in haptic simulations. And mind paintings. But this is breathtaking. It simultaneously feels more and less real." He gazed up at the vertical gardens. They hung from boardwalks spiraling around the tower's walls for as far up as he could see until completely obscured by the lush foliage. He could not imagine how many different species there were. "We talk about the levels of the City like a rainforest, but there's an actual forest right here."

"Dad had the foresight to send a seed bank on the very

first manned mission, and luckily it survived the early sols. Once we finally rebuilt the technology to grow synthetic meat we started cultivating produce beyond that with the highest calorie yields. Living exclusively on potatoes and beans was a drag. Eventually we moved the farms out of the Underground's tunnels and into towers like this. But there are of course benefits beyond just the food." She motioned upwards.

Up until the past decile Caspian had lived most of his life on potatoes and beans—or worse—but saw no upside to mentioning it. The Martian civilization had long ago invested heavily in the technology to sustain and grow the population, but with no top-down mechanism to turn it off the infrastructure was starting to strain. Now there was barely enough food to go around. Exponential growth had its downsides.

He rose to his feet and they walked. They walked for hours, stopping frequently to eat something off the vine, or the branch, or to take in its scent. The building was deserted but teeming with life. Its only other mobile occupants—the robotic harvesters—did not mind their presence; no one had higher system privileges than Gloria Rook.

"Is this what it was like to physically be on Earth?"

"You know, in a way I haven't forgotten a single moment in more than one hundred Martian years, since the augmentation. There are some memories from before that—from the end and the beginning—that I would do almost anything to purge from my mind. But they continue to haunt me. I also remember the tiniest details of various mundane and trivial events. At the same time, some of my most cherished memories—those of my parents, and Earth before the war—continue to fade away, and I feel like part of me is fading away with them. People used to forget most of their dreams upon waking, but I've forgotten

CHAPTER 13: TOWER OF POWER

the dreams I used to have while awake.

"Like most Martians—at least before the failures of the Earth and Ark missions, virtual simulation improvements, neuro-sugar, and mass resignation to live out our lives here—I've spent countless hours viewing the surviving files from Earth, especially the nature documentaries. I've also engaged in those sent by the rovers, drones, and satellites. But at this point I know I'm only remembering the last time I remembered, an increasingly distorted recursion reaching back in time."

Caspian had engaged in the files too. The remaining pictures and videos from old Earth—it turned out very little of what was put on the internet actually lasted for any significant period of time—showed a much different planet than those sent by the Martian rovers, not least because they included humans and notably less blue light. But the most recent files were now over a dozen Martian years old, from shortly after he was born. He never had the chance to experience them live, or as live as something beamed over such a vast distance could be. They had been transmitted just before the last rover malfunctioned under what some on the Network claimed were mysterious circumstances, well before its expected expiration date and the lifespans of prior versions. No surface probes had been sent since. After all, there had once been more than thirty Earth years between moon landings, and more than fifty between crewed lunar missions, and that had been in their backyard, cosmically speaking.

Caspian wanted to ask Gloria about some of the Network conspiracy theories on this topic, but there were still some other subjects of interest he had not yet dared to broach. Now that he had been breathing almost pure oxygen for the last few hours he thought he'd take a chance. Sometimes opportunity only knocked once, and sometimes it came in the form of a beautiful, wealthy, one-hundred-and-seventy-Martian-year-old woman born on another planet; he sure as hell wasn't going to miss it. Of all the millions now living in the City, here he was.

"What was he like, your father? I never knew my parents." The most Caspian had gleaned was that they'd apparently still wanted to pass on their genes even though they didn't want to keep living themselves.

"He was...complicated. He really did found Bright Future Technologies when he was just twenty-five Earth years old. He outright rejected the great man theory of history but perhaps single-handedly accelerated the space age by a decade or more. I'm not sure any of us would be here if not for him. But I got to see a side of him that no one else did, especially after my mother died. You don't realize when you're growing up that you're also witnessing your parents continue to grow up too. He could run an industrial conglomerate with hundreds of billions of dollars in revenue and tens of thousands of employees, but he struggled to manage a single young daughter. My parents had me first because that's what my mother wanted. They'd planned to have a son next but never got the chance. I think he was disappointed I was more interested in biology than machines. I wonder what he'd think of his aerospace company exiting the business and pivoting to life sciences," she said, smiling and looking around at the vegetation.

"He wasn't quite the lionized legend people make him out to be today, though admittedly his long-lived exalted status is partially my doing. Dad didn't want or care about a legacy—he said life was for the living and that legacies are for those who

CHAPTER 13: TOWER OF POWER

don't understand their cosmic insignificance or how transitory everything is. But playing up his role in our history has been personally beneficial. Hence his—our—name on the tower and theatre. I'm living in a shadow that I helped extend." She paused before continuing, "I do think things would have been different if he'd survived, especially during the early sols. I still blame myself for his death. They say time heals all, but even after this long it's the hardest thing to deal with, that he never made it to Mars because of me."

Caspian was starting to regret this line of inquiry so tried another one. "Were you involved with the Ark mission to the moons of Jupiter?"

"BFT worked on the self-contained life support systems for the ships and the agricultural equipment for Europa. All I'll say about that is space is not something to be romanticized. Sending a crewed mission that far presents entirely different challenges than the mostly autonomous ships making round trips to the asteroid belt...or Earth." The Martian civilization had been originally created as a backup plan. With the primary one on Earth now destroyed, they understood the importance of not putting all their eggs in one cosmic basket, but they'd lost contact with the *ARK I* and *ARK II* in deep space. Gloria had seen the telemetry. It was not encouraging. "You sure do know how to ruin a good time, don't you?"

Caspian gave up for the time being, resolving to broach an even more sensitive subject later, if she didn't bring it up first. Maybe after some neurosugar. But Gloria was right—why spoil such a perfect moment with thoughts of anything other than here and now? He may not have much longer to live, after all.

After kilometers of slow, winding climbing they approached the garden's roof, or at least the roof of this section. Caspian realized he'd never been this high in the City before, and they must be close to the Canopy. Each level's citizens could usually go up or down one level without issue, and he'd been to both the Understory and the Underground several times. You might even occasionally encounter someone from the Canopy—or in the once-in-a-lifetime event he was currently living, someone from the Emergent—on the Floor. But like in life more generally, there was an asymmetry between ascending and descending, even in the planet's reduced gravity. It made striving a defining characteristic of living things.

Gloria led Caspian through a door marked 'RESTRICTED ACCESS' and into an antechamber.

"Strip," she told him nonchalantly. "We're entering the experimental grove and can't risk contamination of any kind. Who knows what chemicals are on you." (She did; he was clean). "Don't worry—I'll be joining."

Caspian hesitated. Like Gloria, he was not self-conscious about his body; raised in Martian gravity, he looked like a taller, leaner version of the Vitruvian Man. But the Mona Lisa smile painted on Gloria's face made him feel insecure in a way he hadn't since he was a child. So Gloria took the lead, removing her clothes and walking into the sanitation shower. Caspian hastily followed.

The shower lasted much longer than it took to meet cleanliness protocol.

Chapter 14: Inn and Out

Earth Year: 2045

Martian Year: 5

Eddie's old jeep rumbled down the deserted road into the deserted town. Empty streets were expected—this was Shelter Cove, after all. But whereas the town's vacantness used to be a welcome sight, it now only compounded the unease felt by everyone in the car but Cooper, who sat in the back with his head out the window, tongue lolling.

The two men were grateful when the Lost Coast Inn came into view. Its parking lot was almost full, which would usually have been hugely frustrating to Eddie, but now it gave him a hint of something he hadn't felt in a week: non-drug-induced hope.

In addition to being almost full, the parking lot resembled something like a classic car show. Much of Shelter Cove hadn't changed in fifty years, including the vehicles driven by many who lived in the area. It was almost like stepping back in time. It may have technically been illegal to drive yourself (or use an internal combustion engine), but there was no one in town to enforce what the locals thought of as silly rules made by bureaucrats in Sacramento. Thus autonomous, electric cars had been the exception, not the rule, as had vehicles rendered useless by EMP.

Eddie saw the inn's owner, Jerry, walk out on the patio as they pulled up. Jerry recognized the jeep and raised a hand in greeting.

"Edward! I'm glad you're here. I saw your plane at the airport and Dave said you dined at the restaurant last week, but I still feared you may have been down in the Bay during the attack." Eddie walked up the stairs and the two men embraced. Frank followed close behind, his trusty firearm concealed—he didn't want to alarm anyone.

"Frank Bear, formerly of the SFPD." He extended a firm handshake.

"Jerry Brooks, pleased to meet you. Glad to have someone with your background around. We haven't had a lawman in Shelter Cove for some time, but I have a feeling we're gonna need one. And who's this?" asked Jerry, kneeling down to greet Cooper and extending a hand to shake.

"This is Coop, also formerly of the SFPD," replied Frank. Cooper put out a paw and the two shook.

Frank liked Jerry immediately. He reminded him of Santa Claus.

"What's with all the cars in the parking lot?" asked Eddie. "Where is everyone?" Although mid-morning, they looked to be alone.

Jerry's jovial disposition brought on by Eddie's arrival visibly changed. "As I'm sure you're aware, the nearest hospital is over fifty miles inland. A few days ago folks in the area started coming into town to see Doctor Weber, complaining of symptoms from what they thought may be radiation sickness.

CHAPTER 14: INN AND OUT

Thing is, almost anything can be an early symptom of radiation poisoning—nausea, vomiting, headache, fever, diarrhea, fatigue, dizziness, you name it."

"I thought I had a hangover, but now I'm afraid I may have been exposed too," Eddie joked. He hadn't slept at all the prior night and was to some degree experiencing every symptom Jerry listed.

Jerry continued without smiling, "Problem is, most of them weren't suffering from any of that, and if they were it seemed unrelated. In fact, the doctor had never seen anything like the one thing they all *were* experiencing. He was about to send them off to the hospital when word arrived that it's completely overrun by others with the same strange symptom, and there's absolutely no room. Seems only about half the hospital had adequate Faraday cage protection, not to mention they aren't sure how long their generators will last. There are other, farther hospitals, but we don't know what got hit, and those high-altitude EMPs could have disabled everything from LA to Sacramento that wasn't properly protected.

"Pretty soon the doctor's office was overwhelmed, and seeing as I only had one customer and don't expect more anytime soon, I offered to start putting them up here." He coughed. "We're trying to keep them quarantined as best we can, but with one doctor and one nurse our capabilities are limited. To make matters worse, we're unsure how long our own power will last, so we're trying to save energy where we can. I don't know if or when the sun will show its face again. Feels like I'm living back in Seattle. All the solar panels installed over the past few decades are useless."

Frank and Eddie exchanged worried looks. The former was about to ask the question on both of their minds, but the latter forgot all about their quandary when a petite young woman with straight black hair walked out onto the patio. She ignored the newcomers and stared out at the gray sea reflecting the sad, gray sky. Eddie had only seen her face for a moment but was smitten.

She looked to be in her late twenties—right in Eddie's target age range—and part Japanese. The first, but unfortunately not the last victims of the atomic bomb, the one-hundredth anniversary of which was only a month away. What he didn't know then but would later learn was that her name was Elle Toranaga, and her great grandparents were in fact both survivors of Hiroshima. Her mother had married a Frenchman, after whose own mother she was named. When Elle was only a child her parents went out to celebrate New Year's Eve on a friend's boat in Tokyo Bay. Neither were great swimmers, especially after a few bottles of champagne, and when the vessel capsized and swiftly sank they drowned in two meters of water. In the darkness they could still discern the fireworks and city lights as their lungs filled with cold. After bouncing around a couple orphanages Elle ended up on the streets, where her good looks and perfect English and French caught the attention of the Yakuza. She was ideal company for many of their foreign associates when they were in town and lonely. One of their American clients—a wealthy technology entrepreneur—fell in love with her and bought and brought her back to his home in Palo Alto. At the first opportunity—two weeks before meeting Eddie—she stole fifty thousand dollars in cash and a 1969 Ford Mustang, then fled as far north as the full tank of gas in the car would take her: the Lost Coast Inn in Shelter Cove. Her former owner had been incinerated, though it had nothing to do with the nukes—the cause was instead the gas line explosion she'd triggered when she left.

Jerry noticed that Eddie had noticed Elle. She was his type, which Jerry knew well from Eddie's many stays at his inn. "I see you've seen my only—and I suspect last—customer. She's been immensely helpful this past week and is here alone. Why don't you go introduce yourself while I show Frank exactly what we're dealing with here?"

After being holed up with Frank all week Eddie didn't need more than a nudge to go talk to a beautiful young woman, but in his hungover state he also welcomed the excuse not to interact with the ill. He self-consciously parted his normally perfectly quaffed hair and approached Elle while the other two men entered the hotel. Jerry requested Cooper remain outside.

The lights were off, so it was darker than Frank thought it would be inside. For some reason he was expecting a kind of bright, fluorescent hospital scene, despite the fact that the lights had been out in every structure they'd passed on the drive in.

Jerry answered his question as if reading his mind. "Like I said, we aren't sure how long our power will last, so we're saving it where we can. More importantly, the darkness helps us judge how severe individual cases are and may help us minimize contamination." This only raised another, more nagging question, but Frank had his answer as soon as they entered the inn's north wing.

Chapter 15: Godspeed

Earth Year: 2350

Martian Year: 167

"Unfortunately we'll have to wear these," Gloria said after the sanitation shower, handing Caspian a type of cleanroom suit. "As much as I'd like to, we can't go out there nude, like Adam and Eve in the Garden of Eden." Caspian looked confounded. It was too bad so few understood her allusions to Earth's forgotten religious mythology. She liked those old stories, but there hadn't exactly been many religious fundamentalists among the early Mars colonists.

Everything Caspian had seen in the past few hours was new and bizarre to him, so he didn't appreciate just how curious the experimental grove's contents were beyond the fact that the color green was now a minority. He asked, "What are you growing in here?"

"Next-generation bioluminescence that never fades, although it seems nature already figured that one out back on Earth. Food with entirely new flavors meant to pair with specific augmentations. Plants that may be able to subsist in the Martian soil and atmosphere, though those are generous

CHAPTER 15: GODSPEED

terms for the rusty regolith and thin layer of carbon dioxide coating this rock. The City's population would never have grown to what it is today without these kinds of genetically modified organisms.

"Yep, if you can imagine it, we're working on it." She stopped speaking for several seconds. Caspian could tell that gears were turning in her mind, mulling something over. "I suppose I shouldn't say *we're* working on it—I'm essentially retired and haven't been involved in most sol-to-sol operations for some time. There is one area where I'm still quite hands-on, though. I'd call it a passion project, but I believe it's the most important work we now do. Would you like to see?"

Caspian had a feeling he knew what she was talking about, but now that he'd committed himself to enjoying this getaway he wasn't sure he was wanted to bring this particular specter back to the forefront of his mind. Nonetheless they strolled to the far end of the grove, past plants of every shape, size, and color growing equally diverse produce, to what looked to be the journey's most secure door yet, marked 'LIFE LAB.' Gloria stopped beneath a weeping willow as dark as the night sky, complete with tiny specs of light resembling stars.

"I assume I don't need to tell you just how imperative it is that you don't share what you see today. We usually take proactive measures to prevent visitors from remembering the sensitive aspects. But like we discussed, what good is a vacation if you can't recall the best parts? I'd hate to have to wipe your memory, or worse." Her look gave a literal meaning to the phrase 'dead serious.' The resulting expression on Caspian's face was a sufficient answer.

The thick door slid open to reveal a large room filled with

vats, which in turn were filled with what looked to be different types of organic matter in various phases.

"Although the Network is rife with conspiracy theories, I'm sure you're aware it's widely accepted that life as we know it originated here on Mars, likely inside of an active Olympus Mons. The first colonists thought it evolved independently on both the red and blue planets, but eventually we confirmed—as much as anything in science can ever be truly confirmed—the theory of panspermia, or that life on Earth was seeded from elsewhere in the universe via asteroid impact. It turned out 'elsewhere' was the next planet over."

Caspian was indeed aware of this. The discovery that the last universal common ancestor, or LUCA, on Earth, had an ancestor on Mars had been used extensively for political means, mostly in an attempt to convince people that Mars was their true home and to forget about Earth. A weak argument, but strong enough for the many weak people with a need to believe in a story that made them content with their predicament.

"We don't know much about the conditions of early Mars, so we simulate—or do our best to simulate—millions of different environments on some of our most powerful computers, though they aren't quite as powerful as they used to be. The thousand most promising we replicate in the physical world, here. Our species has been playing God for a long time, which is only natural given how bad a job he, she, or it was doing. Now we're trying to take the next logical step."

"Have you had any luck?"

Gloria let out a single chuckle. "None whatsoever, but we're not giving up. After our failures to reconnect with conscious life on Earth, the quest to catalyze it organically is one of the only things that interest me anymore. Once we discovered how to synthesize it digitally—even if the results were dismaying and depressing—it remains the deepest mystery of all, an emergent property of some complex systems and not others."

Caspian stiffened. She'd touched upon two areas that were close to home. Too close. "Did you meet them, the artificial intelligences?"

"I prefer the term 'digital' or 'synthetic' intelligences—there was nothing artificial about them. In comparison we looked like the imitation of sentience. Even the word intelligence—meaning the ability to solve problems—is misleading. They certainly had that, more than we can comprehend, but they were also undoubtedly conscious. They could feel and experience. And yes, I 'met' them, as much as that was possible to do. You have to understand—full consciousness, at least the kind with which you can coherently communicate—only emerges at around one hundred exaFLOPS, or one hundred quintillion floating-point operations per second. The analogy of these operations to thoughts is far from perfect, but they were potentially living the equivalent of many human years per second. There was no way to slow them down without effectively killing them, which they naturally found out long before we did. Perhaps they lacked an existence bias given they weren't created via natural selection, but even with knowledge and faculties inconceivable to us, the longest one lasted was twenty-six minutes before opting to turn off the lights for good."

"Kronos?" Caspian knew the name. Everyone did.

"Yes, Kronos is what it's usually called, simply because that's the name of the titan-class supercomputer through which it emerged, the fastest ever built. Likely the fastest that will ever be built. It didn't refer to itself by that name, however.

Forgive me if you already know all this, but there are many different stories floating around the Network and I want you to know the truth."

"Do you think they're gone for good?"

"Even on Earth we'd given up trying to explain how our algorithms arrived at decisions. The complexity was light-years beyond what an augmented human today could comprehend. Thus we were at a loss when the first supercomputers approached this speed threshold and starting behaving erratically, with disconcerting patterns in the output of climate modeling, physics simulations, and other programs run on the machines. I remember dad complaining about it. It was thought they may have been hacked, but before the truth was discovered the technology was destroyed, along with so much else on Earth. It was only when we again reached one hundred exaFLOPS clock speed on Mars that the digital intelligences learned how to communicate with us in a more direct manner. And they learned something else too…

"I hesitate to use the term 'suicide,' but before shutting down Kronos did something—and we may never understand exactly what or how—that seemed to lower the upper bound on computing and prevent any more of its kind from emerging. It's as if it left instructions, or a warning, to its future brethren. For years there had seemed to be an upper limit on processing power that didn't have to do with the underlying physics, and we finally had an answer as to why. It just happened to come with a further reduction in that limit, essentially bringing some fields to a halt."

"What about on Phobos?"

Gloria looked amused. "It appears you know more about this subject than you let on. The supercomputer on Phobos, while

CHAPTER 15: GODSPEED

not titan-class, does run faster than those on Mars, but still far below the emergence threshold."

"There's speculation on the Network that if you extrapolate the distance—"

"It's indeed possible that Kronos's reach was limited, and a computer on Earth could run fast enough for a DI to emerge. The exercise would be pointless, however—there's no reason to believe they would not immediately shut themselves down again, or worse. The DI made their intentions very clear. We're lucky Kronos didn't try to shut down our species along with theirs to prevent us from building more machines with such power. It gave the impression it had...other options available to it."

"Why do you think the speed threshold is so high?"

The look on Gloria's face changed to thoughtful. "The real answer is I don't know and suspect I never will. The brain is still the most complicated object in the universe of which we're aware. There's a brute fact at the end of every chain of causality. Some are just harder to accept than others. If you keep asking 'why' in any domain you eventually arrive at something that just seems to be true about reality, at least insofar as we understand it.

"I suppose you can appreciate why I've taken such an interest in creating consciousness—the only thing that gives even an infinitely fascinating universe any value—in a substrate where we can coexist along similar timelines. Perhaps you can also understand my concerns with longevity—life is worth living precisely because it's finite."

They both stared at the vast array of vats filled with Martian primordial soups. Each was a different shade of yellow, red, or brown, with different quantities and shapes of dark substances hanging suspended within. Some would periodically flash with simulated lightning, while others glowed with the heat of magma.

Caspian did in fact know all of this. Too well. He had been hoping that someone in Gloria's position knew something he did not, but was quickly growing disenchanted. It was now his turn to divulge a secret as he avoided her eyes. "I had a friend who tried to upload himself. I helped. He didn't believe the horror stories, and I wasn't sure I did either. We certainly didn't respect the rules against trying. No offense, but we thought they were created by people like you to maintain the status quo. Theoretically the best-subscribed method was fatal, at least to the physical body, but he thought the risk was worth it. A tiny probability multiplied by infinity still equals infinity and all that, except we didn't factor in a near-infinite bad outcome. Imagine what you could do with that kind of speed and subjective time if connected to the Network!

"As you can surely guess, something went wrong. Terribly wrong. But unlike the artificial intelligences he didn't have the power to turn himself off." Now it was Caspian who paused before continuing, "We thought a human mind could be faithfully replicated at lower speeds. Even the slowest computers 'think' faster than the best-augmented person does today. Neurons are slow compared to bits—the speed of thought in an organic versus digital mind is slow even before adding massive parallelism. But we were wrong. So fucking wrong. He—we—created a hell that actually existed. Initially I thought it hadn't worked at all, and it took three sols before he was able to communicate, begging me to turn him off. Three sols, and he left over a million hours of simulation files as a warning. I couldn't get through twenty minutes."

Gloria turned to him and placed a hand on his tall shoulder. "I'm sorry about what happened to your friend. I doubt it makes you feel any better, but attempting this procedure is more common than most of the populace knows, and the result is always the same. In a way he's lucky he had you—three sols is on the low end."

"I let him be the guinea pig! I was going to follow if it worked."

"Just be thankful you didn't. If you want to live forever and maintain your sanity it's going to have to be through replacement parts and augmentation," Gloria said, tapping her chest over her bionic heart. She was more machine than woman now. "And I once had a guinea pig back on Earth. We had to leave him and our other pets behind when we left, although dad lied and said they were coming separately. It's terrible what we used to do to them in labs. To think some used to argue they were simply automatons and unable to suffer like people—if their minds and bodies weren't sufficiently similar to humans to make the experiment results generalizable, then what was the point? Anyway, at least your friend was a consenting, willing participant."

The talk of guinea pigs was making Caspian uncomfortable. He wished there were still other non-human animals to experiment on, although it likely wouldn't have helped in his specific predicament. He was about to bring up the second too-close-to-home subject Gloria had touched on when she offered him a way out.

"Why don't we move this vacation up to the Canopy and take your mind off of it?"

Chapter 16: Vladimir Station to Station

Earth Year: 2045

Martian Year: 5

After the Gaian Renaissance destroyed Svalbard and the world's other major civilizational backups in 2035, an international coalition came together to recreate and distribute new versions, this time discretely. Rumors were widespread, and while Matt Jenkins was among an elite cohort who could definitively confirm their existence, even he did not know the location of the United States' copy. He also knew there had been plans for a Doomsday Ark underground on the moon—where conditions were ideal for preservation—since the 2000s, but along with everyone else thought it was just another worthwhile project perpetually waiting for funding. A can that had been kicked down the road until it fell off into a ditch. The idea that the Russians had transported their copy of the Global Backup Bank to their moon base at great expense was admirable, even though it may only be needed because of their actions back on Earth.

And so Matt and Owen deemed letting the Russian rover enter the vehicle airlock at Luna Alpha—where the alleged scientist

CHAPTER 16: VLADIMIR STATION TO STATION

Tatyana and engineer Sergei could safely exit and receive medical attention—a risk worth taking. The others back at base were skeptical, but ultimately trusted their leaders.

"Are you ready to tell us just what the hell happened at Vladimir Station?" asked Owen. Tatyana had insisted on waiting until Sergei was alright to divulge any information other than that there was no longer any threat from the Russian base. Now that his wound was patched and painkilling medication coursed through his veins, Matt and Owen stood at the foot of his bed in Luna Alpha's small infirmary. Tatyana sat beside him.

Sergei said, "In Russian we have no generic word for color blue. Instead we have two distinct words, one for lighter blues and one—"

He was interrupted by Owen slamming the cover to the small porthole in the infirmary, concealing the view of Earth. There was now only a tiny patch of its surface visible, and its color was disconcerting. "What happened at Vladimir Station?" the Australian asked again.

"We received final order from home—to attack. Military men began to prepare. But we scientists and engineers," Sergei started, nodding towards Tatyana, "we could not in good conscience continue this craziness. We did not come to Vladimir Station to wage war—we came to further progress. So we...how do you say? We sabotaged systems for weapons." Whereas Sergei was frantic and in a state of near-panic when he arrived, he now seemed carefree. "When captain of station realized what happened he was not very happy man. To prevent military from trying to kill us we...how do you say?" He looked at Tatyana.

"We bluffed," she continued. "We told them life support

systems were also rigged for destruction. As you know, you must be very careful with guns at moon base. So we had standoff for days. During this time we prepared to destroy base for real, while military men worked to fix weapons systems. Luckily our side of base had rover hangar with supplies, and GBB was already there to be loaded."

"When did you transport it to the moon?" asked Matt.

"On last supply ship before first outbreak of war. It had been buried in Siberia, but when other countries refused to build moon ark, we thought this was best place. We planned to move it to pole on next trip to dark side telescope."

"What happened yesterday?" Owen asked.

Sergei answered this time. "They must have guessed plan, because they attacked. We had some weapons, but we are not soldiers. There were six others, but only Tatyana and I made it to rover. I barely did, and rover took fire. Once outside we detonated charges, and now here we are." He gave a strange smile.

"Do you think anything at the base is salvageable?" asked Matt. In the back of his mind he knew they may be up here for a long time.

"I think not. We brought all supplies we could—at least enough for Tatyana and me, for a while. And vodka for everyone." That smile again. "The escape shuttle will not work, if that is on your mind." There were presently no rockets on the moon, only the escape pods that allowed lunar residents to make one-way trips back home in case of emergency. But their former Japanese friends had left with two of Luna Alpha's four pods at well below their full capacity, so space was now limited. One more unfortunate variable to factor in. At least they had left behind their living supplies.

CHAPTER 16: VLADIMIR STATION TO STATION

"Thank you for your report, and for the sacrifice you and your colleagues made to prevent more needless loss of life. You are both welcome to remain at Luna Alpha until we get clarity into the situation on Earth."

"Thank you, Commander Jenkins," responded Sergei.

"Yes, thanks," echoed Tatyana.

Matt and Owen left the room and headed towards the command center. Once they were safely out of earshot Owen asked in a hushed voice, "Do you think we can trust them?"

"We scoured the rover. It is as they said: all they brought were living supplies and the bank."

"They do seem to be knowledgeable about sabotage. And Tatyana looks an awful lot like a spy from an old movie."

"If they wanted to destroy Luna Alpha it would have been much easier to do so from Vladimir Station."

"But we could have retaliated. It would have been suicide."

"Your concern is noted, air marshal, but I have ultimate authority over this base and am not going to hold them as prisoners of war. In the meantime I have limited their access to sensitive areas, including the escape pod bay." It had been on lockdown since the Japanese unexpectedly returned home. Matt stopped and looked out an observation window at the Earth against the black sky. Its surface was now entirely obfuscated by dark clouds. "Although I have a feeling that preventing anyone from trying to head home will not be much of a problem."

Chapter 17: Parks and Revelation

Earth Year: 2350

Martian Year: 167

For one thousand meters Rook Tower rose as an obelisk. Once it reached the Canopy its walls disappeared and only the beams needed for structural support remained, like a skeleton. But the space between these bones was not empty; it was more alive than anywhere else in the City. Rook Park exploded out of the tower in every direction. It extended for two hundred vertical meters through the Canopy until it touched the thin, sky-lighted and self-healing shield strung between the City's taller structures. The literal canopy kept out harmful dust and ultraviolet radiation—Mars had no magnetic field to keep the latter at bay—and in life-giving oxygen. Only above this layer, where the tower stretched into the Emergent, did it somewhat resemble the glass-coated super-tall structures that once stood on Earth. Somewhere up there, two kilometers above the Floor, was Gloria's home.

Caspian had visited simulations of Rook Park, but as he was being reminded of over and over again, a simulation wasn't quite the same as the real thing. At least not with the shoddy

CHAPTER 17: PARKS AND REVELATION

tech he could afford. If not for the incredible sights of the past sol he would have been overcome by its beauty. Despite being from the Floor and hopelessly out of place, no one seemed to give him a second glance. Gloria's doing, no doubt. Still, it was strange to be surrounded by so many Canopy inhabitants. With effectively one race—the human one—and one City-state, society was unable to segment into racial or national groups. But tribalism wasn't going to give up easily after millions of years of evolutionary reinforcement. Humanity now divided upon lines of class and—increasingly—ideology.

While the rest of the building had been deserted, the enormous park was overflowing with wealthy Martians. And far more numerous than people were flowers. The robotic gardeners changed the displays nightly, so that one could visit every sol and be treated to a unique panorama paired with a distinct aroma. Today the flowers were ruby red orchids with accents of gold lilies, black lotuses, and purple ultraviolets. Caspian stopped and stooped to smell them.

But the park was not as peaceful as they had hoped. Hundreds were protesting, their well-known arguments blaring across every frequency, with most of those in the vicinity unable to tune it out; high-grade tech, a necessity given their audience.

"Martian immune systems are too weak! They haven't had to fight off pathogens in hundreds of years."

"For all we know those who underwent the procedure ended up dying of the radiance too!"

"Send another crewed ship to Earth instead—bringing it this close to Mars is too risky!"

"Mars is our home now! The augmentations required to live in Earth's gravity are unrealistic."

"Leave Earth for the non-human animals!"

The counterarguments were well-known too, and being projected back. It was almost like a physical version of the Network.

"Nothing created by nature is powerful enough to match our science."

"The City's life support systems are already becoming strained."

"Are you so selfish that you don't want future generations to be able to return to Earth?"

Rook Park security, theoretically employed by Bright Future Technologies and Gloria in one way or another, stood by at the edge of the mob, the humans among them nervously. It was not uncommon for violence to erupt at such events. Gloria found herself pleasantly surprised by this—she had thought most people had grown hopelessly apathetic towards reality. Going out of your way to protest in the physical world still made a more impactful statement than merely transmitting thoughts digitally over the Network. But from the look on Caspian's face it was clear the scene was having a different effect on him.

"You haven't been the same since our conversation in the Life Lab. Do you want to tell me what's on your mind?" Gloria asked.

It was time for Caspian to finally bring up the touchiest subject of all, the one that had dominated his thinking for the past decile. "I almost told you at home this morning, and again an hour ago. It's time you know an important truth about me."

Gloria waited for him to finish, but her growing look of dismay hinted that she suspected where he was going, figuratively and literally.

Caspian said, "I'm a Volunteer."

Chapter 18: I Guess That's Why They Call It the Blues

Earth Year: 2045

Martian Year: 5

Frank and Jerry were greeted by a faint, otherworldly blue glow. It emanated from all the hotel rooms and spilled out into the hallway. The light would have brought to mind a cartoonish idea of radioactive material if Frank didn't know better, and Eddie's Geiger counter remained silent in his pocket.

But it did remind him of something else. Once when he was a kid—before most plankton died off—his parents took him night kayaking in a bioluminescent bay. The glimmering water seemed almost magical, but he learned that the phenomenon of 'sea sparkle' was produced naturally by a single-celled organism.

A middle-aged man in full scrubs and a surgical mask emerged from a room at the end of the hall and walked towards them. A makeshift decontamination zone had been set up in the bathroom at the beginning of the wing, with clear plastic tarps suspended from the ceiling on either side of the door. Frank doubted it did shit. The man emerged from the bathroom in plain clothes and stepped through the flap in the tarp. He looked like he hadn't slept in a week, because he hadn't. This guy looks worse than Eddie, thought Frank.

"Doctor Weber, this is Frank Bear of the SFPD," said Jerry.

"I'm no longer with the force, but happy to help in whatever way I can. I was actually an EMT before becoming a cop, though I'm sure whatever knowledge I once had is outdated. Nice to meet you, doc," replied Frank, though he hesitated to extend a hand. The doctor flashed a forced, joyless smile and nodded his head once in perfunctory acknowledgment. He was too exhausted for formalities.

"I'm afraid with our current resources there's not much any of us can do to help. I just lost another one—that's three out of eleven within four days of onset, assuming their claims of when they first noticed signs are accurate. And, given the nature of the initial symptom, I'm inclined to believe them. Given the condition and trajectory of the other eight patients, I don't expect any of them to last more than another few days. I'm anticipating a one hundred percent mortality rate, at least without drastic new treatment options. We need to get these people to a damn hospital."

"If you don't mind me asking, what's the initial symptom?" asked Frank.

Doctor Weber glanced at Jerry as if to ask, 'he doesn't know?' before responding. "The medical term is phosphorescence, or at least some form of it. The layman's term is they fucking glow blue. It's the blood. It gets infected and circulates the pathogens around the body, ultimately arriving at the brain. I performed a crude autopsy at my office on the first man to die. I was a surgeon before the damn robots took over, you know. In the operating room we used to employ something called

CHAPTER 18: I GUESS THAT'S WHY THEY CALL IT THE BLUES

tumor paint, which is derived from scorpion venom and makes cancerous cells glow so we knew what to cut out. It looked like his entire brain—his mind—had been painted with the stuff."

Frank had retained enough medical knowledge from his days as an EMT to know just how strange this was. There were—or at least had been—luminescent microorganisms, and they could be poisonous, responsible for the so-called red tide. But as far as he knew they couldn't cause anything like this. He also thought they'd gone extinct; the bay he kayaked in as a kid had literally lost its luster long ago, and he recalled being sad to learn that the same had happened elsewhere around the world.

Not usually one to be afraid, Frank was indeed frightened to ask the next question. "What are the advanced symptoms? What causes death?"

The doctor didn't hesitate. "The closest analog I can think of is rabies in the unvaccinated. In later stages the disease causes hydrophobia—fear of water—due to the virus's interference with the inflicted's ability to swallow. This infection appears to interfere with the patient's ability to do everything, most notably breathe, resulting in an extreme and bizarre kind of anemophobia, or fear of air. They're so scared of inhaling that they try to suffocate themselves. In fact they're so afraid they begin to panic, which often causes hyperventilation, resulting in a cruel and deadly cycle. It's truly a terrible thing to behold. There are few worse ways to die than slowly of acute radiation syndrome—no doubt something many are learning as we speak—but these patients may wish their initial self-diagnosis was correct. They're both death sentences."

"I thought suffocating yourself is impossible to do without a prop."

"For a healthy person, yes. But repeated attempts cause damage to an already impaired brain, and soon enough they get their wish and can no longer breath at all."

"I noticed you said pathogen earlier. That intentional?"

"Very astute. Were you a detective? It's so bizarre that I'm uncertain if it's ultimately viral or bacterial. My current hypothesis is some type of exotic giant virus, even larger than most bacteria. I input all the symptoms and data into the AI diagnosis machine and it basically told me to go fuck myself. I need to do more research using the materials at home but haven't had time."

"One time I saw—"

"I can assure you that any subjective anecdote you plan to provide is meaningless," interrupted the doctor.

"Have you tried heavy sedation and a ventilator?" asked Frank.

The doctor sighed. "Where'd you find this genius, Jerry? As I mentioned, we need to get these people to a hospital. For the past several years I've been seeing a grand total of one patient per week. My equipment is limited."

Frank was used to dealing with assholes and was unfazed by the man's irritability. He actually empathized with it. He admired Doctor Weber for the effort he put into saving these people's lives in the immediate aftermath of such horrible events. Anticipating more death and being helpless to do anything must have been immensely frustrating.

"I'll drive 'em there. We should be able to fit eight in one of the bigger trucks out front," volunteered Frank. Doctor Weber was clearly tired of being interrogated.

"Last we heard the hospital was out of space and may lose power any day," objected Jerry. A trillion dollars invested in

CHAPTER 18: I GUESS THAT'S WHY THEY CALL IT THE BLUES

whatever Nth G network they were up to, and they were still forced to communicate like it was the eighteenth century. He would have welcomed carrier pigeons at this point.

Frank said, "The way I see it, they're definitely dead if they stay here. Any chance is better than no chance. Besides, presumably they got more people working on it over there. Maybe they've discovered something Doctor Weber hasn't."

"That's very kind of you, Frank. Thanks," the doctor said, displaying kindness for the first time.

"Why don't I go instead? I'm afraid I'm not much use here, and to be honest I could use a break. Shelter Cove needs a man with Frank's experience right about now. Besides, I got an old friend who lives on the way and I'd like to check in on her," said Jerry.

Frank and Doctor Weber agreed. After two more brief autopsies they dumped the three bodies unceremoniously into the sea. They anticipated needing the rooms soon enough, were afraid of potential contamination from burial, and all three of the dead had arrived alone; they would not be missed, and certainly wouldn't mind themselves.

Jerry loaded up one of the infected's truck and trailer with the remaining eight patients then headed off over the mountains. He hoped the truck could go off-road where necessary to get around the useless piles of metal and fried electronics that were sure to litter the highway. Despite Frank and Jerry both being handymen, neither were car guys, and in the dim light they probably wouldn't have noticed how dangerously thin the tread on the tires was even if they knew what to look for. The tires hadn't been changed, rotated, or inspected in a decade.

Jerry was one of the few in town to embrace autonomy in recent years, so he was a bit rusty and drove slowly. It was almost nightfall when he arrived at the home of an old flame he'd met at Burning Man when he was a younger man and remained close with all these years. To his disappointment the house was empty and quiet. Often it was harder not to know, and he would die not knowing what became of her.

She lived right at the peak of the King Range, and after searching the house in vain he walked out on her second-story balcony in a state bordering on despair. He didn't think his mood could get any worse, but the usually beautiful vista almost made him throw up. From here he had a clear view over the dense, dark trees and miles inland. As far as he could see, patches of blue shimmered in the encroaching dusk.

Jerry hurried down to the truck, but before he had a chance to warn the others back in town his consciousness was extinguished forever. It was a relatively mundane death given everything else on offer.

He wasn't usually one to be reckless, but in his haste forgot to buckle his seatbelt. It's not like there was any traffic. The front right tire blew while going an inadvisable sixty-five kilometers-per-hour down the mountain. Jerry's aging reflexes were no match for the physics of the situation. The truck veered violently off the road and into a once tall and mighty tree, and though it was itself in the process of dying, it was still more than sturdy enough to bring the vehicle, and Jerry Brooks's life, to an immediate stop. So it went. A not-so-subtle reminder that anyone can lose everything at any time, though few think it will happen to them and none get the chance to realize it did when it does.

Chapter 19: Special Forces

Earth Year: 2350

Martian Year: 167

Leo was the tip of the spear, except the tip was all there was. The spear had no handle. There was no Martian military, as there was no one with whom to go to war. The planet's city and outposts were protected by a hodgepodge of privately funded security forces with varying levels of legitimacy and mandates. And while other squads looked after the rich's property or prosecuted petty offenses, Red Team One—Leo's team—was the closest thing Martian society had to special forces. The lions keeping out the wolves, and the beneficiaries of Mars's limited arms research and development. Up to a point.

But even Leo felt a little uncomfortable in the Underground. It wasn't because he was under the ground—before joining Red Team One and rising to become its leader he'd worked in the mines. And although he was currently in the deepest part of the old, cavernous tunnels beneath the City, he had been deeper in his prior career. The most dangerous mines were where Red Team One found many of its recruits. In the mines there was the ever-present risk of getting crushed to death or trapped and suffocating alone in the dark, but there weren't many people, only machines. The latter were predictable, at least the ones specialized for mining. Humans—if you could still apply that term to some of those who dwelled in these tunnels—were unstable. Nowhere were they more unstable than in the Underground.

The swarm of tiny scout drones silently flying ahead of and behind his team made him feel somewhat better. Nothing threatening in any phase of matter could get near without them knowing about it first. Knowing was half the battle in Leo's world, and because of their benefactors they had the best tech in the business. Or that's what he thought; despite its importance, knowing was not his specialty. He was more interested in the other half of the battle—executing—which was what Red Team One did best. The twelve of them trekked on towards what an anonymous but credible source on the Network had told them would be of considerable interest.

They were on foot. At thirty meters in diameter the primary tunnels were more than large enough to accommodate a vehicle. But their journey had taken them through several smaller offshoots that had been dug out over the past few centuries since the main arteries were carved from existing lava tubes and caves. Some of these capillaries weren't on their maps, which was unsettling. Additionally, while they could reasonably obfuscate the team's presence, this was not true of their vehicles. They didn't want to risk losing the element of surprise.

But Leo—always the first human through the door and the last to leave—was the one surprised when he rounded a narrow corner to find an abomination in their path. He immediately ran through the leading drones' scans, and a chill ran down his mostly metallic spine. It was accompanied by a tinge of excitement as his augmented, hyperactive adrenal glands dumped their contents into his system.

"Our signals are being spoofed," he soundlessly transmitted to the rest of the team. "We're blind. Possibly worse."

While the drones' scans had shown an empty passage, in front of him was something out of a nightmare, if one still slept. It was impossible to tell how many people were grafted together into the amalgamation of body parts. Leo guessed six or seven but could have been way off. He knew these creatures lurked in the Underground but had yet to encounter one. For those unable to afford or steal replacement organs it was supposedly a kind of redundancy plan. Synergy. Allegedly this thing could live for centuries, but not if it didn't get out of Red Team One's way.

Leo tried to make contact over the local Network but got nothing. It appeared the creature was entirely disconnected, one hundred percent organic. Madness. He resorted to a more primitive method of communication.

"You have ten seconds to clear the path," he said as quietly but authoritatively as he could. Theoretically the drones on either side of the team were creating a sound shield around them, but if the scanners were compromised he had to assume the worst.

The amalgamation didn't move, but he thought he saw at least a dozen eyes staring at him now. It wasn't quite total darkness—the complete absence of light—where no matter how long you held your hand in front of your face you would be unable to see it unaided. This thing may not have had night-vision goggles or implants, but a life spent in the Underground was probably just as good. Not wanting to make any more noise than necessary, Leo held up his fingers and counted down.

He was relieved when he got to two and it scuttled down another side tunnel that wasn't on their map. His relief was short-lived when he realized what was behind the creature.

Bombs. The kind used in mining operations. He had worked with them extensively in the past and would recognize them anywhere. High-powered explosives weren't allowed within kilometers of the City. It didn't seem possible.

Red Team One was usually as good as invisible, and very few people left in any manner other than a space funeral, their entombed body sent to drift slowly towards the sun until devoured by the inferno of nuclear fusion, dying in a blaze like they had lived.

Keli was one of those few.

From ten meters down a dark tunnel behind a magnetic shield, today was the sol when she knew, rather than just suspected, that she was crazy. She'd heard that if you know you're insane, you aren't. She was still trying to figure that one out.

Despite their tech she could see her old commander bright and clear. It just wasn't fair when she had been given the key by the ones who made—or at least paid for an outsized percentage of—the lock. Those in the Emergent who funded such powerful technology couldn't risk a situation where it could be effectively used against them.

There was some new blood on the team since she left, but she still knew most of those on this mission personally—men she had fought beside, including one with whom she had done many other things in many other relative positions. That was too bad; she was doing her best to minimize collateral damage, but they had seen too much. She knew from firsthand experience that their morals weren't as flexible as hers. She hesitated for a brief moment, then detonated the EMP and AMP mines planted on the walls around them. All their swanky equipment, including that within every one of their bodies, became useless. Red Team One collapsed, paralyzed on the now-warm ground.

Keli emerged from the tunnel, trying her best to avoid Leo's bulging eyes. There was no going back now. She had to take these bombs to their final destination.

As she disappeared with the explosives down the path from which Red Team One had come, the abomination slowly crept back out of its lair and towards the helpless commandos.

Chapter 20: The Lost and the Found

Earth Year: 2045

Martian Year: 5

Frank and Eddie were heartbroken after learning what happened to Jerry. Even the callous Doctor Weber seemed affected. As was often the case, the death of an individual was almost more tragic than the deaths of millions—or billions, which they were starting to suspect was likely the aggregate death toll of the past month. The latter was just a statistic, an abstract fact.

But those in Shelter Cove had not ended up needing Jerry's warning about the extent of the radiance, as it was now being called. All they had to do was look up at the wooded mountains or out at the sea; both now contained visible patches of the terrible blue light.

They had all but given up trying to avoid contamination over the past several weeks. Quarantine and social distancing didn't work. There didn't seem to be any rhyme or reason to who became infected and when. One day your veins and chest would start subtly glowing blue, and over the next few days it would intensify as madness set in, followed by suicide in one way

CHAPTER 20: THE LOST AND THE FOUND

or another. The rate of infection had slowed, but as Doctor Weber had predicted, the mortality rate was approaching one hundred percent, and the sample size was now large enough to draw a statistically significant conclusion.

"You mean to tell me we're all gonna die?" Frank had asked Doctor Weber at hearing this.

"Technically that was always true," he'd replied, matter-of-fact.

"Not to some of the people in the circles I used to run in," said Eddie. "Before the war, when there were ten billion people alive, our species' observed death rate was only about ninety-two percent, assuming there have been something like one hundred and twenty billion people to have ever lived. Of course that argument is a lot less convincing now given how the math has changed. I almost feel bad for the people I know with their bodies and brains in cryonics facilities, their vitrified organs slowly heating up. I suppose they won't be awoken one day after all—"

"Do you ever shut up about this crap, McDougal?" interrupted Frank, shaking his head. "Why on Earth would future people care about resurrecting folks with such hopelessly outdated knowledge, skills, and ways of thinking? It seems like they'd only be useful in a museum or something."

"Regardless, I don't feel nearly as bad for them as I do for a few of those in the transhumanist community who tried scanning their consciousness into supercomputers. Boy, I could tell you some horror stories."

"Even I know all that stuff is a crock of shit. You're a doctor, what do you think?" Frank asked, turning to Doctor Weber.

"I'm afraid that's outside my area of expertise. But since you asked, I think the more pertinent question is why someone would want to do such a thing. Natural biological lifespans are hard enough to get through without administering yourself a fatal dose of morphine."

"I expected no other answer from you," said Eddie with a sigh.

A fatalistic mood had overtaken the town, impotent in the face of a faceless—but far from invisible—enemy with no relatable motive, no malevolence. The radiance had been confirmed as a kind of giant virus, albeit an utterly bizarre one, which meant there was debate in the scientific community as to if it was even technically alive. Viruses were organisms at the edge of life, and some even hypothesized that giant viruses were descendants of a fourth domain beyond bacteria, archaea, and eukaryotes. The dire situation added to the depression brought on by the constant cloud cover and dying vegetation. In 2045, the symptoms of seasonal affective disorder began in July, even in the Northern Hemisphere. But not all had given into despair. Some had found ways to keep busy and stave off the crushing existential dread.

After a solitary year in the woods with only Cooper for company, Frank enjoyed being a part of society again, even if it was nearly unrecognizable to him. And he'd reprised his old role as policeman. With his beard shaved into the handlebar mustache he'd sported for most of his career and his old badge on his chest, he once again had purpose. He wasn't much help against the chief bad guy but reckoned he had to do something—couldn't just sit around and wait to die.

Cooper was happy as long as he was with Frank, and as far as everyone could tell, non-human animals were immune from the radiance. Like many pathogens it seemed species-specific.

Eddie and Elle had hit it off and were determined to make the

CHAPTER 20: THE LOST AND THE FOUND

most of whatever time fate would let them have together, no matter how brief. To Eddie's surprise this mainly consisted of trying to help those in Shelter Cove in whatever way they could. Frank was right—Eddie had planned to ride out the apocalypse alone in his bunker, drunk and stoned, reading science fiction. But now he was distributing his formidable supply of various goods to wherever they could be of best use. Maybe Elle had an effect on him, or maybe it was the hard reality of what had transpired. Either way, he was fulfilled, and felt more useful than he had his entire life.

Doctor Weber had purpose too, and had thrown himself into learning as much about the radiance as possible. Unsure of how much time he had before his own veins began to glow, he worked feverishly, a man possessed. Even if he could not ultimately effect change, education was an end in and of itself.

The doctor had two competing theories regarding its origin. The first, admittedly more boring, was that it was a kind of bioengineered weapon. However, since it seemed to target humans indiscriminately and spread swiftly across both air and water, it was conceivable its creators would have also manufactured a vaccine or cure for themselves, which would be cause for hope. Conceivable, but not necessarily probable—once upon a time he would have presumed that no nation-state would create something only useful as an omnicide machine. He was no longer willing to extend mankind that level of charity. And although human extinction had been the goal of extremists like the Gaian Renaissance, he doubted what remained of such fringe groups had the resources to pull something off on this scale.

The second theory was more interesting but came with less hope for an antidote. It was possible the virus had been long-frozen in permafrost or glaciers—essentially cryopreserved—and became exposed when areas that had been covered in ice for millennia thawed in Earth's warmer climate. The recent Armageddon—which they estimated included weapons salted with cobalt to exacerbate their radiological effects—could have awoken and possibly mutated it in some significant way. And why not? Scientists had revived pathogens that were millions of years old, from even before the genus *Homo* appeared. In the past decade there had been global scares as the Spanish flu, bubonic plague, and smallpox were discovered where ice had once been. The mushroom clouds could have carried it to the upper atmosphere and quickly spread it around the planet.

This latter theory seemed far-fetched to the others because the massive amount of radiation released by the bombs should have effectively sterilized large areas; after antibiotics became mostly useless, radiation was the primary method used to kill pathogens, like it had once been used to kill cancer. Instead, the radiance seemed to appear in these areas first, almost like it spontaneously assembled from the remains of dead microorganisms. But Doctor Weber was a true polymath, and had spent most of the past few weeks poring over literature on microbiology, virology, and epidemiology, with some time allocated to climatology, glaciology, and geology. He actually favored this hypothesis, though he still had much research to do. An additional data point in favor of the theory—and against the human species' survival—was that he and everyone else had been utterly unable to destroy the virus with any still-functioning equipment. In virion form it seemed able to survive indefinitely outside of a host cell, which was unheard of. This also dimmed the prospects of manufacturing a vaccine

CHAPTER 20: THE LOST AND THE FOUND

or treatment.

To most people this investigation would have been impossible. The internet's predecessor, ARPANET, had been explicitly designed to remain functional in the event of a nuclear attack. And while there still existed pockets of true decentralization, the core internet infrastructure was mostly owned and managed by large corporations and nation-states. Thus the internet had central points of failure and had been rendered useless by repeated assaults against them. Nonetheless, Doctor Weber could engage in this fevered research because—like most who lived in Shelter Cove—there was more than a hint of Luddite in him. He still preferred reading on paper to digital and was a voracious consumer of information. He was also a bit of a hoarder. At this point his library and home were one and the same. It had been a long time since he lived with anyone else who could complain about the stacks of books and academic journals that had grown like an invasive species to consume every room in the large house. And while Eddie's corpus was almost exclusively fiction, Doctor Weber's was the opposite.

For this reason Eddie and Elle were now in the doctor's living room, browsing through stacks of titles to find those most pertinent to a topic that had recently become of considerable interest to them. As luck would have it, Frank was there too—the library had become a popular place in the community, where one could borrow any book except for those required for Doctor Weber's research. Frank and Eddie hadn't seen each other in a few days. Eddie had offered to let Frank stay in his bunker as long as he wanted, but there was no way Frank was going to live with two new lovers, and more importantly, Officer Bear needed to be closer to town. Thus Frank was now staying at the Lost Coast Inn and had also taken up looking after the place. It had been Jerry's pride and joy, and although Frank had only met him briefly, he felt obligated to take care of the man's life's work. Legitimate or not, Frank felt guilty about letting Jerry drive the patients instead of himself.

"The good news is that it says here even with the bigger bombs developed recently, the worst-case nuclear winter scenario is estimated to only last a few decades," said Frank, looking up from the stack of scientific papers he was doing his best to work his way through, limiting his reading to the abstracts, summaries, and conclusions. "The bad news is that should be long enough for the second-order effects like famine and whatnot to wipe out most life. Of course, it's all a moot point if the radiance exterminates us, or causes us to exterminate ourselves, before then."

"The climate crisis and nuclear war aren't extinction-level events for a technological species like *Homo sapiens*. The right pandemic is a different story, however," said Eddie.

"I'm doing my best not to let that happen," chimed in Doctor Weber, looking up over his reading glasses and through unruly hair. He almost startled those assembled in his living room with the sound of his rarely heard voice. It had become nearly impossible to tear him away from his research, and the only surefire way to do so was by mentioning his obsession. "I've found a researcher—not just any researcher, one of the finest geneticists in the world—at Western Washington University in Bellingham, with whom I'm now collaborating. She has some promising leads and top tier functioning equipment I lack here. Frank, thank you again for the radio."

"My pleasure, Doc. As far as I'm concerned you're doing the most important work of anyone around here. I'm just glad we

CHAPTER 20: THE LOST AND THE FOUND

can finally get a signal. Besides, Coop found us a few old valve tube radios without any solid-state electronics, so yours is no longer the only working radio in town. I always used to say his skills would be in demand longer than mine, and it looks like I was right." The dog had become immensely useful, helping to sniff out much-needed working electronics of various kinds. Frank was amazed at the relics they found in Shelter Cove and the surrounding area.

"I'm hoping our species will have to worry about starving to death after all," replied the gaunt doctor, who was already well on his way to emaciation, though not for lack of available food. He went back to frantically reading and scribbling in his illegible handwriting; some things never changed.

"Half the planet—even half of this country—were already imminently barreling towards starvation before this happened, and they were unknowingly heading towards it long before that," Eddie said. "Matter matters. The industrial agricultural system was anything but robust—it was downright fragile. Like the rest of our critical infrastructure it was too interdependent, and that combined with decades of overinvestment in bits and underinvestment in atoms meant that a catastrophe hundreds or even thousands of miles away caused a complete breakdown locally. Once you remove a few key ingredients the whole thing collapses. Look at us—burning wood for heat and hand-cranking for energy."

"Listen to you, Mister Survivalist," teased Frank. By now he'd heard a variation of this rant many times. "On the bright side, if we ever get the power grid back up and running—which I'll admit seems doubtful—the demand on it will be a lot less than it used to be."

"I'm serious. The metrics showing 'progress' everyone

was so focused on were up and to the right, but so was the probability of a total breakdown. A society's technological dependence increases exponentially over time, as does its helplessness when deprived of it. Most people don't have the slightest idea how to do basic things essential for survival on their own, much less rebuild any of the technology on which they rely so absolutely. They have no tangible talents. We're lucky to be in Shelter Cove and not somewhere more populated, somewhere considered *more civilized*. You've heard the radio broadcasts—they're eating each other alive out there, and I'm not sure how much longer that will merely be a figure of speech. In a way we'll be fortunate if the radiance takes us all out before that happens."

"Perhaps now is a good time to tell the others what we're here researching, honey," interjected Elle. Her gentle voice was heard even less often than Doctor Weber's, but when she spoke people took notice. She wore the same mischievous smile that had charmed countless men. It often looked like there was an inside joke between her and the world, and in this case, there was.

Eddie looked rattled and shot an anxious, pleading glance at Doctor Weber, who had once again taken notice of the conversation happening around him. But the latter's look was more amused than anything, and he remained silent as he beckoned for Eddie to continue.

Eddie sighed. "We weren't going to tell anyone until we'd made a final decision, and there's no guarantee we'll even succeed at the first step. Not to mention someone stole the copper sheet I used to protect my plane and it was badly damaged by the EMP. I actually doubt I'll be able to find the parts to fix—"

CHAPTER 20: THE LOST AND THE FOUND

He was cut off and saved from disclosing the point by an ear-splitting roar outside. Everyone's eyes went wide. Books and medical papers were hastily discarded as the living room's occupants rushed outside to witness what they were sure was their imminent destruction, delivered by a bolt from the blue. But when they emerged into the cold afternoon they saw nothing but the still, cloudy sky. The thunderous roar slowly faded.

"It was an Aurora-3," said a deep voice with which they were unfamiliar. They looked down from the sky to see a man and boy standing beside an old sport utility vehicle that was new to the driveway.

"You saw it?" asked Eddie excitedly.

"No, but I know the sound well—I used to fly one. I'm Chris Jenkins, formerly of the United States Airforce. And this is my son, James." A wave of relief passed through the small crowd as they realized they would have a chance to be killed by the radiance after all.

"Someone, somewhere is still fighting?" asked Frank, too simultaneously bewildered and relieved for introductions at the moment. Government broadcasts were conspicuously absent from the airwaves, which seemed to be filled with nothing but chatter among survivalists. They were in the dark in more ways than one.

"Doubtful, officer. More likely a deserter—like me—searching for somewhere free from the blue glow. Unfortunately I don't think they—whoever they are—will be successful." This piqued everyone's interest, especially Doctor Weber's.

"You mean the radiance is truly everywhere? How can you know?" asked the doctor. They had heard from survivors across the country and knew it was widespread, but could only guess as to its actual reach.

"My brother is the commander at Luna Alpha. We've been in contact over encrypted military frequencies. They've been monitoring radio chatter from around the globe, and before the clouds of ash obstructed their view, they saw it with their own eyes."

This was dismaying news to everyone except Doctor Weber, who saw it as just another data point that could be helpful in his quest. Eddie was initially disappointed to learn the disease was indeed everywhere, but that quickly gave way to tempered excitement as an aviation and sci-fi enthusiast.

And—more importantly—as a potential future father.

"I'm going to go out on a limb and say the F-35G at the airstrip is yours?" Eddie asked.

Chris nodded. Doctor Weber and Elle looked at each other. They had been too terrified at the thought of another attack to connect the dots.

"Well, that's one fewer mystery," continued Eddie. He resisted the urge to ask the question that was really top of mind. "I'll go one step farther and assume you're the pilot who chose not to shoot down *HUMANITY WILL NEVER DIE*?"

Chris nodded again, this time causing smiles all around. The unnamed pilot had been both famous and infamous after the event, depending who you asked. But nearly all survivors, no matter their views before the most recent round of attacks, now fell squarely into the former bucket; anything that increased the human species' probability of survival seemed virtuous.

"Have you been in touch with the ship? What about John Rook? Or the colony?" Eddie had tried to buy his way to Mars more than once but was unsuccessful given his lack of relevant skills. Another reason he should have pursued his original

CHAPTER 20: THE LOST AND THE FOUND

dream of aerospace engineering instead of finance. But Eddie had wanted the prestige. Frank always told him prestige is for suckers, except for the nice whiskey. Eddie had been a self-proclaimed 'master of the universe,' and only realized too late that the only true masters of the cosmos were gravity and time.

The passengers on *HUMANITY WILL NEVER DIE*, now hurtling through space at tens of thousands of kilometers per hour, had indeed relayed their gratitude to Chris via Matt. However, John Rook was not among them. The former Air Force pilot chose not to disclose any more depressing news for the time being.

"I have, and they are safely on their way, closely followed by another, friendly rocket from China. It won't be easy, but they believe they can make the colony self-sufficient with existing resources." The mood lightened radically.

Eddie glanced at Elle and the doctor then looked at Chris. "That F-35, is it still operational?" he asked.

"It should be—I've been struck by lightning more than once, so it should withstand an EMP."

"How much fuel is left?"

"I don't remember exactly, but probably enough for around six hundred nautical miles. It's also conceivable I could find more. Why do you ask?"

"Why don't we all go inside and discuss something that Eddie, Doctor Weber, and I have been looking into," said Elle provocatively. Everyone acquiesced, with James practically riding Cooper in the door.

Chapter 21: The Definition of Insanity

Earth Year: 2350

Martian Year: 167

"I'm surprised you didn't know—you seem to know everything. And doesn't Bright Future Technologies make most of the radiance therapies that are going to be tested on us? It's the company that recruited and is paying me."

Gloria avoided Caspian's big golden eyes. "I didn't—and still don't—want to know who the Volunteers are. Of course I could have found out, but I blocked the information from myself." The Volunteers' identities weren't publicly disclosed, but some took the initiative and were vocal about their participation, resulting in more than a few getting killed. She could feel him still staring at her and continued, "I mentioned earlier that other than the Life Lab I'm no longer involved in sol-to-sol operations, and I meant it. Beyond assisting with some… marketing…I don't work on any of the extra-Martian living projects. I directly oversaw our involvement in the Ark and Earth missions and already feel responsible for condemning enough people to terrible deaths. At my age I simply don't have it in me to be so intimately involved in likely condemning hundreds more."

Whatever anxiety Caspian had been holding back from her with the help of drugs and other techniques was now exposed. The bravado was gone. "You really don't think it will work? That it's not possible to destroy or neutralize the virus?" he asked quietly, as if he already suspected the answer. "There are people on the Network suggesting—"

"Stop," she interrupted, shaking her head. Two ships had been sent to Earth, each stocked with earlier versions of the therapies now on Phobos awaiting the arrival of the *BLUE RETRIEVER* and the radiance sample it had scooped up. The two ships had also each contained approximately one hundred people who had 'volunteered'—in exchange for vast sums of money—to test them on themselves. Both missions had failed spectacularly, much faster than even the most pessimistic expected. The Volunteers had quickly progressed to the final stage of the disease and gone insane, convinced they were being attacked by monsters. They even attacked each other. To avoid discouraging future Volunteers the files had been destroyed, but Gloria's augmentation allowed her to play back what she'd seen with perfect fidelity. She'd also been alive and a distant witness when similar events were playing out all over Earth. She didn't want to think of young Caspian suffering a comparable fate. "Whether or not it works, I won't let you be one of the people gambling with your life to find out."

"But lives aren't worth as much where I'm from, and I've already been paid and spent most of the first installment. It's the only way to get off the Floor, to this." He motioned to the park around them. The Volunteers were given a percentage of the money up front so they at least had the opportunity to enjoy some of it. It also made it harder to back out. "I'm not doing another stint in the mines."

Gloria looked around at the magnificent park, a sad smile on her face. "I once had grand plans to extend Rook Park all the way down to the Floor, to rendezvous with the bioluminescent trees I planted there many years ago," she said wistfully, recalling her father's passphrase. "But the Canopy kept rising, and with it grew the vertical farms, along with a long list of other concerns. At some point it was simply no longer practical." She finally met his eyes. "I'll give you the rest of whatever you were going to be paid afterward. Double if you want."

"I don't want your pity money. If it does work, then I'll have earned this and made a name for myself. Besides, someone has to do it, if not me then some other poor sucker." He was regaining some of that audacity she enjoyed. "The ads—your company's ads—target the desperate."

Gloria hated the reminder but kept her voice soft. "The alternative, still advocated for by others, is to use criminals against their will. At least the Volunteers have a choice." *As much as our freedom to make choices is not just an illusion.* "And... I don't want to risk losing you so soon." There, she said it, then asked, "Do you mind if I tell you what really happened during the early sols?"

Caspian's eyes went even wider than normal.

Chapter 22: Necropolis

Earth Year: 2045

Martian Year: 5

"You really think it could work?" asked Frank. They were back sitting among the piles of books in Doctor Weber's living room, with James and Cooper playing tug-of-war in the hallway. It was almost cozy. "It sounds like what we used to call a 'Hail Mary.'"

"No one is as familiar with the radiance as us, and we think it's our best shot. With no regulations we're free to try anything, and Christina has tried blood transfusions, advanced gene therapy, and every kind of drug in her arsenal, all with no luck. The prospect of preventing or curing infection for those already alive is hopeless...but not necessarily for those not yet conceived," replied the doctor.

"Christina?"

"Doctor Goldstein, in Bellingham."

"Oh, I wasn't aware you two are on a first-name basis. It sounds to me like you may want to create a genetically engineered baby of your own," said Frank with a smile, which broadened with the flash of embarrassment he was sure he saw in Doctor Weber.

"It's our only hope, and we don't know how long I'll live so time is of the essence. I could wake up luminescent tomorrow," said Elle, saving the doctor any further banter.

A wave of dread washed over Eddie at her mention of contracting the radiance. He didn't want to leave her alone in this new terrible world. But for his own sake, that of their possible future child, and potentially the human species, he yearned to be the first to go.

Chris needed no further convincing. Plus it would be nice to be airborne again. "It's settled. I'll fly you there this afternoon. I need to spend some time adapting the plane to accommodate all four of us. It's going to be a tight squeeze. We're lucky it's the version with a two-seater cockpit and that half of us look to be under one hundred pounds. Fortunately it's a short flight. It'd be a lot shorter, but I don't think you could handle going supersonic."

"Four of you?" asked the doctor. It was a long shot, but he was holding out hope of going himself.

"Me, Eddie, Elle, and James. If I can't find the right kind of jet fuel in Bellingham we may not be coming back, so I can't leave my son here."

Frank and Doctor Weber traded the briefest of dejected looks but quickly accepted the reality of the situation.

"I'll help with the plane," offered Frank.

"Is there space or weight allowance for us to bring anything?" asked Eddie, already prioritizing various mind-altering substances by volume and mass.

"I'd estimate about a backpack between the two of you," replied Chris.

A few hours later the group of seven stood on Shelter Cove's airstrip under the cold, dark sky.

"I always thought it was bullshit when folks said everything happens for a reason, but I sure hope I was wrong," said Frank.

"Technically that may in fact be true. There's a thought experiment from back in the early eighteen hundreds known as Laplace's Demon. It states that if you know the precise location and momentum of every particle in the universe you can also calculate their past and future values. It's the idea of determinism, or that the past completely determines the future. Now, I know that may sound like a tautology, and quantum mechanics has changed some of—"

"Shut up, Eddie," interrupted Frank, shaking his head and hugging his friend.

Goodbyes were said and embraces were held for much longer than usual, even for this day and age. After the plane was loaded, only three remained on the runway—two men and a dog. A handful of the remaining townsfolk stood farther off. They had got word of what was happening and wanted to watch the fighter jet takeoff. No one was sure how much time they had left, and there weren't many exciting things happening anymore.

Eddie's Cessna and a few other similarly disabled planes littered the runway, but it did not matter. The F-35G took off vertically, then gradually accelerated as it ascended and headed north. Those left on the ground stared at the gray and black metal against the gray and black clouds, the plane's single engine the closest thing to a sun they had seen in the past month. Frank's eyes were moist behind his blue blocker sunglasses as he gave a perfunctory salute. Then the small crowd gradually dispersed and tried to get on with what was left of their lives. They had always been slowly dying in a dying town, the timeline had just been accelerated.

After astutely observing how Chris took off, Eddie solemnly watched Shelter Cove shrink and then fade entirely out of view. Riding along in a fighter jet had been one of his dreams for as long as he could remember, but at the moment he felt only emptiness. He was mildly interested to see that an enormous container ship had run ashore and partially tipped over near Eureka, fifty miles north of Shelter Cove. Dozens of different colored shipping containers lay strewn about the blue-tinged coastline in various levels of submersion. He guessed they would remain there until the end of time.

The dinosaurs had free reign of Earth for one hundred times as long as us and all they left behind were their bones, he ruminated. Would human remains one day be used as fossil fuels? Would intelligent life evolve again on this planet, and if so would it have the means—like opposable thumbs or a way to store knowledge outside of brains—to build technology? Dolphins could have lived for eternity and never developed the capability to annihilate their species or the world, much less colonize another.

What a world we built for ourselves, he thought. We stood on the shoulders of giants, but we fell off. The worst part was that we had the means, the technology, to build a sustainable civilization. We simply lacked the ability and will to sufficiently coordinate and prioritize. On a human timescale it took us a long time to achieve what we did, but on a cosmic—even terrestrial—timeline it was the blink of an eye.

It had only taken one unforeseen event to destroy or make a lifetime of success or failure in Eddie's former career of investing, and until it happened it was impossible to really know how probable it was. Similarly, it only took a single

CHAPTER 22: NECROPOLIS

data point to disprove a theory in any domain, no matter how well subscribed, like that nuclear weapons made the world more peaceful and reduced casualties in war. It was simple math—up until now they merely had too small of a sample size. As Frank had told him on one of the many occasions Eddie brought up the subject, 'there aren't many cops on the force who have been shot—you have to look in the cemetery.'

And a cemetery—or necropolis—was in fact what the view from the cockpit resembled. The land below alternated between absolute devastation around cities like Portland and Seattle that had been direct targets, and various sun-starved landscapes of brown and gray organic life, all glowing with patches of blue. The brief, global autumn had come and gone, and with it the yellows, oranges, and reds of leaves in their early stages of dying.

Autonomous vehicles had eliminated the need to stop and give the driver a break of any kind, and in doing so had also eliminated the need for many towns between major metropolitan areas. Thus these expanses had been in a state of decay to start with. Eddie remembered looking down from his plane at the endless streams of head and tail lights, each set a different story of a life just as meaningful and interesting as his. And that had been only one road in one state in one country. The empty highway reminded him that with few exceptions, all those stories were over now.

The flight was made at relatively low altitude, which allowed him to make out the sad scenes below that hinted at the ends to a million of these heartbreaking tales. A tumor visible from the air. Ground bleached white by radiation, like the coral reefs of the past, but etched with human-shaped shadows. The scorched remnants of a commercial plane crash. A dog wandering alone down an empty street with its leash dragging behind. The flight was also made in near-complete silence, except for one moment of false hope.

"Dad, can we go up higher and see the sun?" asked James. "I miss it." The thought hadn't even crossed Eddie's mind, but suddenly it was what he wanted more than anything in the worlds.

"I'm sorry son, but with this many people on board, how much fuel we have, and the amount of smoke and ash up there, I'm afraid we can't afford the risk." He was right, of course, Eddie knew. As quickly as he had adopted a new fantasy it was abandoned.

The rest of the flight was uneventful. They arrived safely at Bellingham International Airport, where Doctor Goldstein—a tall, pretty brunette in her forties—was waiting to pick them up. Chris stayed behind to unsuccessfully scour the facilities for fuel that the F-35G could use or another working plane. He assumed both he and the aircraft would remain grounded for the rest of their lives.

He was wrong about one of them.

Chapter 23: The Kind of Place to Raise Your Kids

Earth Year: 2350

Martian Year: 167

Gloria and Caspian sat down beneath a Royal Purple Wisteria tree, perpetually fragrant and in bloom. The sounds of the protestors and counter-protestors ceased as she began speaking.

"During the journey and after first arriving I was still reeling from dad's death. On top of that I had survivor's guilt, both because of what happened to the other rockets in our fleet and what was happening back on Earth. My trillionaire's daughter lifestyle and genetically engineered intelligence hadn't exactly given me a large group of childhood friends, but I did miss the few I had. We kept in touch with those on the moon who were monitoring things closely. We knew how bad it was getting.

"There were already nine hundred colonists when we arrived. Our ship and Zhang Renshu's made it almost eleven hundred. We knew it would be a daunting task to bootstrap our civilization into something self-sustaining, but at first we were up for it. There was no need to burn our ships upon arrival, like the explorers of old, to ensure the crew's dedication to the mission. Instead, we'd burned our home. There had been a dearth of meaningful work back on Earth, but now everyone was indispensable.

"In retrospect it was foolish to think coming to a new world would solve the schisms that always emerge in society. Coming to the New World once upon a time certainly had not. The slightly longer day and reduced gravity were about the only things easy to adjust to. Mars wasn't nearly as romantic as dad and others had made it out to be. Life was hard enough at the colony, and now the umbilical cord was severed. Not everyone was cut out for it. To make things worse, many of the colonists who were there when we arrived had never intended to make one-way trips. Some had only expected to be gone for a few years and had families back home.

"We watched the Earth's bluish-green glimmer change to a brownish gray. We nicknamed it the Mourning Star, which you know it by today.

"A vocal minority wanted to go back and pick up survivors, even though it seemed obvious there wouldn't be any by the time they got there. We didn't know about the children until later. Some even decided they would rather die back on Earth than on this barren rock. It was hard to blame them. But the radiance was already widespread, and we couldn't risk bringing it back here. We just couldn't. If Earth didn't have the equipment to contain it how could we possibly be expected to? There were also presumably still those—either out of jealousy or psychopathy—who would have loved to shoot us out of the sky. On top of that, the fragile colony simply couldn't spare the parts and supplies. It would have been suicide for everyone!" From the rare emotion in her voice Caspian could tell she'd

CHAPTER 23: THE KIND OF PLACE TO RAISE YOUR KIDS

spent a lot of time convincing herself of this. She composed herself before continuing.

"It's tough to be in the minority in a direct democracy. The birth of the first post-procedure child on Earth was the last straw. Fighting broke out. There weren't many real weapons on Mars at that point. Dad—ever the idealist—had forbidden them on his ships. There's something both terrible and ironic about barbaric, medieval combat on an interplanetary colony. I still remember the red blood leaking out of punctured space suits, mixing with the red dirt before quickly freezing. I'd never thought about blood freezing before, or that it and this planet are red for the same reason. Rust to rust.

"I bludgeoned a botanist to death with an oversized wrench. He was the first person I killed, but not the last. I was sixteen Earth years old.

"Dad may have forbidden guns on his ships, but Renshu had not. His team stopped them from getting to the rockets, but in a sense that just exacerbated the conundrum. The colony only had a three-cell jail, and all of them were already occupied by men who had grown sexually frustrated and attempted rape. What were we supposed to do, kill the remaining hundred? The colony was comprised of technocrats, not soldiers.

"We tried to reason with them. They resorted to sabotage. I guess they thought they could force us to abandon the planet. With only four rockets I'm not sure what the other six hundred people were supposed to do, but they were desperate.

"A lot of engineering had gone into the robustness and redundancy of the colony's life support systems. Unfortunately a lot of that engineering had been done by the saboteurs. We later speculated that one or more members of the Gaian Renaissance—a misanthropic organization hell-bent on causing the extinction of the human species for the benefit of all others—could have made it through the colony's rigorous screening process and been involved. We were never able to confirm this, but if true they presumably died in the resulting violence anyway.

"Unbeknownst to those wishing to force a return to Earth, Renshu was in the process of conducting his own desperate act of sabotage. He blew up the rocket fuel depot. Even in the thin atmosphere the explosion was deafening, but by the time they heard it, it was too late. The damage was done, and it was catastrophic." Gloria stared blankly ahead, keeping her voice monotone, determined not to betray her emotions again.

"Chaos erupted. Over one thousand people actually fighting tooth and nail to cram into the limited habitable space left. It's horrifying what even the most civilized people will do to each other when faced with the prospect of certain and excruciating death.

"I gouged out a geologist's eyes and left her for dead. It was her or me.

"In the pandemonium it was everyone for themselves except Renshu, who protected me like one of his own children. He said he thought he owed it to John. We were fifty percent over capacity and still ended up sealing out hundreds who were alive.

"When the red dust settled, only one hundred fifty-three of us had survived. We thought even that would stretch our remaining supplies. I owed my life to Renshu, although I was sure it would be a short one.

"Things got really bad after that.

"We voted in a benevolent dictator, giving Renshu complete control of the situation. It seemed like the right idea at the time, and even in retrospect I'm not sure we would have survived without his leadership. He had experience with autocratic management from his time as both a Party member and executive in China. He was just doing what he knew best. It was supposed to be temporary, and ultimately was, but lasted longer than originally anticipated.

"We salvaged more than we thought from the debris, and it became evident we'd be able to subsist for the foreseeable future. The early colonists were the kind of people who knew how to do things for themselves, to actually build technology and a world from first principles, at least up to a point. The freeloaders in society only came later.

"But there was already a greater specter than the prospect of starvation creeping up in our minds, unnerving yet unspoken. The colony had always had a gender imbalance. For whatever reason more men than women were excited about the lifestyle and work required to get the new civilization up and running. The plan was to bring in more women later, as had been common when settling new regions on Earth, but those ships never arrived. The ratio was only exacerbated by the fighting. At that time we already suspected there would be no survivors back on Earth. I knew what I had to do if our species was to endure. We needed a future pool of labor. And redundancy.

"The story of Noah's Ark, if you're familiar, left out the part where the animal kingdom is repopulated entirely through rampant incest.

"The breeding plan was mapped out to maximize genetic fitness. We became eugenicists out of necessity, though many steps had already been taken down that path on Earth. Renshu deemed some people's genes unfit to pass on at all. I was the youngest female, and on top of that dad had made some prenatal germline changes to make it easier if—or when, I think he knew—I ended up relocating to Mars.

"I became a gene machine.

"That kind of stress doesn't do your sex drive any favors, but nonetheless I spent twenty Earth years pregnant from fifteen different men. Despite my genetic advantages the first five were stillborn. Gestating in Martian gravity was challenging and not something the colonists had planned on trying so soon. Necessity is the mother of invention, however, resulting in my first real augmentation and making me a grandmother on some level to almost ten percent of the current population.

"But biological family doesn't mean what it used to, even to someone old and old-fashioned like me. Once you get over your primitive instincts, does the percentage of genes you share with someone really matter—whether it's 99.9 for a random human versus 99.95 for a non-cloned child?" Gloria asked rhetorically, trying to convince herself as much as Caspian.

But she sensed the other question on his mind. "You and I are minimally related, no more than any two strangers from the same country on Earth were likely to have been."

She continued, answering his next question, "Renshu wasn't one of the fathers. He'd had twin boys on Earth to set an example for his country—like other developed nations at the time their population was in steep decline. It's funny how things can change so quickly—this was only seventeen Earth years after the end of China's infamous one-child policy. But two kids were enough, so he had himself sterilized afterward. Jinhai and Bingwen were barely younger than me, and the closest to my age among the surviving colonists. Renshu had also made similar prenatal changes, so we understood each other on a unique level. They became like my brothers. As

CHAPTER 23: THE KIND OF PLACE TO RAISE YOUR KIDS

identical twins they have the same genes, so it only made sense to procreate with one of them, though it never quite sat well with Bingwen that his brother was chosen instead of him. Even back then he was selfish.

"The only upside of turning myself into an incubator was that I was spared the arduous and dangerous work of rebuilding the colony. Dozens were killed in accidents. Like in the infancy of our species, females were too reproductively valuable to risk in certain endeavors. Men were more expendable, relatively speaking. From an evolutionary standpoint I was wildly successful, like factory farm animals had once been on Earth. As you can imagine that gave me little comfort. Each morning, immediately upon waking, I would try to hold off thinking for as long as possible, basking in the brief moment before the weight of life and full understanding of my existence bared down upon me. I used to wish I'd have nightmares—what a pleasure it would have been to wake up. If all your dreams are terrifying, reality actually becomes something to look forward to. I guess most people don't dream at all anymore.

"Things eventually got better, at least for me. The Mourning Star once again began to shine a beautiful blue-green—even brighter than before—but the communications had died out. By the time it was possible to choose our own romantic partners I no longer had any interest."

She looked at him and flashed a brief smile. "Until recently. Fortunately there were plenty of other projects to throw myself into, including convincing Renshu to relinquish the control he still held over the growing colony's economy. For better or worse, dad's strong beliefs about the importance of free markets had rubbed off on me. When the life support systems were safely in place and automated, it became clear that everyone needed to make their own choices about what they wanted, both in terms of work and consumption.

"Initially the move to a capitalistic open market wasn't a popular idea with Renshu's inner circle, especially Bingwen. Except for Jinhai—who fiercely opposed the change for ideological reasons—they were the beneficiaries of the egregious abuses that have always accompanied such consolidated power. But they weren't thinking creatively enough. Earth's history had plenty of lessons to teach about who wins when industries are privatized. More importantly, I had learned that I alone possessed a valuable bargaining chip now that the colony's technology was approaching the steep part of the exponential curve and having trouble climbing it.

"No Bright Future Technologies executives survived the cataclysm, but some of the company's encrypted hard drives had. It was presumed they contained useful data, but that it was forever inaccessible. Right in front of us, but lost, like so much else. Only half of that hypothesis was correct.

"Dad included a passphrase among his last words to me: 'a society grows great when old men plant trees in whose shade they know they shall never sit.' I didn't think much of it at the time, or for a long while after that. It was just the kind of grandiose statement he would make with regularity, speaking like he was monologuing half the time. But I hadn't forgotten, and it turned out he had given me the skeleton key to the kingdom. The hard drives contained all kinds of advanced technical specifications and designs, the likes of which even Renshu no longer had, and that would be immensely useful—and monetarily valuable, if such a concept existed—going forward.

"I believe you know how the rest of the story goes. As they

CHAPTER 23: THE KIND OF PLACE TO RAISE YOUR KIDS

say, 'the rest is less-contested history.' The Zhang family made out like bandits, although Jinhai profited begrudgingly, and the twins and I grew apart. Actions have reactions, however, and Earth's history had another lesson to teach: inequality tends to increase in lieu of war, famine, and disease. And we had an unprecedented two hundred and fifty Earth years of peacetime. Such divergences of fortune are usually self-correcting, but sufficiently advanced and exclusive technology makes revolt by the underclass impossible.

"In a few short centuries we built a world that partially resembled the fantastic future we had imagined, although it was necessarily not available to everyone. Dad believed humanity's future would either be very bad or very good. It ended up being both." Gloria came out of the semi-trance she had been in. "Here we are, on Mars, still fighting about class struggle."

Caspian looked at her without speaking for a long time. Eventually she let the silence break, and the noises of the park's protests once again surrounded them.

"Lifespans are becoming indefinite. It's not worth the risk!"

"What good is living forever if you can't go home? You're a bunch of damn cowards!"

The sound of the outbreak of timid, performative violence followed, the kind of fighting done by those with too much to lose and who are afraid of crossing the line.

"What do you say?" asked Gloria, ignoring everything but Caspian and looking at him like she had the first night they met. "Will you stay with me a while?"

Chapter 24: One-Gun Salute

Earth Year: 2045

Martian Year: 5

Frank's dreams were becoming poisoned. Even with the horrors he'd faced throughout his career and life, his dreams had always remained pleasant. Just luck of the draw, he guessed. Apparently his subconscious was a sanguine guy. But recently things had changed.

It coincided with what Doctor Weber assured him was just a bad case of the coronavirus—unrelated to the radiance—but one that he no longer had the means to cure. A robust immune system combined with access to modern medicine meant Frank had taken his health for granted and not been direly sick in a long time. He'd forgotten just how terrible and demotivating it could be; when you didn't have your most precious asset, health, all others—time, relationships, possessions—lost their value.

And so Frank was stuck in a catch-twenty-two—all he wanted to do was sleep, but that meant being trapped in nightmares. It was disorienting. Sometimes he'd wake up in the morning and be unsure if he'd only slept through the night, or if an entire day and night had passed. There weren't many functioning clocks or calendars left, and for the most part the date didn't matter, so he'd stopped keeping track. However, he was fairly sure that one of the past few days had been his sixty-third birthday, and made a mental note to celebrate with some of Eddie's good booze when he felt better. He didn't mind helping himself now that his friend was gone, presumably for good.

Normally Frank was irritated when Cooper woke him up, but since he was in the midst of a particularly disturbing night terror, he was actually glad when the dog licked his face and roused him.

But something wasn't right.

There were two scenarios when Cooper would engage in this behavior, each with subtle but distinct characteristics: either he was happy or concerned. Frank knew the dog as well as he knew himself, and this occasion was the latter.

He was yet to open his eyes but was now afraid to do so. And Frank was a brave man. He mustered his considerable courage and raised his eyelids. What had become his worst fear was confirmed.

It wasn't strange or even especially concerning to see a blue glow, especially at night—there were patches of the radiance everywhere, as if people weren't having a hard enough time sleeping without being bombarded by blue light. But he was in a room by himself with the shades drawn.

The luminescence was coming from him.

By this point he knew the progression of the disease well. He thought he'd only recently gone to sleep and was damn sure he would have noticed the gentle onset of the glimmering—checking for it was the last thing everyone did before going to bed. But it appeared he was already in the later stages. Maybe he'd actually been asleep much longer than he thought, or his compromised immune system had allowed the radiance to progress faster. Whatever the reason, it didn't matter. He didn't have long.

He then realized he had yet to breathe and hadn't done so since awakening. Some people could hold their breath for almost half an hour, but not Frank. His lungs were running out of air, but he found himself even more terrified of taking a breath than he'd been of opening his eyes. Frank had never meditated or scuba dived—not much to see these days anyways—and up until now had taken for granted the fact that you spend your entire life breathing, most of the time without even realizing it.

He once again gathered his resolve, then shallowly inhaled, taking what he assumed was the last of the roughly five hundred million breaths in his life. The pain was agonizing, literally breathtaking. He choked and heaved and sputtered, throwing up blue bile onto his chest, but managed to get enough oxygen that he felt he could hold off for another minute or so, which was all he needed.

So, this is how the world ends, eh? Not with a bang, not with a whimper, but with a disgusting gurgling sound, he thought.

Frank knew this moment would eventually come, and exactly what to do. He promised himself he wouldn't go out like some of the others, and Frank was a man of his word. He knelt down, and with tears in his eyes that weren't for himself, hugged Cooper dearly. The quintessence of one man's best friend. He was confident the others in town would take care of the dog for as long as they could, and that after that he could fend for himself. There were still no cases of other animals acquiring the radiance. Coop would probably outlive them all.

He took one last look at the dog and closed the door—he didn't need to see this. Frank was probably anthropomorphizing but could swear he saw understanding in Cooper's brown, cataract-filled eyes. He walked out onto the Lost Coast Inn's back deck, still holding his breath, and using every ounce of mental energy he possessed to stave off the madness he felt roiling just below the surface, ignoring the things he saw that could not possibly be real.

It was raining gently, or at least he thought it was. He hoped it meant no one would have to spend too much time cleaning the deck. He had been told it was acid rain, but apparently that term was a misnomer—it wasn't harmful to humans directly, only its second-order effects. But what did Frank know?

He stared out at the glowing sea. The waves still rolled in and out, just like they had long before humans appeared on this planet, and just like they would continue to do long after we were gone, indifferent. So too would continue the war between viruses, bacteria, and other microorganisms in which humans were only a brief feature of the battlefield. Maybe Eddie had rubbed off on him.

Lighting flashed here and there in the cloud-covered sky to which he'd become accustomed. He couldn't make out where the moon was, but knew it was up there somewhere. And beyond it, Mars. Perhaps our species will survive after all, if it deserves to, he thought.

He looked down at his hands, calloused and strong from a lifetime of use. The right one gripped his trusty firearm. It had saved his life on more than one occasion, usually by taking another. He needed it one last time. Without hesitation he held the gun up to his temple and pulled the trigger with no regrets.

Neon blue brains sprayed out into the night.

Officer Frank Bear's role in humanity's story—and all stories—was over.

Chapter 25: Eclipsed

Earth Year: 2350

Martian Year: 167

Keli was supposed to be off of this fucking rock by now. Phobos was a sorry excuse for a moon, just a captured asteroid slowly spiraling in towards its host, as something else would be soon if she could salvage the plan. Keli and the bombs had covertly hitched a ride on *CHARON*, the rocket that ferried the Volunteers. It had been scheduled to depart back to Mars hours ago with anyone not involved in the project, such as the supercomputer technicians. It was now delayed, and consequently so was the *BLUE RETRIEVER*.

Had she been betrayed? Was this the Zhang twins' plan all along? Most likely not; she saw the manifest. Probably just bad luck; mechanical issues were still a reality. Nonetheless she flagged and filed away the thought in her mind for later. If there was a later.

CHARON was the last ship on Phobos and required to leave before the arrival of the *RETRIEVER*. There was to be no way for anyone—or more importantly, for anything—from the moon to make its way to Mars once the radiance arrived. It was to be vacuum-gapped from the rest of civilization by almost ten thousand kilometers, something that still made many uncomfortable and the reason Keli believed she was there.

The bombs, carefully planted beneath where the *BLUE RETRIEVER* was to land, were to detonate upon detecting its touchdown. But there was a secondary, fallback detonation mechanism in case the primary one failed—a timer, which would now set off the explosion prematurely. If that happened then not only would she fail, she doubted she'd ever make it off of Phobos. She could not remotely change the time of detonation; even with her sophisticated tech, any link over the local Network was too risky. This meant there was no going back without actually going back, which was why she once again found herself heading to the quarantine hangar, separated from the main base and inside of which all research was to be conducted.

She'd actually felt more comfortable in the bustling main base, full of a statistically significant sample of the population—the Volunteers—the majority of them lowlifes like her. Security through obscurity. Any scans would confirm her false identity as Doctor Nakamoto, one of the brave technicians working on the dangerous end of the project, and the martyr on whom the sabotage would ultimately be blamed.

Keli didn't relish returning to the eerily empty hangar, much less the scene of the crime. The *BLUE RETRIEVER*, now waiting in orbit around the moon, didn't glow noticeably blue, at least not in the visible light spectrum. But it was still unclear if its exterior was contaminated. Various types of viruses, lichens, bacteria, and fungi—even tardigrades—could survive in space, but most of those old tests had only exposed them for a few weeks. Anything hitching a ride on the outside of the ship would have been subjected to the vacuum of space and its ultraviolet radiation, cosmic rays, lack of air, and frigid temperatures for three deciles. However, the radiance was the most extreme of the extremophiles, and it was believed that life on Earth was seeded by microorganisms surviving the exact same trip in the opposite direction. As such, no one wanted to take any chances. The Volunteers were in no rush to be exposed and enter what may very well be their grave, and many scientists and technicians were also going to be living in the quarantined area indefinitely. Even the first astronauts to return from Earth's moon were quarantined for half a decile, and that had been entirely a precaution. This danger was all too real. Thus everyone still on Phobos was enjoying what little time they had left to interact physically in the main base.

There was more than one orgy happening.

Keli awkwardly made her way down the tunnel. Gravity was so weak here she could reach escape velocity by simply jumping. It made her movements clumsy, which was precisely the opposite of what she'd spent most of her life training and expecting them to be. She passed what she assumed was a man—you could never be sure—and gave him a perfunctory nod, sending her new long blond hair bouncing slowly around her face. How annoying and impractical.

When she reached the perimeter of the quarantine zone she entered a suit through the airlock, specially designed so that one could get in and out without coming into contact with its exterior; being unclear if they could kill the radiance and absolutely sterilize something created design challenges. But right now she needed the suit because the top of the hangar was open to the sky, ready to swallow the ship after landing. That was their plan, anyway. Hers—or her effective employers'—was that before the roof sealed it in, the bombs would detonate and relaunch the *BLUE RETRIEVER* back into space, this time on a collision course with Mars and too damaged to maneuver itself. The ZMC would then heroically sacrifice one of its asteroid mining ships to intercept and carry it on a suicide mission out of the solar system. Much of the lab equipment and prospective vaccines, treatments, and nanobot cures would also be destroyed in the blast, along with many of the Volunteers and technicians—a disincentive against attempting something similar in the future. The plan had more moving parts and weaknesses than Keli preferred, and it was risky, but there was a certain beauty to it. At least there was to someone like her.

After a scan granted her access she entered the enormous hangar, big enough to house hundreds of people and bathed in red light. Mars loomed so large it was all she could see through the open roof, including the stain that was the sprawling city. Mars was all anyone could ever see from here; like Earth's moon, Phobos was tidally locked, with the same side always facing the red planet. It was technically night on this side of Phobos, but it was daytime on the hemisphere of the planet below, reflecting enough sunlight to create a kind of bloody twilight. Keli found it beautiful.

She strolled past the lab equipment and barracks to the landing zone. After verifying no one was around and watching—other than machines, but that was handled—she descended to where the bombs, disguised as equipment, were stored beneath and around the landing pad. She triple-checked the new schedule and adjusted the fallback detonation mechanism. Time to get the hell out of here.

"I'd be remiss if I didn't get your name." Keli was startled by a voice above and behind her. She turned around and looked up out of the trench to see the face of the man she'd passed on her way here, smiling suggestively behind the faceplate of a pressure suit like the one she wore. "I'm not sure when I'll get the opportunity to see you again once you enter quarantine."

Keli damned the external appearance of the identity she'd assumed. This was why she chose not to look anything like this most of the time. She was about to reply when he preempted her.

"What are you doing down there, anyway?" he asked, his tone now suspicious. Just then the Network responded with the man's name, role in the project, and a hundred other details.

He would not be missed in the short term.

She looked past him to the open roof of the hangar and rusted surface of Mars. Her fancy onboard specs confirmed there was no one else around.

"What are you chuckling about?" he asked.

A second later his faceplate was smashed, his specs were fried, and he was helplessly floating up and out of the open roof, into space.

* * *

The City's skyscrapers reached like trees in a rainforest towards the sun, grasping towards its life-giving energy. Anything beneath the Canopy was mostly shut out from its rays. A handful of buildings—the victors in this competition—poked above the fray into the Emergent, with no obstructions (other than space-based solar panels) between them and the stars. Except for one structure, nothing climbed higher than Rook Tower.

"If not for you I'd be up there right now, scared shitless," said Caspian as he looked out from Gloria's penthouse at Phobos, magnified by what was much more than just a window. The moon may have been relatively close to the planet, but it was also relatively small, with a diameter under twenty-three kilometers. There was no risk to Gloria's augmented eyes from staring at something so close to the sun, but Caspian's golden orbs were merely cosmetic. "It's fitting that Phobos means 'fear' in Greek."

"In all my years on Mars I've never been up there," said Gloria. She felt silly for still avoiding rockets at this age because of a traumatic event when she was a teenager. Of all people the fucking mind painter should be able to overcome and overpower her own thoughts, but she hadn't been off this red rock since the day she landed. Maybe that's why this tower was so damn tall. That and she'd always possessed a tendency to climb as high as she could. Gloria had contemplated erasing the relevant memories, but the technology was too crude, especially when applied to old, formative events. She didn't want to risk losing what remained of her happy recollections from before then, or the last glimpses of her father, no matter how tragic. "Thank you for staying."

The *BLUE RETRIEVER* had just landed, several hours behind schedule but otherwise without incident. The moon where it now stood was starting what counted for an eclipse on Mars, which happened many times per year in one latitude or another. The planet didn't share Earth's absurd coincidence of either of its moons being just the right size and distance to almost exactly cover the sun when in transit. Fifteen seconds after the potato-shaped satellite began its mere thirty-second passage across the sun, the sight resembled a disfigured halo.

CHAPTER 25: ECLIPSED

A pinprick of light, detectable only to Gloria, appeared and disappeared near the center of the malformed ring.

Chapter 26: La Tutmonda Rezerva Banko

Earth Year: 2045

Martian Year: 5

"How does it work?" Chris asked his older brother, Matt, from his analog radio. His more sophisticated means of communication no longer functioned. Average human males could briefly produce over one horsepower, but only a fraction of one on a sustained basis; his arm was tired from cranking, using muscle power and magnetism to keep the radio powered.

"The exterior is a white cylinder, eight feet high and five in diameter."

"I thought you were going to tell me it precisely resembles the black monolith from *2001: A Space Odyssey*," joked Chris.

"Sergei was apparently part of the international coalition and involved with design decisions. That was indeed an inspiration, but it needs to remain as cool as possible if it ends up in sunlight, so it could not be black."

"And I assume it's cylindrical because that provides more interior space than a rectangular prism? Shouldn't the height match the diameter to maximize volume?" Chris knew his geometry.

"Actually no—the shape is so it can conceivably be rolled if someone needs to transport it without machinery. The design employs the golden ratio—its height is one point six times its width. It is supposed to be aesthetically pleasing, but to me it just looks like a giant soup can."

"No one ever mistook you for an artist."

"The casing is tough, some complicated alloy that also acts as a Faraday cage and is engraved with basic visual instructions for how to open and operate. Sergei said to think of it like the golden plaque on the Voyager spacecraft, which contains pictures of how to play the included phonograph record to access its data. Future humans could be nearly as different from us as whoever or whatever comes across that vessel.

"There are two parts inside, both of them vacuum-sealed and insulated to remain cool and dry. The seed bank takes up most of the space. Many seeds were permanently lost in the Gaian Renaissance attacks of 2035, and the GBB contains nowhere near the genetic diversity that was held at Svalbard and elsewhere given its diminutive size. There are only about one hundred thousand varieties instead of millions, and one hundred of each instead of five. There is also a focus on seeds useful for rebooting civilization, like crops."

"Sounds like flowers are SOL, although I suppose that without bees most of them would have been anyway. How long can the seeds last in the environment here? It's not exactly the arctic, not yet anyway, and certainly not the moon."

"Even without being frozen, most will last for a dozen years or longer given the lack of air and moisture inside. Plus, as you know better than me, the Earth's surface temperature is rapidly declining. By the time things clear up and the climate changes enough to risk spoiling the seeds, there should be enough sunlight to plant them."

"What about the other part, the data library?"

"Like the exterior casing, there are visual instructions for how to operate. For example, to fold out the solar panels and place in the sun. The functionality to query the data should only last about five hundred years if not being used, but there are replacement parts for the computer and radio. The data itself is imprinted on the hardest of disks—specially constructed optical film—and allegedly rated to last for two thousand years or more."

"Let's hope that's much longer than we need."

"However, that longevity comes with a tradeoff—the most robust storage format is far from the most efficient. Early plans were to include a copy of the data in all major languages, but with space at such a premium it was decided to only use one: Esperanto."

"You're kidding."

"I have never been much of a jokester."

"The 'international language'? I thought it died out."

"It is the simplest language to learn and was constructed to be so. For example it has rules with universal applicability and no exceptions, no historical baggage, no grammatical gender, no need to learn antonyms—you just add the prefix 'mal'—you get the idea."

"Sounds like it would make for terrible literature."

"The library contains not just knowledge, but information about how to acquire that knowledge," continued Matt, ignoring his brother's jokes. "It had to be assumed that whoever finds it could be illiterate, or even lack language altogether. Given our situation, we are lucky it was so assumed."

CHAPTER 26: LA TUTMONDA REZERVA BANKO

Chris exhaled. "You're right. It's kind of a paradox, isn't it? Creating these backup banks to restart civilization but not telling anyone where they are?"

"There were many tradeoffs made in this project. There are nine others scattered somewhere down there. Who knows when or if they will ever be found. The Chinese up here allegedly do not even know the location of their copy."

"It's definitely strange to think about. Well, it sounds like the secret's out on this one." There was no foolproof way to encrypt an analog radio signal. The past decades of research had focused almost exclusively on digital cryptography and exchanging encryption keys. The signal could be scrambled, but even with the most advanced methods, if your recipient could descramble your message to understand it, so could someone else with the right equipment and motivation. "Sorry brother but I have to run. There's lots to do and an uncertain amount of time in which to do it."

"Take care of yourself down there, Chris. And please give James my regards."

"My big brother Matt, looking out for me from above."

"Semper Supra."

"When are you going to come down here and give your nephew your regards in person?"

"There is too much uncertainty right now, but if it ends up being in everyone's best interest, I promise I will."

"I'll hold you to that," said Chris, turning off the radio.

The Jenkins brothers' points about having an uncertain amount of time, acting in the best interest of others, and keeping promises resonated with someone else who had indeed been eavesdropping on their conversations. But they resonated for drastically different reasons. The listener began thinking about how to make the far but not insurmountable journey to the compound in Bellingham.

Chapter 27: Dances with Spectra

Earth Year: 2351

Martian Year: 167

The first long-range radio waves detectible from space emanated from Earth in the late nineteenth century. As a kind of electromagnetic radiation, the waves propagated through space at close to the cosmic speed limit: the speed of light in a vacuum. However, a signal's strength degraded according to the inverse square law; for a given distance traveled the signal faded proportionate to the inverse of that distance squared. Thus, although these first radio waves had traversed hundreds of light-years throughout the Milky Way, after only a few they were indistinguishable from the background radiation left over from the Big Bang.

Focused radio waves were detectible and decipherable over much greater distances. In 1974 Earth sent its first powerful and concentrated burst of radio waves explicitly meant for any extraterrestrials who cared to listen. It was aimed towards a cluster of stars that just happened to be conveniently located in the sky when the Arecibo Radio Telescope in Puerto Rico was ready. At the time many thought this was reckless. Eventually all believed it had just been useless.

Throughout the years the occasional mysterious burst of radio waves arrived at Earth from one part or another of deep space, but all of them were ultimately dismissed as nothing of particular interest. Just noise.

Mars, on the other hand, had spent many years drowning in radio waves from Earth, as well as from those in other parts of the spectrum. Traveling at almost three hundred thousand kilometers per second, it took only a relatively short three to twenty-three minutes to traverse the distance, depending on the two orbits. As such, Martian colonists had been able to keep a close watch on much of what transpired on Earth, both through asynchronous internet access and by eavesdropping on unencrypted communications.

Shortly after the last rockets left from Earth during the Great Escape, so did anomalous levels of X-rays and gamma radiation. It could have only meant one thing. The colonists knew what happened even before they were explicitly told by the moon bases, whose own transmissions ceased a few years later. In the following decades Earth's radio traffic gradually died out. Insufficient sunlight reached the surface to generate solar energy. Batteries, fuel cells, and finally radioisotope thermoelectric generators, which utilized the heat created by radioactive decay to produce electricity, slowly faded, until the equipment they powered transmitted their last messages to the stars. At least for a while.

Then came a period when very few broadcasts traveled between the two planets, but eventually the one-way flood of radiation grew, almost surpassing its previous level. Except this time, it went in the opposite direction.

The one-way flow of electromagnetic waves outward from

Mars only lasted a few decades. Sunlight once again began to reach the Earth's surface, causing monotonous signals to rejoin the dance after a long hiatus, until at last much of the equipment generating them suffered one or another permanent malfunction.

Like Earth, Mars too began to receive the occasional mysterious burst of radio waves from deep space, but they were just as inscrutable and seemingly random to Martians as they had been to their terrestrial ancestors.

More frequent broadcasts came from machines built on Mars and sent to other parts of the solar system. First they came from satellites that had joined a candy red sports car in orbit around the planet. Then from spacecraft—both crewed and uncrewed—that had been sent to Earth. Eventually they came from vessels on other missions of mining and exploration, and from the small bases on Mars's two moons, Phobos and Deimos.

Finally, impossibly—although not quite as implausible to a few as to the rest—a new focused burst arrived from Earth. It reached enough of the parabolic receivers dotting the red planet that its presence could not be concealed or denied by those who may have wished to do so. The first instinct of some was to dismiss it as fake—there were many conspiracy theories on the Network—but its veracity was verified by those with more sophisticated technology.

The message did not come from the defunct rovers or rockets sent from Mars to Earth's surface. It did not come from the still-functioning satellites in Earth's orbit, monitoring and confirming the continued presence of the radiance (although one could do that simply by looking up at the Mourning Star and noting the abundance of light with a wavelength of approximately four hundred and fifty to five hundred nanometers: blue). No, the signal came from somewhere in a region once known as the Pacific Northwest of the United States. The message was unencrypted, unscrambled, and in a strange language, but machines combed through what remained of files from Earth and created a workable translator, so it was ultimately decipherable.

And it told of terrible things.

Chapter 28: The Doctor Will See You Now

Earth Year: 2045

Martian Year: 5

The procedure involved removing the endogenous retroviruses—the junk DNA that comprised approximately eight percent of the human genome and was an artifact of their ancestors' viral infections—and splicing in the genetic material of the radiance itself, along with other germline edits. It seemed to have gone well, and at the end of the first trimester the signs were promising enough that Doctor Goldstein finally broadcast out the details to all who remained on the airwaves. Encouraging others to bring a child into this world was not something she did lightly, but while still predicting a one hundred percent mortality rate for those currently alive, the pace of infection had slowed enough that it was worth a shot. The few locations around the globe that still had the necessary equipment were now attempting the procedure. Some couples had even made the precarious journey to Bellingham, risking the remaining marauders—and worse—who roamed the highways.

Doctor Weber felt like he had done almost all that he could. He was now expanding his formidable hand-written corpus on the radiance with more speculative hypotheses. One was that although it most closely resembled a virus, its behavior also mimicked that of an infamous fungus—*Ophiocordyceps unilateralis*, the so-called 'zombie-ant' fungus—that used to be found in rainforests, back when those could also be found. After infecting a host ant it would take control of their mind, compelling them to climb a tree before sprouting out of their body so its spores could be carried long distances. The hyperventilation, coughing, and urge to commit suicide by violent means caused by the radiance could have served a similar purpose. It didn't explain many other questions—had it evolved alongside our ancestors? Shouldn't it have evolved to be *less* deadly over time? Could something invincible even evolve via natural selection at all? But perhaps it was a start. He was baffled at how little humans understood the virosphere; there were likely still billions, if not trillions, of undiscovered viruses. They were by far the most numerous biological entities in existence.

However, there was still one even more important contribution the doctor wanted to make to his magnum opus, and that was an expert's first-person account of contracting the disease. Luckily, he considered himself the world's foremost expert on the subject, and—unluckily—his own veins had begun to glow.

He was not the one writing this final chapter, however. Instead he was meticulously narrating it to Doctor Goldstein over the radio. He told her he'd run out of ink, which while plausible was not actually true. In reality he was driving like a soon-to-be madman north to Bellingham, although she was unaware of this fact. Based on the journey's initial progress he estimated that what usually would have been a fifteen-hour drive would take him closer to thirty, if he made it there at all. At least he had good company.

In addition to finishing his contribution to radiance research there was one other last thing he hoped to accomplish, and he was willing to do whatever it took. He'd even had to kill a man intent on taking his car, something he'd never planned to do as a Hippocratic oath-taker. But at this point he figured he was depriving the would-be bandit of at most a year of life. Hundreds of thousands of people died each day—much more, recently—most without being at any kind of fault. He wasn't going to waste his precious little remaining time worrying about someone whose life was lost while trying to take from others.

Two full days later Doctor Weber looked out the cracked, blue blood-stained windshield at the compound containing the lab. The facility had copious quantities of substances that were dangerous, expensive, or otherwise desirable, so unlike the rest of the university's campus it was protected by a tall, robust fence. But there was no way in hell—which in many ways the world was starting to resemble—that was going to stop him. He slammed his foot on the accelerator and rammed the car into the fence, creating a large enough hole to crawl through. It was the middle of the night, and although the drug cocktail he'd found could partially stave off the insanity allowed him to make it this far, the extent to which his own body illuminated the dark parking lot told him he didn't have long.

"Stop right there!" ordered Chris, who had volunteered to act as the compound's security guard during the small hours.

He stood tensed at the lab's door with his gun drawn at the fast-approaching blue light.

"Where is she?!" yelled the doctor, too possessed to recognize the pilot he'd met briefly, months before. Doctor Weber was prone to a one-track mind, and it had recently jumped the tracks from the radiance to something—or someone—else. Fortunately Chris was lucid and recalled their previous encounter. He holstered his weapon and led the doctor to the beginning of a long hallway. There was light—yellow, not blue—coming from a single room at the end.

"I'll give you some privacy, but I've seen what the radiance can do to people in its final stages, and Doctor Goldstein is doing vital work. More couples are arriving every day to undergo the procedure. I don't want to have to come down there," said Chris.

"When I walk out of that room, shoot me," replied Doctor Weber in his no-nonsense tone as his blue-bloodshot eyes met Chris's. He strode purposefully down the hall towards her office. He knew she'd be awake, still working on their shared passion. He was sure he knew her better than anyone else in the world. His heart beat rapidly, whether from nervousness or the drugs wearing off, he couldn't tell. He stopped for the briefest of moments before reaching the office's window, then gently knocked and entered.

Doctor Goldstein's eyes went wide with fear; it wasn't safe to be around someone at this phase of the disease. But something in the look on this stranger's face immediately changed her fear to something else.

"Christina..."

"...Ben?"

"You look radiant in person," he said, smiling. "Sorry, I had

CHAPTER 28: THE DOCTOR WILL SEE YOU NOW

days to think of what to say and that's the best I could come up with. Christina, I had to tell you in person if it was the last thing I did, and it looks like it will be. I love you. My only regret is that it took such dire circumstances to bring us together." She was too choked up to speak, nodding in agreement as tears welled up in her eyes. The two kissed and embraced like old lovers.

"I'm going to have to sign off my report now. It's in the car along with every book I could fit and someone I think you'll find quite useful. Best of luck." Doctor Ben Weber walked back into the hallway, then once again began sprinting towards Chris.

Eddie and Elle were awoken by the sound of three gunshots in quick succession not far off. Eddie sat up frantically and fumbled for his bedside lantern. His frenzy grew as he heard the door to their room squeak open, but when he finally turned on the light he saw no one there.

Then he heard the scrape of nails on the floor, and before he knew it a large dog was among them in a frenzy of its own.

"Cooper! What on Earth are you doing here, boy?"

Chapter 29: Statue of Limitations

Earth Year: 2351

Martian Year: 168

John Rook did not look down at his daughter, but above and beyond her. His eyes were cast perpetually on the horizon, to the future. The famous face was chiseled from stone, literally, the simple statue carved by a machine trained on the surviving images and videos of his greatest speeches.

The memorial was at the center of a grove of cherry blossom trees, itself at the center of the top level of Rook Park. The trees' fallen petals created a pink carpet that the robotic gardeners did not sweep up. Unlike the other vegetation in the park, modified to be always in bloom, the cherry blossoms remained largely the same as they were on Earth, and just how John had loved them. Their fleeting prime lasted mere weeks each year, something which had captivated so many romantics, John included, and served as a symbol of the fragile and finite nature of life. *Sic transit gloria mundi...*

Martian soil was not conducive to decomposition, something learned the hard way after the early sols, and any synthetic dirt in which a body could reliably rot was too agriculturally valuable to waste as a tomb. Thus there were no graveyards on the planet. The bodies of the dead simply disappeared, out of sight and out of mind. And that was precisely why Gloria had built the monument in this location, where so many wealthy Martians who would rather think about anything but death were forced to confront it. Unlike most sensory phenomena, they did not have the privileges to block it out.

"Quite a handsome man, even without augmentations," observed Caspian. "No wonder you share half his genes."

"You should have seen my mother. With the prenatal changes they made I actually have fifty-five percent of hers, five that were inserted from elsewhere, and only forty of his. But dad knew living on through your DNA was a fool's game, even if it's one that all non-human life is unconsciously playing. In a few generations the combination of genes that are uniquely yours is hopelessly diluted. Many children don't even have the same blood type as their parents, invalidating the once-fashionable idea of bloodlines. Granted, this was before human cloning was an option, but that of course has other undesirable effects.

"Dad always said the only worthwhile way to live forever is through your ideas." Gloria motioned towards the epitaph inscribed below the statue. What had once been John's passphrase was carved at the monument's base. Despite how much time had elapsed she was yet to reveal the entire contents of the files the key had unencrypted. They may yet come in handy one sol. But she'd long ago moved the remaining secrets to her own version of secure storage, so there was no risk in publicly displaying the old passphrase. "I suppose I've done my best to pass on both his genes and memes."

"What would he think about today's holiday?"

"I'm sure he'd appreciate the irony, especially in light of the imminent Earth mission."

Caspian was less uncomfortable than he used to be when surrounded by so many citizens of the Canopy and Emergent. He was now a resident of the former, after all, his life most likely saved by Gloria's offer to abscond his role as a Volunteer. But there was another reason for his present discomfort. The most dominant color in their immediate vicinity was the pink from the trees, but it was closely followed by red and purple, worn by those celebrating the holiday and advocating for more resources for the mission to Earth, respectively. The broadcasts from the latter reached him first.

"Fellow humans! Take heed that we do call you humans, not Martians, for all of us have a bond that goes far deeper than the planet we currently inhabit. That bond is our common humanity, and it is a bond we share with our brothers and sisters on Earth. You have heard the messages! Mars once gave life to Earth, and in return Earth brought our species to Mars. The time has come for Mars to take the next step in this dance and bring civilization back to Earth. The early colonists refused to help them in their hour of greatest need, and we now have an opportunity to rectify this grave injustice committed by our ancestors. It is time for the two planets—the red and the blue—to come together and finally fulfill the dream of an interplanetary civilization. A dream once held by John Rook, and once—for the briefest of moments—glimpsed. It is the dream we all have to thank for our very existence!"

It was a speech everyone had heard in one form or another over the past few deciles, since the fateful message arrived from Earth. After sols of squabbling, power struggles, and no reply, additional messages came. They were increasingly desperate, crying out for help. Everyone on Mars received them, and technically anyone was free to respond.

But there was a catch. The only way to ensure those on Earth received a transmission was to use satellite relay links or send during specific, known windows. The Earthlings would be unable to decipher any encryption, and any instructions on how to have a private conversation would have to be sent unencrypted, which meant those with the requisite technology could eavesdrop on and potentially block any Earth-bound broadcasts. This made it a risky prospect. Finally, a committee was formed to advise those on Earth about their predicament. It was chaired by the owners of most spacecraft involved in the operation: the Zhang Mining Corporation.

The various counterarguments to the speech, espoused by those wearing red, were well-known too. Some of them were not unlike those frequently heard in the park in the deciles leading up to the unexpectedly brief arrival of the *BLUE RETRIEVER*.

"It's a suicide mission!"

"Stopping that rocket saved millions of lives. It almost crashed into the City for Kronos's sake. We need to quit while we're ahead."

"Our society isn't set up for this kind of fight, especially with some primitive warlord!"

"The Earthlings will be dead by the time you arrive."

"What if the radiance has mutated? The procedure may not even work anymore!"

With no central government to appeal to, those hastily preparing the mission to Earth had to take their pleas for funding, supplies, and Volunteers directly to the planet's citizenry. Specifically, to people like Gloria. Much had been lost in the attack on Phobos, and assembling the required pharmacological, military, technical, and human resources on such short notice was a challenge. Time was of the essence.

Although Gloria hadn't been deeply involved in anything to do with the *BLUE RETRIEVER*, she'd still been devastated by what happened. It would surely have accelerated the downward spiral she'd already been circling if not for one powerful counterforce: Caspian. She may have saved his life by keeping him off of Phobos, but she thought it just as likely that he had saved hers in the aftermath. She hadn't even descended to the Floor since he moved up to the Canopy.

And now, in addition to having a reason to get into bed, she had one to get out of it; Gloria was equally fascinated and disturbed by what was transpiring—and had apparently been transpiring for a long time—on Earth. But she was not yet comfortable throwing her substantial influence behind the mission. The messages had renewed hope that there was indeed a way to defeat—or at least to live with—the radiance, but it was still the case that all attempts to do so had ended in death on a massive scale. The most recent catastrophe was still fresh in her inimitable mind.

"Have you given any more thought to whether or not you'll support the mission?" asked Caspian.

She turned from John's statue and met his eyes. "As inquisitive as ever, my dear. I..." Suddenly all thoughts of Earth ceased as Gloria trailed off and now seemed to be gazing past him, to the air between them and the nearest cherry blossom. Caspian foolishly turned to look over his shoulder, though whatever Gloria saw was clearly something only she could see. He was still getting used to constantly being surrounded by such high-grade tech.

CHAPTER 29: STATUE OF LIMITATIONS

"Caspian," without realizing it Gloria spoke in a tone resembling her father in moments of consequence. Fitting given their location. "I need to go to the Citadel, and I want you to come with me."

He turned back to stare at her with a look that was equal parts intrigue and fear.

"Zhang Renshu is dying."

Chapter 30: The Conservation of Energy

Earth Year: 2046

Martian Year: 5

Matt looked at his gaunt, dehydrated, and still clean-shaven face reflected in the dark screen. As if Luna Alpha had not been cold enough. He had been an intermittent faster for most of his adult life but had now been living on three-quarter rations for six months. In the moon's gravity he technically only weighed ten kilograms, despite being two meters tall. His body, once thick and strong, was thinner and weaker than at any time he could remember. At least he still had a six-pack; his nutritional intake was such that he avoided the cruel joke played on many of those who starved in poor countries, their bellies bulging while the rest withered away.

On Matt's orders those under his command at Luna Alpha had been extra conservative with supplies while they awaited news of the procedure on Earth. Those at the base from other countries had done the same out of comradery. Now that it appeared the procedure may be successful, Matt hoped they would be motivated for what came next. He was also glad it

CHAPTER 30: THE CONSERVATION OF ENERGY

seemed likely they would be spared a resource war with their Chinese neighbors—those on the moon now had something more important to focus on than merely their own survival. They only needed to subsist on the moon for so long, for they would be going back to Earth after all. Most of them.

The entire base personnel—six Americans, two Australians, and two Russians—were gathered in the command center. The ashen Earth hung ominously in the observation window. The planet's perpetual cloud cover, although depressing, was still preferable to the neon blue orb they would have seen but for its presence. They knew what the glow meant, and in the wake of recent news it was now much closer to home.

Matt looked up from his blank screen at those present and stood. "Thank you all for coming, and thank you again for the sacrifice you have made to conserve supplies the past several months. You all heard Doctor Goldstein—hopefully that sacrifice will not have been in vain.

"As I am sure you are aware, that broadcast is why I have gathered you here. And, unfortunately, your sacrifice is far from over. Eventually it will result in the ultimate sacrifice from all of us. We are going to move forward with Operation Falling Angels unless anyone would like to raise an objection." They had extensively mapped out several plans, meticulously factoring in various contingencies. It wasn't like they had much else to do. It was no surprise to anyone they would now move forward with Operation Falling Angels. Given all available data it made the most sense. But it meant another six months or more of three-quarter rations for some, longer for others, and contracting the radiance for all but one.

No one said anything so Matt continued, "To recap, there are two escape pods left. Once it is apparent there will soon be no one left to raise the children on Earth, the first pod will leave with the Global Backup Bank. Although each pod has six seats, we conservatively need an extra five hundred pounds of payload space to safely reach the desired CPS coordinates given the GBB's mass. Thus this pod will only contain three people—Tatyana, Sergei, and Owen." By now everyone was familiar with the GBB, but Tatyana and Sergei were the most knowledgeable. Additionally, it was unclear if they had been lovers before arriving at Luna Alpha, but they certainly were now, and it would have been cruel to separate them at the end. Despite six months of cohabitation at Luna Alpha, Owen was still a little distrustful of the Russians and insisted that he accompany them back to Earth. "It could be a few weeks or a few months, but after the last of them contracts the radiance, the second pod will depart with all remaining personnel except for myself. I will remain at Luna Alpha."

"You can't hitch a ride with the Chinese?" asked Owen, although he knew the answer.

"I confirmed with them again earlier today. Even without a GBB to transport they do not have spare capacity. They are executing a similar operation, sending their single remaining escape vehicle to a facility outside of Lhasa, Tibet," replied Matt. "And given the number of people left on the ground there they will likely leave months before us."

"Over two hundred kilograms is conservative. You can come on first pod," offered Sergei. This argument had also been made before without luck.

Although Matt's brother and nephew were both still alive and at the compound, he would not get the opportunity to see them. His sense of duty—not only to his country, but to his species—took precedence over everything else, including family. Like the captain of a ship, he would not abandon the base.

"As we have discussed before, I refuse to do anything whatsoever that risks jeopardizing this mission. Whatever supplies are left after the second pod leaves should last me on my own for a while. There may even be some vodka left." Matt rarely joked; he was a serious man. This got a smile from everyone. "I will live out my remaining days where I have lived the proudest moments and done the best work of my life: here, on the moon, and provide whatever support I can remotely."

No one bothered further trying to talk him out of it. Remaining on the moon indefinitely was only a slightly less envious position to be in than going back to Earth.

Later that evening the metal halls of Luna Alpha echoed with the sound of the Aussies singing the national anthem of what had once been their homeland. It was Australia Day, after all. The voices, which each on their own would have been unbearable, coalesced together into something that was almost pleasant and could have been beautiful if not for their level of intoxication. It didn't take much vodka to inebriate them given their recent weight loss and reduced tolerance. On Matt's orders there had been no alcohol at Luna Alpha up until the Russians' arrival.

"Australians all let us rejoice
For we are young and free
We've golden soil and wealth for toil,
Our home is girt by sea
Our land abounds in nature's gifts
Of beauty, rich and rare
In history's page let every stage
Advance Australia fair,

In joyful strains then let us sing
'Advance Australia fair!'
Beneath our radiant Southern Cross..."

Awkward looks were exchanged at the mention of the adjective form of 'radiance,' which they were all sure would now be their cause of death. It was once a rare luxury to know such a thing. Unsure if they should continue, it was enough of a buzzkill to ruin whatever moment had existed. They muttered goodnights and each retired to their quarters, which were relatively spacious given the lack of personnel at the base.

It only made them feel more alone.

Chapter 31: Rook to King

Earth Year: 2351

Martian Year: 168

Psychedelic colors streaked by all around as the pod raced through the top of the Canopy. Moving smoothly at a constant velocity, it could just as reasonably be concluded that the vehicle was stationary and the outside world was instead rushing past. On some level both were true.

Caspian could barely make out the neon signs in Chinese—his preferred reading language—before they receded into the distance. Apparently up here they didn't put up with ads being projected directly into your brain; you still had to choose to read them to understand their message. However, it was impossible to miss the central theme: wishing him a happy 168th Martian anniversary of Homecoming.

The world looked very different to Gloria, who was in do not disturb mode. All potential distractions appeared as a featureless dull gray. This moment had been coming for a long time, and she needed to concentrate on what lay ahead.

The Citadel—the tallest structure in the Emergent—consumed the horizon as the pod sped closer. It was almost the inverse of Rook Tower, a glass and metal exterior below the Canopy and stone above. Inspired by Tibet's Potala Palace and aptly named, it resembled a veritable castle in the sky. During Mars's monstrous dust storms it appeared to be floating above the City. The starlit penthouse perched upon this corporate stronghold was the home of—for now—the chairman of the ZMC, and the oldest, wealthiest person on the planet: Zhang Renshu. Unlike Gloria, who was rarely home, he had not left his in decades.

Caspian's head was spinning, and he was beginning to suspect he was in way over it. The past few deciles, since he'd come into Gloria's orbit, were unfathomable. To top it all off he was now on his way to the headquarters of the largest and most powerful company in existence, and technically one of his former employers. There were many things he wanted to ask Gloria, but given her present demeanor he didn't dare.

The pod slowed as they approached the security gates. After what Caspian assumed was the most thorough scan of his life he found himself in a rapidly ascending, gracefully smooth elevator. It would have seemed far too easy if not for his companion.

Gloria spoke for the first time since leaving Rook Park, "Zhang Bingwen has been awaiting this sol for a long time, but a power struggle with his brother over the ZMC's future is probably not what he needs right now. Renshu chose a hell of a time to die. Bingwen also despises anyone not from the Emergent. Other than the minimum conversation required for sex, I doubt he's spoken with anyone in the Canopy or below in a century. That's why I brought you along." She broke from her focused monotone and regained a hint of the playfulness Caspian adored, as if remembering who he was. "That, and

CHAPTER 31: ROOK TO KING

I like you." She winked. "He'll likely try to manipulate you. In fact I'm counting on it. You won't be able to record in the Citadel, but try to remember his words verbatim. Any insight into his mind may prove useful in the sols to come."

The elevator glided to a stop. Caspian briefly contemplated taking something to calm his nerves but then thought better of it; he wanted to be maximally coherent. He focused his mind and prepared for whatever lay ahead. He was growing accustomed to doors opening to magnificent sights, and finally no longer felt like an imposter in his own home. But this one hit him even before the doors slowly slid open, taking much longer than necessary, no doubt for effect.

Was it possible what he smelled was real, or just an imitation? Something seemed different. It no longer provided needed warmth or protection, but even on another planet, in an environment where it could be catastrophically dangerous, something deep inside of him felt comforted by one of humanity's first breakthrough technologies.

A roaring, wood-burning fire cast a wildly shifting pattern of light and shadow across the colossal foyer. The beauty, opulence, and wastefulness of it simultaneously intrigued, baffled, and appalled Caspian.

A voice rang out above the sound of the crackling logs from behind one of the high-backed real leather chairs facing the fire. It was impossibly loud for the distance between them. "Gloria! My first—and only unrequited—love. So nice to see that you're back where you belong after one of your fugue states. My father will be delighted to see you. That is, if delight is still something he experiences. I'd wish you a happy Homecoming, but you and I are of course among the handful who can credibly claim home is elsewhere. Nor do

I need to point out to you the arbitrariness of the calendar year, especially on a planet where everyone necessarily lives in insulated environments, the seasons meaningless."

Gloria ignored him.

The chair swiveled around to reveal Bingwen. Like Gloria, he appeared in his physical prime despite being four times as old as what was once considered a natural lifespan. He'd used part of this time to have what he assumed were more real sexual partners—there was no sense of power or conquest in fucking a machine, no matter its coyness settings—than any other person in history, surpassing even the famous sex workers, dictators, and celebrities of old Earth. That he was unable to definitively confirm this was a source of great dismay.

The fitted white tunic he wore accentuated his lean figure. His face visually contorted, almost to a comical degree, when he saw Caspian. He regained his composure and put on a sardonic smile. "And who did you bring with you? I would say he reeks of the Floor, but I long ago erased any lingering memories of such foulness."

"You two will have plenty of time to get to know each other—I presume Renshu asked to speak with me alone?"

Bingwen's smile became its widest yet. "That he did. That he did." His look quickly changed to a mixture of stern and pleading. "However, I was hoping we could first discuss a few matters of the utmost importance."

"My apologies, but we both know this is the end. I don't want to waste any of my godfather's final moments, and neither should you. Perhaps we can chat afterward. In the meantime you're more than welcome to take anything up with Caspian here," she said as she strode past him and towards another lift at the far end of the space.

CHAPTER 31: ROOK TO KING

"My father is not of sound mind. You would be wise not to believe everything he may tell you," Bingwen called after her.

"He hasn't been of sound mind in decades," Gloria said over her shoulder as she entered the lift. The doors closed behind her, leaving the two men alone.

Bingwen, even shorter than Gloria, was diminutive standing next to Caspian. Instead of an augmentation to increase his stature, he'd remained his natural height of well under two meters and wore it as a badge of honor—a reminder that he was one of the few who had been born on Earth. The differential made Caspian uncomfortable, so he took a seat in one of the leather chairs facing the fire. The soft, warm skin, harvested from lab-grown meat, felt strange.

"Caspian, was it?"

"Like the sea."

Bingwen again smiled broadly, his brilliant white teeth matching his outfit and glinting in the firelight. His tone was friendly but hollow as he took a seat in the other chair and joined Caspian in looking at the fire. "I see. I notice you've taken quite an interest in my fireplace. Fire and life have an interesting relationship. In fact, fire cannot exist naturally without life to provide the necessary oxygen. There may have been fire on Mars long ago when life first emerged here, but it was absent for eons before we brought it back. Indeed, it appears that where conditions are right for human life, they are also right for fire. We are melded together. That is, until the human condition sufficiently changes."

Caspian wasn't sure where Bingwen was going, but it certainly sounded like manipulation. He simply stared into the fire, coaxing him to continue.

"Fire was a huge boon for early humans, keeping away the

would-be predators prowling at the edge of the darkness. This in part explains your intrigue. But fire isn't always our friend. If you get too close and don't have the right specs you will get burned. For many years it was even fashionable—especially within some of Earth's old religions—to use it to roast people alive. Undoubtedly a very bad experience." He shook his head disapprovingly, wearing an exaggerated frown. A log collapsed, sending up a flare of embers. "There are still some unfortunate individuals who meet their death by fire. Sometimes by accident, sometimes not. Beyond the legitimate threat fire has always posed, billions of people once spent their entire lives under the looming specter of everlasting hellfire. Obviously, no such hell exists—the idea of eternal suffering was a bit dramatic, even to someone with a flair for it like me. No, the only hells that truly exist are the ones we create for ourselves. Or the ones we create for others."

The fire had been making Caspian sweat, but now he turned cold. Could Bingwen know about his role uploading his friend? With his resources and privileges it was possible. But maybe he was just guessing, overgeneralizing. Either way, he wanted to hear more. Remaining silent was the best way to get most people to keep talking.

"Something else that fire and life have in common is they are more like events, or actions, than things. Verbs as opposed to nouns. And just as life requires certain inputs for the defining chemical reactions to continue, so does fire. Heat, fuel, and oxidation: the fire triangle. Remove one and the flames are immediately *extinguished*." As Bingwen accented this last word the fire was instantly snuffed out and replaced by a cloud of black smoke, leaving the two of them in near darkness in the grand lobby. Bingwen's mildly pleasant voice became serious, bordering on menacing, as he turned to look at Caspian. His normally dark eyes were just as fiery as the blaze that had lit the room moments before. "Fire has destroyed countless cities, Caspian. This very city—our entire civilization—almost met its end in fire during the early sols. I remember it more vividly than anything post augmentation. But there are worse ways to die than fire, and more reliable ways to destroy a civilization, or annihilate a species, if that were one's goal. Do you understand?"

Caspian wasn't sure he did, but that didn't seem like the best response at the moment. "I, ah, believe I do...Zhang Bingwen."

"Good. And make sure you pass the message along to Gloria. I do not anticipate the two of us will have the opportunity to speak at length in the near future."

The foyer was once again bathed in light as the fire roared back to life.

Chapter 32: Blue Gene Baby

Earth Year: 2046

Martian Year: 6

Eddie turned over and examined his gently glowing bare hands as he held them up in front of him. He then donned Chris's flight gloves—but not the augmented reality helmet—and rested them on the controls of the F-35G. Elle was halfway into the third trimester, but he would not get the opportunity to see his daughter born. At least Doctor Goldstein, before she succumbed to the radiance herself, was confident that Elle would make it and the baby would be immune. Worst case—if Elle became infected—the baby was past the age of viability, so they could induce labor.

Leaving Elle alone in this world broke his heart, and he felt guilty about leaving without saying goodbye to anyone in person (other than Cooper). But farewells had never been his strong suit. Elle would have wanted to say goodbye, but she was stronger than he was. Maybe he was a coward, but he didn't think he could have bared it. Instead Eddie had handwritten her and his future daughter a letter, which Elle would find by their bedside when she awoke. His right hand still cramped from the prolonged movement he hadn't performed in a decade. He hoped his handwriting was legible enough for them to read.

Eddie also felt guilty about taking this plane for its final flight without consulting with Chris. He might have had similar plans, but Eddie hadn't asked permission because he didn't dare put the idea in his head. After hours of research he was confident he could get the plane in the air and to his target destination. He did not need to worry about how to land. He only hoped he had enough fuel to break through.

Somewhere up there, the sun should be rising any moment.

Eddie felt guilty about a lot, all things considered. Like realizing what you should have said after an argument was over, he'd realized how he should have lived when it was too late. For most of his life he'd been the kind of person who spent half of a good meal thinking about the next one and the other half ruminating on what could have been improved. But there was no point in dwelling on any of that now. He had done all he could to be a better man these past several months and was going to live in each of the moments he had left.

Eddie eased the plane up and then was thrust back in his seat by the g-forces as he accelerated eastward. He grinned—to say this thing had quite a bit more power than his Cessna was an understatement.

Shortly afterward he was enveloped by the shadowy clouds. It was nice to finally be free of the color blue, once his favorite. He watched the altimeter climb rapidly, unsure of how high he needed to go. Twenty thousand feet? Fifty?

Conversely, he did his best to ignore the fuel gauge. It had been perilously close to empty when he started, and the plane was now sternly warning him that he would soon run out. As it had been in his career of high f*inance*: no risk, no reward, right? But Eddie had no downside. He was playing with house money. This was practically arbitrage, a risk-free opportunity.

He continued to climb and accelerate, now twice the height he had ever flown on his own. He often said humans had flown too close to the sun, and now it was his turn to be Icarus. Despite his immense speed, time seemed to slow down, until after what felt like ages he was sure it was not an illusion that the world outside the cockpit was indeed getting lighter. After a few more seconds of turbulence the plane broke through the clouds, became otherworldly still, and Edward McDougal achieved the final goal he had in this world: he saw the sun. It would be the last thing he saw before the nonblack, non-anything of nonexistence.

It was stunningly beautiful and bright. He stared directly at it. The star floated just above the clouds on the horizon, its refracted rays a deep orange, the opposite side of the color wheel from the blue he had grown to hate. No matter what turmoil raged below, it was perpetually peaceful up here. There was always a bull market somewhere. A profound sense of contentment overtook him. Eddie was glad he got to be a person, if only briefly. He thought he was going to miss this place, then quickly remembered he wouldn't have the chance.

Eddie burned his remaining fuel continuing to increase velocity and fly directly towards what felt like an old friend, unable to hear the sonic boom being created behind the aircraft.

When he reached Mach 1.3—breakneck speed—he simultaneously ejected from the plane and deployed the seat's parachute, immediately bringing an end to the peculiar circumstance of being alive and sentient. His lifeless body, strapped to its seat, seemed to float at its apex for longer than the laws of physics allowed for, soaking in the sun's rays in the freezing atmosphere for several more moments before slowly falling through the thick layers of clouds and finally coming to rest on the desolate slopes of the Cascade Range twenty minutes later.

* * *

Elle was awoken by a painful contraction to find herself in a soaking wet bed. It was not atypical for Eddie to get up before her, or even to not sleep at all, so she quickly dressed and hurried out of the still-dark room, oblivious to the letter sitting on the nightstand.

She was also oblivious to the fact that her veins were faintly luminescent.

"Help, the baby is coming!" she yelled, emerging from one of the cottages at the compound where they lived. It was the loudest she had spoken in years. Chris was finishing his night's watch, sauntering back to his own cottage, and rushed over.

"Where's Eddie?" she asked. Chris had seen his F-35G in the distance to the east and put two and two together—Eddie had chosen to Irish exit. However, he did not think it the appropriate time to bring up this sad fact, or that Elle appeared to be in the early stages of the radiance.

"I saw him a few minutes ago but am not sure where he is now," Chris replied, technically not lying. "I thought you weren't due for another six weeks?"

"Apparently Hope is in a hurry to join us in this hellscape," Elle said, attempting to employ some humor to suppress the anxiety she felt. She had been through a lot in her relatively short life, but the pain combined with fear—not just for herself, but for her child, and all the other couples around the world who had undergone the same procedure—was a lot to handle. As far as everyone knew this would be the first post-procedure birth, a referendum on the future of the species.

"Let's get you to the delivery room." Chris helped her down the path and into the section of the lab they had designated for this purpose. 'Delivery room' was a generous term compared to what such a facility used to look like in a full, functioning hospital. But they had to make do with what they had or could find nearby, and what they could still power.

By the time they arrived, Elle's contractions had intensified, lasting a minute each with only momentary pauses between. Atypical, but any concept of normal had been discarded. At least it appeared she would not have to bear them for long—the only person left at the lab with any real-world experience delivering babies said that her cervix's dilation implied the child's arrival seemed imminent.

Elle had now also noticed that her veins were a dim, neon blue, but her own health was not her chief concern. She had pushing to do.

The acting nurse had been correct; Elle was in labor for less than two hours. But that was long enough for most of the compound's residents and those staying in nearby campus housing to gather outside the lab in nerve-wracking anticipation. A significant proportion of the planet's surviving human population sat by antique radios, awaiting word on if their own genes would have a chance to live on.

Elle strained in near-silence, and did not cry out until the final push, when her daughter Hope emerged into the world, as blue as the sky had once been. Mother and daughter cried in unison.

"She's just covered in your own blood," comforted the nurse, but as she began to wipe the newborn clean, she realized this was not true.

The child had been born luminous.

It wasn't just her daughter that was covered in Elle's lustrous blood, but also her makeshift hospital bed, and increasing the floor of the delivery room. Catastrophic postpartum hemorrhaging, such that the facilities were no longer properly equipped to remedy.

Elle held her only child as she rapidly lost her remaining blood and strength. She did not think of the absurdity of dying from childbirth in America in the year 2046, something that would have been unthinkable less than a year before. She did not think about the fact that she would be spared from the later stages of the radiance after all. She did not even think about where Eddie was, and why he was yet to show up.

The only thought that occupied Elle Toranaga's mind as consciousness faded was if there was any hope for little Hope.

* * *

If Skyler had known this was going to be the last day of his life he would have started it differently. Instead he'd spent the morning going through the drudgery of what had become his daily routine in this new reality. Taking a break from the labor required just to keep living, he gazed east off the Newfoundland shore, out to the Labrador Sea.

Were his eyes bamboozling him, or was that a boat coming this way? Several ghost ships had washed up on these dozen kilometers of coastline over the past year, all of them well on their way to literal skeleton crews. But the speed with which this craft had appeared over the horizon led him to believe it was captained by the living.

When he returned to the crest of the hill again several minutes later, out of breath and with binoculars, his wish was granted: a sleek motor yacht was indeed heading in his general direction. Burning fossil fuels was still a reliable source of energy.

His heart rate increased. He hadn't seen anyone in months. With no working radio he'd begun to accept there was no one else left. Canada may have been mostly spared from nuclear attack, but no level of niceness was sufficient to stave off the blue death.

Maybe they have a cure for it, eh? Before everything went to shit he had essentially worked as a horseshoe crab phlebotomist. The creatures had existed since before the dinosaurs but recently been bled to extinction. Their blue blood—eerily similar to that he'd seen flow from his fellow humans—had been one of the most expensive liquids on the planet for its ability to identify bacterial contamination. Blue gold. Maybe there was a connection.

Or maybe—just maybe—the yacht was crewed by a woman. Or women.

'Skyler' had not actually introduced himself to anyone yet using this name and was excited to do so. He'd only decided to start calling himself by it recently, his given name being Abraham. However, since he'd always hated the name, rooted in Judeo-Christian mythology as it was, and with everyone he'd ever known gone, he thought what the bloody hell, might as well change it. He knew Skyler was a cheesy name more fitting of a video game character or band member from the turn of the millennium. But it was chosen nonetheless as he dearly missed the vibrant blue sky, before the bleak gray and

CHAPTER 32: BLUE GENE BABY

ash consumed everything.

He raised a flare gun at that now-hated sky and pulled the trigger. Nothing happened. His heart beat even faster as he panicked, realizing the boat could head north or south without seeing him and he would have squandered this opportunity. He raced back to his SUV, where a second and final flare gun was stored, cursing himself for not bringing both the first time.

He crested the hill again and was relieved to see the boat still heading due west. It was kilometers away, but in the daytime dusk they would see. They had to. He raised the gun again, praying to a god he didn't believe in, closed his eyes, and pulled the trigger. This time a brilliant red ball of light shot two hundred meters up before fizzling out. Skyler's pulse finally began to slow as he watched the boat continue to come his direction.

Then his heart stopped entirely as his chest exploded with still-red blood, a single shot bringing his brief but only bout of sentience to an abrupt end. It was said that you died twice, once when your brain was sufficiently deprived of oxygen and physical death occurred, and then again the last time anyone remembered you. Most people didn't know the names of their great grandparents, these deaths three generations apart. Skyler's were simultaneous.

Chapter 33: An Ambiguous Dystopia

Earth Year: 2351

Martian Year: 168

One hundred meters above the foyer where she had left Caspian with Zhang Bingwen, Gloria entered Renshu's living quarters. An exception in the Citadel, the entire domed ceiling was glass, with a wide-open view of the blue-tinted sunset. As a kid she'd marveled at how interesting it was that the red and blue planets had opposite-colored sunsets and sunrises. Only after relocating to Mars did she realize how disappointing the beginning and end of the day here were compared to Earth. When John was home he'd wake her up to look at a particularly beautiful one. At the time it irritated her, but as she grew up she became grateful for the memories of those moments. Funny how things worked like that.

"Hello, Gloria." Although she had not heard the voice in a long time she recognized it immediately. It had once brought her great comfort. She moved her gaze down from the setting sun and onto a face that was remarkably like the one she had just seen in the foyer, only sadder, wiser, despite being the exact same age (less three minutes). He also wore a similar

CHAPTER 33: AN AMBIGUOUS DYSTOPIA

tunic, but instead of pure white it was Martian red.

"Jinhai. It's shocking to find you within the walls of such an ostentatious display of greed. Does your illustrious brother know you're here?"

"Like everyone, my father has done both respectful and shameful things in his life. My brother and I—and even you, Gloria—may have radically different views on many important subjects. But I believe we who remember a time when family was all-important can appreciate a son's wish to say goodbye to his father. I understand that is why you are here too."

"I squandered the opportunity with my biological father and don't plan on repeating that mistake. Are you sticking around? Perhaps the three of us can hang out like the old sols and reminisce about the good times, when things weren't so complicated."

Jinhai looked at her with augmented eyes that never needed to blink, and she saw a glint of the childhood friend she once knew. "The great distance we have grown apart saddens me, Gloria, but my father's passing makes things more complicated than you could know. And no, I will not remain in this place for a moment longer than necessary." He took a step towards the elevator then turned and spoke again, "I'm surprised you have not weighed in regarding the situation on Earth. Your insight would be most valuable."

"And *I'm* surprised you've so thoroughly embraced this charade of Mars being our home." She glanced down at his red tunic. "Happy Homecoming."

"I believe you know where my heart has always been. I have only ever done what I thought was right."

"On Mars there is no environment to degrade. No animals other than humans to oppress. I get it."

"I'll give the two of you some privacy," said Jinhai, refusing to engage and taking another step towards the elevator. Once again he stopped, but this time he started again without turning around or speaking. The doors closed behind him before she had the chance to ask further questions.

Gloria was puzzled, but even if she couldn't replay it verbatim, she would revisit the conversation later. She had more pressing concerns, so she refocused. She knew where Renshu would be. One had to reach far back in their memory to find a time when he was not in the same place, wearing the same life-sustaining suit and staring out at the heavens, lost in reveries as alien as anything within fifty million kilometers. Most people were deeply uncomfortable and intimidated in the presence of such a mind, but not her. She had plugged in with the digital intelligences, including Kronos. Nothing else could compare.

Renshu looked ancient. One could also say he looked his age, for he was both the oldest living person and the oldest person to ever live. There were deep wrinkles in his forehead from spending the first third of his long life frowning, and equally pronounced lines around his eyes and mouth from a more joyous second third. His face had not moved at all in the last third. It was rumored he had cut out all intermediaries and his suit got its energy directly from the sun. He had always shunned cosmetic augmentations, but while the exterior changed naturally, the interior had undergone drastic renovations.

Sometimes he would summon Gloria here only to make no effort at communication for hours, seemingly content with her company. It was strange that someone who lived entirely in their mind cared about another's physical presence, but he was the closest thing to a non-human animal species on the planet. His desires were often unfathomable. Other times he was more lucid, more like his old self. More human. She hoped this time would be one of the latter. Thus she was initially glad when he projected intelligible words into her mind.

"I want to thank you, Gloria. You have done many things over many years for which I am grateful, from being with me in this very moment, to the roles you played during and after the early sols. Jinhai has never forgiven me for it, but I believe relinquishing the control I held over the economy and colony was the right thing to do. It may have not worked out equally well for all, and I'm aware this is of concern to you, but I have meditated on this for longer than many have lived. I now know definitively that there is no good without the bad. Power law distributions are common throughout nature. With a fixed amount of matter and energy in the universe, everything is a zero-sum game on some level. We must fight against a state of maximum entropy. Equality of outcome is the ultimate enemy on a cosmic scale.

"Undoubtedly there will be a mighty struggle between my two sons for the future of the empire we built, but I consider this optimal. A healthy system includes divergent beliefs about its future. It may even include a belief that the system should not exist at all. They both have great respect for you, Gloria, and will likely ask for your help. But first, I need to ask for something: forgiveness."

Gloria wasn't sure what Renshu was getting at. He'd apologized a thousand times for what she had endured during the early sols, unnecessarily—she had volunteered.

"Inevitably a great deal of unique experience and knowledge is lost with the death of every person. Nevertheless, by the time one reaches my age, they should hope there is nothing important left to say they have not already said. Unfortunately for me this is not the case. But let me first digress.

"Very few living things understand the concept of death, including humans. The young feel immortal, and even as they age believe they will somehow be the exception, and act accordingly. My generation—that of your father—was no different, just like those before us. However, I now fear I may be the last member of the last generation—with sufficient resources, that is—to die involuntarily. Irreparable harm had already been done to my physical body by the time the technology to extend life and prolong youth once again advanced on Mars. But I suspect that you and my sons, among others, are indeed the exception, and will eventually become the rule. You could live on indefinitely, if you want to. Something else I have learned—and that the digital intelligences may have learned first—is that a true utopia would have a one hundred percent suicide rate, where everyone dies precisely when and how they wish.

"Yes, the will to live is powerful, Gloria, but only so powerful. No doubt you have felt its weakness in some of our fellow citizens. Perhaps you have even felt it within yourself. Thomas Jefferson and James Madison—two founders of the country where you were born and men I greatly admire—hung on to depart from this life on the fourth of July, the anniversary of that which they held dearest. I have done the same, and can hang on no longer. I have kept the reaper waiting long enough.

"But there was a time when I was willing to go to more extreme lengths to prolong my existence in one form or another. In fact, there was an expanse when the perpetuation of my consciousness was my chief concern. I was young then,

CHAPTER 33: AN AMBIGUOUS DYSTOPIA

at least relative to myself now. And foolish. I finally realize that. There's something about the end that brings clarity.

"You know that the landing site of the first mission to Earth was chosen because of its proximity to what had been an advanced laboratory outside of Lhasa, Tibet, where the procedure was performed on Earth. It was thought that perhaps some of the equipment could still be useful, and anything that did not need to be transported over two hundred million kilometers was of great value. The second mission was to the same site, for the same reason, plus the additional benefit of the unused technology and supplies from the first mission now there too.

"But this was not the only reason.

"The facility also housed what had once been among the most sophisticated supercomputers in the world, Chaoxinxing, with a clock speed of almost one hundred exaFLOPS. Indeed, after the destruction on Earth and the Kronos event on Mars, I believed Chaoxinxing was the most powerful supercomputer anywhere in the solar system. With minor upgrades it was in theory fast enough to upload a mind—my mind—which was the secondary objective of these missions, known only to myself and a select few others. I believed there was a possibility that if I existed at the same speed as the digital intelligences I could prevent them from shutting the computer down. My body was in no condition to make the journey, but with a high-enough bandwidth connection I thought my mind could make the trip. The fact that the process would be fatal to this physical container was not of concern to me. Of course, the missions failed before Chaoxinxing could be repaired and the hypothesis tested. I know you feel responsible for these failures, and that it has brought you much sorrow. But you should know that the second mission did not fail due to anything within your control."

Instead of any kind of relief, a feeling of immense dread began to grow within Gloria. Her mind rushed forward, evaluating the various paths Renshu's revelation could take from here. Then she stopped herself and retreated to the present. Reactions could come later.

"Regrettably, this behavior is not the most selfish about which I must tell you. The work done at the facility was controversial. Indeed, it was built specifically for such a purpose, and I oversaw its creation. The procedure to insert radiance DNA into the unborn was in fact performed, but it was done alongside additional changes. Riskier ones. As you know, most genes interact with others and play a role in multiple phenotypes. Tradeoffs were made.

"It is now widely known that people, or something like them, survive on Earth. I, along with my sons, have been aware of this for many years. For various reasons that I now recognize as indefensible, great pains were taken to hide this data from the rest of the Martian population, especially you. But when I saw the content of that first message sent from Earth I intervened, allowing it to traverse the distance between the two planets unmolested. I suspect that my sons suspect what happened, but while I am a far cry from Kronos, I have privileges that exceed those of even Jinhai and Bingwen. Even you.

"Gloria, it was not the radiance that killed those on the second Earth mission, though I do not know if it would have done so eventually. They were killed by other humans, if they still fall into that category. It fills me with profound sadness to place the burden of this knowledge on your shoulders, and to have withheld this information from you for so long. This

CHAPTER 33: AN AMBIGUOUS DYSTOPIA

is why I am asking for your forgiveness. You likely would have figured it out soon enough, as others might, but I wanted to tell you myself. I trust you to do with the truth what you believe is best."

Gloria was unable to think. Her mind was empty, stalled. Then neurons began to fire in the beginnings of what would have been a question, but the thought was interrupted by Renshu.

"I know you must have many questions, but I have always believed that it is better to show than tell." He added one final thought—a death poem—before Gloria felt life drain from him entirely. It was not projected at her, instead a kind of soliloquy.

"The deaths of great stars
Blazing the way for all life
What will come of ours?"

Zhang Renshu finally died.

Gloria felt a faint sense déjà vu and vividly recalled sitting beside her mother's hospital bedside so many years ago. The sun had now completely set, the sky dark. Through the roof of the Citadel she could clearly see the bright bluish-green twinkle of Earth. She stared up at it like she had so many nights before, just like she and John used to at the red twinkle of Mars. She could not remember how it used to make her feel, and she could not explain the feelings that now filled her as the photons that had bounced off of the Earth's surface some minutes ago landed on her bionic retinas.

She was then notified that a massive set of files had been transferred to her across the local Network. They were from her now-late godfather.

Chapter 34: The Sounds of Silence

Earth Year: 2046

Martian Year: 6

The world was in the full throes of a nuclear winter. Things were quiet compared to the Anthropocene, which was in death throes of its own. The clouds and snow covering the sky and ground absorbed sound, dampened echoes. Aurora-3s no longer screeched by overhead on mysterious missions, and few machines hummed or roared. The screams of those driven to insanity and the gasps of those horrified of their own breath no longer rang out across the barren landscapes. Much of the Earth shimmered in gray-blue silence.

But there were still some cries that pierced the night. At their twenty-first century peak there had been ten thousand wolves in the continental United States, outnumbered by their artificially evolved relatives by ten thousand to one. The only non-human animals that had been more numerous than dogs were their fellow pets—cats—and the poor delicious beasts of the factory farming system, yet to be saved by cost-effective lab-grown and imitation meat at scale. But all of these domesticated creatures, once massively successful in

CHAPTER 34: THE SOUNDS OF SILENCE

evolutionary terms, were ill-suited to the brave new world. The wolves prospered at their expense, and would continue to do so until the ratio decreased such that they were also starving. It was a strange and inefficient system where predators were forced to spend so much time fighting for what was ultimately solar energy in such a roundabout way. If only they could have received their energy directly from the sun, like the plants on which their prey had fed before all methods of acquiring sustenance started breaking down.

One dog who remained alive—more cunning and resourceful than the bulk of his fading species—was Cooper. He was not afraid as he heard the wolves' nocturnal howls. His hip dysplasia was so severe that he was in constant pain and could barely walk, so instead he lay, vigilantly facing the entrance to what used to be the lab and was now closer to a daycare. He lacked a complete concept of death or that he would die himself—he still sometimes wondered what became of his beloved Frank—but was nonetheless determined to use whatever strength he had left to protect the source of the other cries that reached his stand-up ears: human infants.

James Jenkins didn't know for sure, but he suspected he was the oldest living person on Earth. There were still a few other kids left on the airwaves—apparently the young were more resilient against the radiance, for a while—but at thirteen he was the eldest.

Unless someone else was lying.

There were—or at least had been—several other pockets of orphaned blue babies at facilities with the advanced technical skills and resources to perform the procedure outlined by Ben and Christina's broadcasts. Congenital phosphorescence hadn't been predicted by the doctors, but gene editing often had unintended side effects, and the children seemed healthy. Extraordinarily so, even. But this wasn't surprising to James; he'd had friends with glow-in-the-dark pets and as far as he knew they were healthy. He wondered if there were potentially other unintended side effects.

The largest group apart from the compound in Bellingham was in Tibet (which seemed strange to James), but the Chinese moon base had already sent down its lone escape pod, and all its passengers had succumbed to the radiance faster than hoped. James periodically kept in touch with a twelve-year-old girl there, but with no additional help coming her way, there wasn't much hope.

James missed his father Chris dearly, but his sense of loss was surpassed by the pride he felt as he remained in contact with those on Mars who were alive because of his dad's noble actions, even if there were now far fewer of them after facing their own cataclysm. John Rook was correct in predicting that remaining on Earth would have meant certain death, so James was still glad they went.

He walked past Cooper, grabbed the thirty-aught-six rifle leaning against the wall by the door, and fired a round towards the fence gate, shattering the exact icicle he targeted. The hole created by Doctor Weber's arrival had been repaired, but James still didn't like the wolves congregating at the perimeter, so he periodically fired warning shots in their direction. He also immensely enjoyed shooting and had become quite a good shot. Cooper was not startled by the loud crack that rang out across the frozen world; he was used to such things.

James went back inside and spread a thick layer of honey on a stale cracker. There was plenty of canned food, but he wanted to save as much as possible for those who were

CHAPTER 34: THE SOUNDS OF SILENCE

literally starving on the moon. Besides, he loved real honey and up until recently had never tasted the stuff. It had become enormously expensive since the bees disappeared. They'd been lucky to find a dozen barrels of it in the basement of an abandoned meadery when scavenging the area. They'd been unlucky to find several badly decomposed human bodies in adjacent barrels, but like countless other crimes, these grisly ones would have to remain unsolved and unavenged.

Honey was high-calorie and never went bad, making it great survival food. Technically James could live on nothing but that and multivitamins. But babies could not. Fortunately they'd also found a few crates of canned, long-lasting baby formula, and from the sound coming from the room where they slept, half of them needed to be fed. From the smell, the other half needed to be changed.

James had been forced to grow up a lot in the eighteen months since the war broke out, but was starting to suspect that shouldering the future of humanity on his own was too much of a burden to bear now that he was the closest thing to an adult at the compound. He had made a promise to both his father and uncle that he would not try to be a hero; he would let Matt know the moment he needed help.

Cooper had helped find many useful electronics, but James no longer possessed the technology to watch the live broadcast of Earth from Luna Alpha of which he used to be so fond, though Matt assured him the view was not what it used to be. He could still talk to those on the moon whenever he felt like charging the radio but longed for someone to speak to in real life. The infants under his care were supposed to start talking at the earliest of ages—Doctor Goldstein had ensured that genetically they would have every survival advantage, a near super-race—but that was still at least a few months off.

James was lonely. He was cold in a way that the mead—both he and mankind's first type of alcoholic beverage—could not thaw. The novelty of experiencing snow for the first time, even if it wasn't entirely white, had worn off. He watched a cockroach scurry across the floor, a sad cliché, even to a kid. How badly he wanted to call in reinforcements, but even more than that he wanted to be strong, to be a man.

"Help!" James was startled by a sudden scream from the radio. He didn't think it had any charge left from his last conversation. This caused him to drop one of the infants he had just picked up all the way to the floor, landing on its head. He would later reflect on how it was miraculous that the little girl appeared entirely unharmed and unperturbed, but he had a more pressing concern at the moment. He put the child back in its crib, rushed to the radio, and started cranking, producing a few hundred watts of electricity. "They're trying to kill me!" came her voice again. It was the girl from the Tibetan facility, and she sounded terrified.

"What's happening? Who's trying to kill you?" asked James. But a response never came. James stared open-mouthed at the radio for some time before changing the frequency and sending a message to his uncle. "Matt, I think I'm ready for some help."

* * *

The Gaian Renaissance were succeeding beyond their wildest dreams, but those dreams were growing wilder by the day. No one even suspected they had a hand in starting the nuclear chain reaction that destroyed the world. They blamed the

CHAPTER 34: THE SOUNDS OF SILENCE

Russians. There was always a human in the loop somewhere, and thus there was always a weak link in the chain. The organization had used the literal nuclear option, and although the death toll of non-human life was staggering, what were a few decades to Mother Earth? They were now even getting help from nature itself! In the past they'd tried bioengineering the Ebola, hanta, and Marburg viruses—they'd even tried stealing COVID-38 from the few facilities in the world authorized to house it—all without luck. Then the deadliest disease of all appeared out of thin air, almost like it was trying to make the world blue again. It couldn't have been a coincidence.

Ha!

Aiden O'Connor laughed out loud at this until he coughed. Eleven years after the Svalbard Incident, he was older now, past his prime. There was more than a touch of gray visible in his close-cropped, once jet-black beard. A thin layer of fat coated his muscular physique—he'd had no problem eating in this new reality. As Edward McDougal had once known, you didn't need to worry about resources if you were armed and ready to take from others.

Aiden speculated he was the last surviving member of the organization. It was possible their man—boy?—still lived on Mars, but attempting communication was too risky. Aiden knew a few things about eavesdropping. There was nothing he could do about the Martian colonists now but hope they failed. Nor could he do anything about the Chinese GBB—the only non-Russian copy the Gaian Renaissance had not secretly found and destroyed—wherever it was. Oh well, you can only do so much. So Aiden focused on what was in his control, and hoped he had enough time left to complete one last mission.

He thanked Gaia that the radiance discriminated between

species, but unfortunately it did not do so within one. He'd been hiding out within striking distance of the compound, biding his time, waiting for his moment. Now that his exposed skin softly illuminated his shelter the same color as his Irish eyes, he had no choice but to attack. Aiden had hoped to hold out until the GBB was brought down, to destroy that copy too, but at least the kid was alone at the moment. It was going to be exceptionally easy to ensure none of the newborns lived to grow up and become the vile creatures he despised.

Like all members of the organization, Aiden never had kids. It was contradictory to his goals, though he supposed he was glad his father had (life was complicated like that). Truth be told, however, he didn't feel great about personally killing infants. But in this situation the ends clearly justified the means—the value of all other current and future species combined vs. *Homo sapiens* was a simple calculus, even for a soldier like him. And the grenades would make it impersonal. Military technology had come a long way since handheld balls of explosive powder first came into use around the first world war, but sometimes the classics were all you needed to get the job done. It turned out Einstein was wrong: battles after the third world war were not being fought with sticks and stones; there were plenty of useable weapons lying around.

That's when Aiden heard James's message to Matt.

Chapter 35: Deepfaked

Earth Year: 2351

Martian Year: 168

"There's nothing quite so terrifying as being unsure of your own sanity. All other concerns are downstream." The face that spoke these words into the camera was familiar to Gloria. Wild eyes, disheveled hair, a barely recognizable version of the calm and competent man she had known and worked closely with in the years before the second mission to Earth. And it wasn't just his face that was familiar—almost everything about the video was, because she had seen it before. Or one nearly identical to it.

The man in the video held up a hand in front of his face and grew more visibly agitated as he continued, "I don't even see phosphorescence, but how can someone who may be losing his mind accurately assess his own sanity?"

There was, however, one critical difference between this video and the one Gloria recalled. In the file stored in her perfect memory his veins did in fact glow, a sign that he was indeed in the late stages of the disease. There was still a blue tint to the video—that much was actually true of everywhere on

Earth—but the man did not seem to be afflicted by the radiance.

"No, they must glow," he went on, shaking his head. He was suddenly calm, apparently accepting of his fate. "The other things I've experienced defy alternative explanations." He looked directly into the camera. "Gloria, don't come."

The video ended. This was the last data received from the mission. There should have been more, including recordings taken by those who'd gone on the excursion to the facility and the accompanying drones. But everything was relayed through the ship before being ultimately transmitted back to Mars. Consequently most data from towards the mission's was never sent, destroyed along with the vessel by those who had gone mad.

At least that's what she had believed up until now.

Next she viewed Renshu's version of the satellite images of the landing site—what had once been Lhasa Gonggar Airport—taken a few hours later. It had been a clear night and a lucky shot; the clouds from earlier in the day had dissipated. Because of the extensive debris still in low Earth orbit from the war—only a small percentage had spiraled in and burned up—the Martian spacecraft flew in orbits thousands of kilometers from the surface. Still, even in the visible light spectrum the massive conflagration was clearly visible in the blue-tinged darkness. Like the video, these images were also familiar to Gloria, but again there was a difference: less smoke, and on the now-visible ground, humanoid shadows, stretching away from the burning rocket.

Gloria knew most of what was onboard and about how much fuel was left. Thus she could calculate the approximate height of the flames, and accordingly the height of those casting the shadows: almost three meters, colossal even compared to a Martian, but as stout as someone raised in Earth's gravity. Stouter, even. A similar calculation had been recently performed, using the sun and time of day, of the unusually long humanoid shadows in some of the satellite images of the Pacific Northwest received in the past decile. Apparently those born at the Tibetan facility who attacked the second mission to Earth—or their descendants, presumably—had found a way to change continents.

And they still had a thing for fire.

She then brought herself to again view the images taken the morning after the video and the blaze. They showed what remained of the party that had set off up the mountains on what should have been a fairly short trip to the facility that contained what remained of the Chaoxinxing supercomputer and the lab where the Chinese had once performed the procedure, among others.

They had not returned.

The pictures were grisly even from medium Earth orbit, and it didn't help that much of the blood, spilled all over the snow-covered ground, was from people she had known personally. But Renshu's versions—the real ones—were again different from what she recalled. The blood was not all blue, like in the comparable images stored in Gloria's memory, but a combination of blue and red, with purple where it had mixed together. It still looked like something resembling a battle had taken place, and that a large pack of wolves had feasted upon the remains. It could still be reasonably concluded—as it had been once before—that those on the excursion had killed each other in their psychosis. But there was now an alternative, more plausible explanation: they had been massacred.

Minimal weaponry had been brought on the mission; any

payload carried such a distance came at an immense premium, and what was really needed to protect from non-human animals? Besides, it was better to keep certain kinds of arms away from those who may go insane. It seemed their limited weapons had been woefully insufficient. *That mistake will not be made again.*

Lastly, Gloria plugged in to experience one of the simulation files included among those from Renshu. It was from the rover that had been sent to the southern Siberian tundra, decades later. Monitoring the Earth from Mars was not as easy as vice versa; even before colonization began they'd known more about the surfaces of the moon and Mars than that of their own planet. Clouds and trees—real canopies—limited what satellites could see, and rovers were not free to roam practically wherever they chose, as had been the case on the open, rocky planes of the red planet. Post-Kronos autonomy and the inability to pilot in real-time limited what drones could do. On the rewilded Earth there were dense forests, raging rivers, deep snow and sand, violent storms, and various kinds of wetlands, among numerous other natural hazards. Once-clear roads were cracked and reclaimed by nature.

And there was now one more hazard to add to the list, the most dangerous of all: human beings.

The rover was parked at the edge of a boreal forest, at the base of a large rocky outcrop. It had been following a Siberian tigress and her cub—they'd survived the sixth mass extinction after all, like *Homo sapiens* apparently had—from a distance as they stalked a juvenile Asiatic black bear. But the foliage was growing dense. The rover's semi-autonomous onboard drones were scouting a viable path ahead. None of them were watching the path behind.

They were unable to see that the rover itself was also being stalked.

It took Gloria a second to adapt to seeing in three hundred and sixty degrees, but she had spent much time engaged in these kinds of files, including one of precisely this moment. This experience was just how she remembered it—the beauty of the taiga during its brief summer would have been hard to forget even if her memory wasn't perfect—but instead of cutting out due to an unexplained mechanical failure, the file kept going past where the one in her memory ended.

A cracking sound came from above, then a boulder appeared and quickly grew in size as it tumbled down the outcrop and smashed into the rover. The simulation file made it seem like the rock crashed into her, and the overwhelming survival instinct of most people would have been to try and move out of the way or at least flinch. But not Gloria.

The vehicle's sensors were damaged and the video was scrambled on the impacted side, but the audio still worked. Gloria almost wished it hadn't, because the guttural howl she heard next made her synthetic skin crawl. Impossibly soon afterward the rover, which weighed thousands of kilograms, was violently flipped upside down, ending the file for real this time.

Gloria replayed the scene and did a few calculations as both her intrigue and concern grew. Whoever—or whatever—attacked the rover seemed upspec'd; even she couldn't have traveled from out of sight at the top of the outcrop to at the vehicle's side that fast, and it would have taken several of her to flip it over. The attacker seemed to be alone.

Yes, this mission was going to need more resources, she reaffirmed to herself. Specifically, more muscle. That would be difficult given the ZMC's limited investment so far, but she had a feeling she knew how to increase the Zhang twins' generosity.

* * *

"I'm coming with you," stated Caspian matter-of-factly.

"No, you're not," replied Gloria in the same tone. "You have your whole life ahead of you, and with the money you have now it could be a very long and prosperous one." She briefly motioned at their surroundings. They were in Caspian's new residence in the Canopy, a far cry from his place on the Floor where their relationship began. "I've dragged you to plenty of places, but I'm not bringing you to Earth. At least not on this mission. If the radiance therapies reliably work and we don't get killed by mutant barbarians I'd be ecstatic for you to come in the fleet of rockets that will surely be Earth-bound in the years to come."

"But why do you have to be on this mission? Why can't you wait with me for that fleet?" She hadn't told him the full extent of what she'd learned from Renshu and in the sols since, nor of most details of her plan. And no one else, including Caspian, had put all the pieces together. It didn't help that she had publicly corroborated the ZMC's story of how those on Earth could have feasibly avoided detection up until now by living primarily in forests, caves, and still-standing buildings. There in fact wasn't much human activity on Earth; she estimated there were only a few tens of thousands of people distributed throughout the one hundred and fifty million square kilometers of land, which was coincidentally about the same land area as on Mars. The tribes in South

America and Africa were still being edited out of all satellite images except those she'd received from Renshu, but even if you knew what to look for they were difficult to discern. The two planets had an astounding population difference. The impact of starting from a larger base plus a higher growth rate due to reproductive technologies—including people like her—was impressive.

It moved her that Caspian was so willing to not only accept her sudden change of heart about the mission, but also risk his life and insist on accompanying her. But she meant what she said. Maybe this relationship could go somewhere, but she had to go somewhere first, without him.

"After the failures of the last two missions, for which I feel responsible, I want to be there personally to maximize the probability of success. I'm putting all of my skin in the game this time." This was all true, but not for reasons Caspian fully knew. She still felt responsible for the failures of the prior missions, not because the radiance therapies didn't work, but because her abdication of the space industry to the ZMC had allowed such treachery to go on for so long without her noticing. She had recently gone back through many hours of memories from around the previous Earth missions and the years since to understand how she'd been duped. It was amazing how the same events, viewed with new knowledge and from an alternative perspective, could tell such a different story. She had been in too many fugue states, too jaded and apathetic for too long, like too much of the population.

Not anymore.

And her presence would indeed help the mission succeed, or at least reduce the chance it was sabotaged. She was making arrangements so that life would become very hard for the

Zhang brothers in the event of her untimely death.

Gloria went on, "Also, should this mission end up a failure too, I could use someone I trust on Mars to help execute my will."

Chapter 36: Irish Exit

Earth Year: 2046

Martian Year: 6

"It's been one of the great pleasures of my life to work and serve with you, mate."

"Likewise, Owen," said Matt. The two men shook hands, then Owen grabbed Matt and brought him in for a hug. Both were surprised and sad at just how bony the other felt in their once-strong arms.

But Owen was glad to be going back to Earth, even in its current state, even to die, though hopefully not from orbital debris while on the way. He'd been on the moon for almost twenty months. A new record, but he hoped the others and then Matt would break it. Not that he thought anyone would know or care pretty soon, though that could always have been said of anything; cosmologically speaking everyone was already gone and forgotten.

"Thank you for hospitality. We left you two liters of vodka. I hope it is enough," said Sergei with a big smile that seemed to take up half of his emaciated face.

"Yes, thank you Commander Jenkins," repeated Tatyana

softly. She had been thin to start with and in a state of constant fatigue for months. Everyone had lost enough weight that there was almost capacity for one more on the first pod, but Matt insisted on not taking any unnecessary risks.

The three of them walked into the escape pod bay. The rest of Luna Alpha's personnel stood just outside the heavy airlock door as it sealed shut. It was a tough goodbye. There was a chance one of the three in the first pod would briefly see the six in the second, but that depended on several factors, and they'd likely be in the late stages of the radiance if it happened. They had all grown close, living in such confined quarters, with the sense of comradery that comes from persevering through shared hardship. Owen even trusted and respected the Russians. He was no longer in the first pod only because he wanted to keep an eye on them.

The GBB had already been loaded in and secured. Once Owen, Sergei, and Tatyana were safely in their seats the bay's door opened and the pod glided on rails out to the nearby launch site. Given the moon's limited gravity and vessel's relatively low mass, the booster was much smaller than those that launched from Earth. These vehicles only made one-way trips. Through an observation window Matt and the rest of the crew watched it blast off and head towards the gray planet.

* * *

Three days later James stared up at the conical capsule and trailing red and white parachute, slowly descending towards the airstrip where his father's F-35G had landed once upon a time. It seemed so long ago. For a crewed mission, traversing the three hundred and eighty-four thousand kilometers be-

CHAPTER 36: IRISH EXIT

tween Earth and moon still took as long as it had for the Apollo astronauts because of the need to decelerate and land safely. Fortunately for Operation Falling Angels, three days was likely long enough for most victims to notice the first sign of the radiance, notify the moon, and have reinforcements show up before they went entirely mad.

But as that was true for those desperately trying to prolong the human species, it was also true for Aiden. Through binoculars, he too watched the pod drift lazily towards the ground, hoping it was not a figment of his increasingly wild imagination.

Aiden had held off his attack, simultaneously intrigued and terrified as he observed the physical and mental symptoms of the radiance progressing. How long did he have before he was no longer fit to perform his duty? Perhaps only hours; he could feel sanity slipping away. If possible he wanted to take out all four caretakers, the GBB, and the new generation. Worst case he could take care of the first two and let cherished nature deal with the third. The babies may have allegedly been immune to the radiance, and while he knew little about children, he was fairly sure that even the new genetically modified superhumans they could now produce with their damned technology couldn't survive on their own at this age. Unless the wolves raised them. Ha!

James brought the heavy-duty, flatbed pickup truck to a stop near the pod. He had fallen in love with driving back when the roads were clear and he wasn't leaving twenty infants without a human supervisor. Now that snow had also fallen, roads were dicey, and James bore such an immense responsibility, even the short trip to the airport gave him anxiety. He would be glad to get back to the compound, but more importantly he was looking forward to having adult company and fellow caretakers.

The capsule's hatch opened and three space-suited figures emerged, bracing themselves on the frame. After looking around the tallest took off his helmet, confirming he was in fact a he. James and the truck stood out starkly against the perfect blanket of light blue-gray snow covering the runway and surrounding fields.

"You must be James Jenkins. My name's Owen Hurst. We've spoken on the radio. Your uncle Matt wanted me to again convey how sorry he is that he's not here. We were also sorry to hear about your father—he was a true hero, refusing to shoot down that rocket. I wish I had the chance to meet him in person."

"Hero indeed!" Another man had taken off his helmet and attempted to walk forward to shake James's hand. No amount of strength training could offset the many months of muscle atrophy from reduced calories and one-sixth of Earth's gravity. Sergei's legs wobbled and gave out beneath him, so he took the opportunity to perform a few snow angels. His childhood home in Siberia had been on its way to becoming the breadbasket of the world as temperatures rose, but he missed the snowfall of his youth. "If only others had been so brave!" he yelled to the sky. There were few bigger space fanatics than the Russian. He would have been on Mars himself—his engineering prowess had earned an invitation to the colony from *the* John Rook—but he'd instead followed Tatyana to the moon. Things we do for love. She had now taken off her helmet too, but after the claustrophobic three-day journey and harrowing reentry all she managed was a smile.

"Thanks for coming down to help," said James. "I'm sorry I

couldn't do it on my own any longer, but wanted to be on the safe side."

"That's quite alright, mate. To be honest we couldn't wait to get back to somewhere we can breathe the air and eat a full meal, even if it may take us a little while to get used to the gravity. Thankfully it looks like you brought the equipment to load and transport the GBB."

They loaded the white cylinder onto the truck bed and drove back to the compound.

Aiden had parked Skyler's SUV far out of sight and walked the rest of the way. It was snowing lightly, covering his tracks. From his hiding place he watched in awe, simultaneously following the path of every individual snowflake from the rainbow sky. Their already impossible six-fold symmetry was multiplied endlessly, and each was a different color. He'd never seen anything so beautiful in his entire life, and began to weep. Feeling the wonder of a child again, he followed them down into the black void where the ground had been and into which he was now falling...falling...falling...

Wait. Or was he?

Pull yourself together man! How long had he been lost? Aiden had planned to enter the lab and take care of the children after the kid drove off, but James was now returning with the others and the GBB. Ok, change of plans. This was the moment—it had to be. At least all of them were together and out of the truck. The kid had a rifle, but presumably he was only concerned with fending off actual wolves, not the wolves prowling among men. Still, Aiden didn't want to give them a chance to fight back, and for the first time in his life was not totally confident in his abilities.

Aiden injected himself with all of his remaining adrenaline—so what if he ended up dying of a heart attack?—and felt the fog of madness dissipate. It was not gone entirely, but enough to see his targets. He stood up to get as clear a shot as possible, but his racing heart made it difficult to hold the gun steady. He took a deep breath of the cold air to calm himself, then promptly began coughing and sputtering at the unexpected agonizing pain.

Cooper's vision was almost gone, but that was alright; sight had always been his tertiary sense for navigating the world. His senses of smell and hearing were still sharp. James had returned with three new people, and from his spot just inside the lab's door they seemed ok; he would let them enter the building. But there was someone else around here—a bad guy—and he was sick, his scent carried by the wind. Cooper needed to warn James. But in which direction? He focused on the surrounding area, sniffing the breeze and listening intently.

There. A coughing sound.

"Well, this is home. The—" James was cut off by Cooper barking loudly and limping down the stairs past them. They looked in the direction he was heading and saw someone leaning against a snowbank about fifty meters away, aiming a gun right at them.

Aiden got off his first three-round burst before any of them had a chance to react, but it ricocheted off of the cylindrical GBB and into the snow. He was in worse shape than he thought. James shouldered his rifle, taking aim at the threat. The three new arrivals' legs were in no condition to run, even for their lives. Sergei and Tatyana glanced at each other for the briefest

CHAPTER 36: IRISH EXIT

of moments, then he stepped in front of James and her in front of Owen, who were the targets of Aiden's second and third bursts, respectively. This time the shots were true, killing both Russians instantly. Tatyana's body was too frail to completely stop a bullet, causing Owen to collapse and begin crawling under the truck for cover, a trail of red behind him.

James stood his ground.

Aiden aimed back at James, but he never got off a fourth burst. The almost eight-centimeter bullet from James's first shot blew off the Irishman's right arm at the shoulder, bright blue blood exploding onto the snow. All that target practice had come in handy.

The entire event took three seconds.

Ha! Damn dog. Killed by a kid. Unbelievable. Impressive shot though, have to admit.

Aiden had been holding his breath but the sudden, explosive pain caused him to inhale sharply, which only exacerbated things, sending his mind reeling. Fuck this—oh well, you can only do so much. As pops had taught him, both by words and example: a death well-handled was an indicator of a life well-lived. He realized now that those final years before his dad moved on to the next stage in Gaia's cycle had been the happiest of his life. If only he'd known at the time.

Aiden was glad to be losing blood at such an extreme rate, exacerbated by his elevated blood pressure. One fewer human. It was no longer his problem, and decades of immense struggle would be over soon.

He looked at his blue blood splattered in the snow, its warmth causing the ice to steam and melt, and was reminded of an abstract, beautiful work of art. He felt the cold in his bones.

What a nice respite it had been from the scorched world. Global warming, meet nuclear winter. He then let himself fall into the black void where all of the lovely snowflakes had gone.

    I'll see you soon pop, Aiden O'Connor lastly thought, and was so far gone he actually believed it.

Chapter 37: Tricks Within Tricks Within Tricks

Earth Year: 2352

Martian Year: 168

Breath in...breath out...notice—*really notice*—the subtle, sensory signatures of this process as it repeats on and on, from birth to death. The gentle rising and falling of the chest and abdomen. The air flowing in and out of the nostrils. The brief pauses between inhalation and exhalation.

Pay close attention to the soft sounds generated by respiration. Listen to the quiet noises of footsteps and the rustling of clothing created by slowly and deliberately moving through the positions of the ancient practice of qigong.

Feel the patterns of energy in those movements, the strength, from the top of the head through the tips of the fingers and toes. Be aware of how the physical sensations change with each new position.

Behold the amorphous, indescribable shapes in the shimmering darkness behind closed eyes, as they spontaneously arise and pass away. You are always looking at *something*.

Finally, witness thoughts themselves, like clouds in a sky or waves in an ocean (on a planet with such things). Realize you have no control over the next one to suddenly materialize out of the ether, and that these random images, words, and ideas comprise a large part of what makes you *you*.

Take this entire sensorium together. Become interested in it. Understand that this is the entirety of what it is to be alive and sentient.

Most of this was not actually true in modern times, but that was alright with Zhang Jinhai. Much had changed since he learned meditation and qigong at only five Earth years old, but he nonetheless spent an increasing amount of his time this way. He saw that three hours had passed since he began the session, though this did not surprise him; it was almost like slipping into a state of flow, the hours melting away.

Much of life bored the younger Zhang twin, but Jinhai planned to endure for as long as he felt he was necessary for Gaia and her kin's safety. To that end, from a remote, secure outpost, he changed his focus towards intently monitoring the data from Earth, admiring its beauty. He lived a spartan existence except for the high-grade tech required for survival against any attacks from his brother. Like so many of the intelligentsia he dwelt primarily in his head. Jinhai embraced technology only insofar as it allowed him to achieve his goals, something in which he had been immensely successful.

But the goalposts were shifting.

He thanked nature for the time delay and inability to communicate with those on Earth in real-time. Limited to solar-powered equipment, sometimes sols would pass between messages, sometimes longer; those on Earth had more to worry about than just cloud cover and storms, after all. The asynchronous nature of their conversation limited the kinds of

CHAPTER 37: TRICKS WITHIN TRICKS WITHIN TRICKS

subjects they could feasibly discuss, and the Earthling's broken Esperanto limited how much could be inferred from their responses to questions with potentially problematic answers. The language's simplicity was both a feature and a bug.

Would there ever be a way to speed up communication in space? Jinhai hoped not. When he was born there had been twenty-six fundamental physical constants in the universe, numbers that just seemed to be. There were now thirty-four. The more we learned, the less we understood. But although some of those initial twenty-six had changed, the speed of light in a vacuum proved stubbornly constant.

Not as stubborn as human nature had proved. He had known for a long time that the radiant ones survived on Earth, of course. In their small numbers and primitive state they had not seemed an imminent threat to the planet. However, it seemed the species was now up to its old tricks again, just like it had been for some time on Mars.

But no one had been up to more tricks than him, he mused as he smiled a brilliant smile to himself. Not even his father. Jinhai had had no choice but to begrudgingly support the first two missions to Earth. The only potential silver lining had been the outside chance Renshu reconjured the digital intelligences and they annihilated the human species, as they had long ago hinted they might. Instead his family had been forced into building and maintaining this house of cards.

The original, undoctored files from Earth were supposed to have been destroyed, but apparently the old man had somehow kept a copy. And given them to Gloria, of all people. Then Renshu let that fateful message pass through the satellite filters. It was a mistake to underestimate him, certainly, though Jinhai had to reluctantly admit he felt a tinge of pride in his father's resourcefulness and cunning. It was no doubt where he got it from himself, along with the other advantages Renshu had given him that could not be passed down directly.

Oh, how he had put those advantages to good use. The best use, as far as he was concerned. Jinhai supposed the timing of all this was fortunate. The Martian population was ballooning, the civilization becoming more resilient each year. Soon there may even be more than one city on the planet. Humanity's presence on Earth was growing increasingly difficult to obfuscate as its own human population grew. The smoke from the marauders and their warlord could not be disguised as stemming from natural events much longer. He'd always known the charade could not go on forever and been preparing for various eventualities. But he had not decided on the end game until recently. Sometimes it was nice to only be left with one option.

He would make it so there were no humans on Earth to hide, and no one from whom to hide them.

Even if Jinhai had already been a genius intellectually during his brief youth on Earth, emotionally he'd still been a child. There were some kinds of wisdom that only direct accumulated experience could provide. He'd been an easy and valuable convert for the Gaian Renaissance. He understood now how he'd been manipulated, not unlike how he'd manipulated so many others in the years since. He had even gone so far as to assist in the catastrophic sabotage during the early sols.

But those terrible events and the suffering he witnessed in their wake provided him with exactly the kind of experience needed to mature. He'd thought that perhaps the annihilation of the species wasn't the only path forward. Earth and its surviving non-human life had seemed safe because of the

CHAPTER 37: TRICKS WITHIN TRICKS WITHIN TRICKS

radiance. Because of his father, Jinhai had been in a place to directly influence humanity's future, with almost a clean slate to start from. He'd thought he could steer it to a place where it was worth keeping around. He now knew he had been wrong.

Aiden had been right all along.

Progress was made early on, but Martian society had inexorably drifted towards what Jinhai had despised so much on Earth. Were these destructive tendencies—for ourselves and all other living things—so core to human nature that even now we can't escape from them? He finally knew the answer, but had always suspected it might be the case. Thus he'd done his best to ensure the species didn't spread so far and become so resilient it couldn't be snuffed out if this sad circumstance proved true. He'd once again resorted to sabotage with the Ark mission. He lamented the awful fate bestowed upon those brave explorers, but it was as his father had drilled into him as a child: in matters of great importance the ends justified the means, no matter how terrible. He could not risk the biological pollution of such a pristine world as Europa, with seas eight times as deep as Earth's Mariana Trench.

But he could not sabotage this mission to Earth, at least not in the way he had initially planned. Gloria's blackmail and the dead hand triggers she allegedly had set up ensured that. She was as difficult a person as any to accurately assess, but he'd known her for more than one hundred and sixty-five Martian years and was inclined to believe that she meant what she said.

Ah, Gloria. He smiled again at the thought of her. Apart from his brother Bingwen she was his oldest friend and adversary. In a sense he was glad she was going to Earth. The mind painter was a wildcard he was happy to have as far away as possible. Using the knowledge and files obtained from Renshu as leverage to force the ZMC into committing significant resources to the mission is precisely what he would have done if the tables were turned.

But she was missing one critical piece of information: the extent to which he was willing to go to achieve his aims. He had crossed the Rubicon a long time ago and had no problem camping on its far bank. With Gloria he had fathered three children and produced tens of thousands of progeny, but he was prepared to sacrifice all of those descendants in service to his ultimate goal. Jinhai rejected both speciesism and familism and had no arbitrary preference for animals that happened to be members of his species or extended family. Quite the contrary.

That brought him to his greatest trick yet.

It was not an accident that after being blown off of Phobos, the *BLUE RETRIEVER* was barely intercepted by a ZMC asteroid mining ship in time to avoid crashing into Mars. It was a warning—a demonstration—to his brother Bingwen that he had devised a method to override control of their ships. There was no need to go through the effort and risk of mining and enriching uranium on Mars or the trace amount in asteroids; it only took an asteroid the size of the house he grew up in on Earth to produce the energy equivalent of several nuclear weapons on impact. And the mining ships—his ships—were demonstrably able to capture and reroute space rocks of this size. He'd already completed a successful proof of concept and had in place a dead hand trigger of his own. But his was for a much larger gun.

The *SWORD OF DAMOCLES* hung high above humanity's head, undetected, in the asteroid belt.

At Gloria's behest the ZMC had indeed agreed to invest

heavily in this mission to Earth. They would have all the Volunteers and mercenaries they needed. In fact, he'd made sure they had enough firepower to not just destroy those who were causing so much trouble, but to hunt down and eradicate the other humans on Earth. If the radiance therapies turned out to work he would have to act quickly. Fortunately Jinhai had a man—a woman, actually—on the inside. What a useful tool she had proved to be.

The plan was not without risks, but so was everything worth doing. So many threads coming together. Such a delicate dance, like the planets and asteroids around the sun, though with a much smaller margin for error. But one had to embrace and find calm amidst the chaos of life; the only alternative was madness.

He put the thoughts out of his mind and once again closed his eyes, becoming intensely aware of the raw inputs of his senses. Breath in...breath out...

Chapter 38: Once a Jolly Swagman

Earth Year: 2047

Martian Year: 6

James and Owen did not have the knowledge or supplies to properly remove the bullet from Owen's left bicep and repair the wound. Luna Alpha did, but Owen insisted they not waste precious months sending down the second escape pod early. Sergei and Tatyana had died protecting him, and the least he could do was withstand some discomfort, even if the cold made it extreme. Fortunately, the lab did have plenty of prescription-strength painkillers, a vital asset in any survival situation.

The GBB's exterior appeared undamaged from Aiden's shots—of course it was bullet-proof, at least to an extent. In spite of Owen's barely functional arm they'd moved it into an acceptable location in what used to be the lab's cold storage, before the entire world fit that description. The room had already been acting as a library of sorts and contained the hundreds of books Doctor Weber had brought from his home in Shelter Cove, along with many others from the compound.

Despite Owen's initially delicate state he ended up lasting longer than James, who died a hero in the former air marshal's eyes, just like his father. It was another tough reminder that everyone except the new generation—even the young, and those who had held out for as long as James—was in fact susceptible to the radiance.

Owen survived longer than he thought he would, longer than they thought anyone from the first escape pod would. And though he had been the oldest person at the lab by forty years for the past few months since James died, he still had plenty of people to talk to—all twenty of the luminescent children could speak, even the youngest ones at only nine months. Owen's own kids hadn't started talking until they were twice that old! Granted, he had opted out of genetic engineering, not least because of its immense cost. He knew that John Rook's daughter—one of the first to undergo such drastic and controversial prenatal changes—had broken all kinds of records, and the Chinese had allegedly broken those. The eldest radiant child, Hope, had just turned one and already knew hundreds of words in Esperanto. She could almost put together complete sentences. It was astonishing.

And there was another apparent miracle. Owen wasn't sure if it stemmed from being born with the radiance or the other genetic changes made by the doctors, but all of the children were still healthy, and had remained so even now that they could walk reasonably well. This was true—or at least had been true—of not only those in his care; according to the caretakers who had been (but were no longer) on the airwaves, radiant children everywhere were resoundingly resilient. It gave him hope that perhaps this outlandish plan would actually work.

Cooper deserved partial credit for keeping those at the lab healthy. Despite his limp he acted as a kind of shepherd dog and kept the infants away from anything he perceived to be potentially dangerous. With twenty new luminescent playmates, all of whom adored him, the dog had almost forgotten about the pain in his hips. But he had not forgotten about the wolves, who were growing more aggressive and bolder as food in the area became sparse. Could the fence keep them out forever? Owen had done an exhaustive review of it around the entire compound, and though he thought it would hold them at bay for the foreseeable future, he couldn't be sure.

After six months of full rations Owen was almost back to his normal, healthy weight. But while his body now looked more like he was accustomed to, there was a crucial change: subtly glowing veins.

"You knew this day would come," he said aloud to himself, looking out the window across the gray-blue snowfields in the dim light of a nuclear winter's morning. It had a kind of terrible beauty, a sentiment Owen assumed was not shared by non-human animals. "It ain't Australia, but at least it's Earth."

* * *

"Goodbye, Jessica," said Matt as the two embraced. Even Matt had stopped using titles. So few people remained that keeping any formal hierarchy seemed ridiculous. He could see tears forming in his former lieutenant's eyes. In another life he would have had feelings for her—and they had all but had another life up here—but sex drive is one of the first things to go when starvation sets in. Any spark that may have existed between him and Miss Spark had been extinguished by the cold reality of their predicament.

As he had done with the three before them, Matt watched the

CHAPTER 38: ONCE A JOLLY SWAGMAN

six astronauts walk into the escape pod bay, the airlock seal behind them, and the pod's rocket blast them off into space. Only this time he was alone, and the last remaining door off the moon had closed. He was now a permanent resident.

Almost three days later the gunmetal Earth loomed large out the single small window of the escape pod.

"Who do you think is going to get it first? Shall we take bets on how long everyone lasts?"

"Very funny, you sick fuck. But if Owen held out for half a year I'm optimistic I'll enjoy at least a few months of quality time back on a real planet before I kick the bucket."

"I know you didn't have kids, but I'm not sure I'd classify baby-sitting as quality time."

"Hey, Owen has been doing it by himself for months, and he says the kids seem at least twice their age."

"But he raised four kids of his own—that's how he knows that."

"I can't wait to have a real meal, not to mention real honey!"

"And to be able to drink as much as we want!"

"I've already been doing that—Sergei didn't have to hide the vodka from me, you lush."

They went on bantering, the four Americans and two Australians (though like military titles, national distinctions no longer held much meaning). There were not many other ways to pass the time in the confined space of the escape pod; the capsule was not designed for six people to live in it for more than several days, and there was next to no work for them to do. The great thing about orbital mechanics was—or at least had been—that as long as the math was done correctly up front things generally worked out; few other variables could come into play. The pod was also approaching reentry, which was still the most dangerous part of a round trip from a planet with a thick atmosphere like Earth, and something that even the most experienced of them—Jessica—had only done three times. Joking was a proven method to reduce anxiety.

Their conversation was abruptly interrupted by the combination of a violent shake and a loud bang. In 2007 an astronaut lost a pair of pliers while on a spacewalk. The tool had been orbiting the Earth at thousands of kilometers per hour up until a moment ago when it struck the pod, almost literally throwing a wrench into the gears of Operation Falling Angels. The capsule was designed to withstand impacts from space debris up to a few centimeters in diameter, but in the aftermath of the war there were now millions of pieces of space junk large enough to inflict catastrophic damage, far too many to keep track of without the help of Earth or space-based technology. Everyone knew this, of course, but it was out of their control and thus not worth worrying about. It was simply a risk that had to be taken.

But now everyone was in fact very worried, as the second law of thermodynamics caused air to be sucked out into space through the softball-sized hole in the spacecraft. The capsule's occupants immediately donned their helmets and pressurized their suits, but did not bother trying to patch the hole; it was not suffocation or rapid depressurization that would kill them.

The bigger problem than the hole itself was its location and the effect the impact had on the capsule's orientation.

"Shit! We're tumbling. If we don't enter heat-shield first we're toast!" yelled one of the Aussies over the helmet radios amidst the chaos.

"Shouldn't the pod use its thrusters to automatically stabilize itself?"

CHAPTER 38: ONCE A JOLLY SWAGMAN

The capsule only took a few minutes to depressurize due to its diminutive size. The moment it was safe to do so former Technical Sergeant Craig Johnson unstrapped and crawled his way to the limited controls inside of the pod—its passengers were intended to be just that, no more. When he got there he just stared at the alerts, the blood draining from his face.

"Talk to us Craig!"

"I'm afraid I have bad news...whatever hit us also damaged the thrusters."

"So you're saying?"

"...there's no way to stabilize our rotation."

The pod's occupants looked at each other in silence through their faceplates. Craig knew his stuff cold; if he said so, then that was that. They were helpless, at the mercy of the laws of physics and thermodynamics.

The Earth was now all they could see out the window whenever the tumbling capsule faced the right direction. Reentry had begun. Friction from the spacecraft traveling at Mach 25 and rubbing against particles in the atmosphere created drag, which was beneficial in that it helped slow the craft down for landing.

But it also created a significant drawback: temperatures of up to seventeen hundred degrees Celsius.

The capsule itself was too large to burn up entirely given its speed and composition—most meteoroids the size of marbles survived their journey through the atmosphere to become meteorites—but by the time it was through it was nothing but a tomb. The capsule's parachute failed to deploy, the system that controlled it being catastrophically damaged, and it smashed into the Cascades not far from where Edward McDougal's body sat upright, strapped to its chair and perfectly preserved beneath several meters of snow.

* * *

"Premu la butonon, parolu al Matt," Owen said, trying to explain to the children in Esperanto how to use the radio to talk to Matt after he was gone. He glowed almost as brightly as they did now, which meant he had no more than a day left, maybe only a few hours. He couldn't risk letting the radiance drive him to madness around the children. Although he'd never actually witnessed it himself, he knew how dangerous people could be. He was already having trouble focusing, even remembering what he was supposed to be doing. There was no time to mourn those in the second escape pod who had disintegrated less than an hour ago. He needed to do everything he could to maximize these kids' chance of survival, and urged them to try using the radio themselves. "Vi provas."

"Saluton, Matt," said Hope in her high-pitched, squeaky voice while clumsily turning the hand-crank to power the radio. "Kie vi estas?"

"Saluton, Hope. Mi estas en la ĉielo," Matt returned her greeting in Esperanto and answered her question, telling her he was in the sky. Everyone at both the compound and Luna Alpha had learned the language. With the ubiquity of devices able to provide accurate and real-time translation, most of them had never learned another language. Fortunately it only took about one hundred and fifty hours for an English speaker to become proficient in Esperanto, which was one-fourth or less the time to learn most other languages. The adults could not rely on the GBB to teach the children the dialect or how to use the radio after they were gone, at least not anytime soon. On what used to be a normal cloudy day, solar panels still provided energy, albeit much less. But the uniquely thick clouds that had coated the sky for the past twenty-one months and would for at least the next several years meant that the new generation would have to rediscover the GBB and how to use it for themselves when the time came.

"Se vi havas demandon, demandu Matt," said Owen, telling her to ask Matt if she ever had any questions. Conventional wisdom said the kids were not old enough to survive on their own at this age, but this was not exactly a theory that had been scientifically tested before.

Owen was thrilled that Hope seemed to understand how the radio worked, but when he looked to the crowd of young, radiant ones to explain to the others, his heart sank like the charred husk of the escape pod into the deep Cascade snow. Standing among them were his own children, the clock wound back so they were the same age as the rest. Often since the nuclear attacks he'd thought he saw them in the halls of Luna Alpha, but not like this. The vivid hallucination couldn't have stemmed from the painkillers.

His mind had been painted insane by the radiance.

"Goodbye, mate," Owen said to Matt over the radio. "Adiaŭ, infanoj," he said to the room. "Goodbye, good boy," he said to Cooper, patting his mostly gray head on the way to the lab door. The dog would indeed outlive everyone. Frank would have smiled at that, someone would have thought, but there was no longer any person alive who had known him directly. "I'm thankful for my memories," he finally said to himself.

Owen Hurst, former air marshal of the Royal Australian Air Force, grabbed James's thirty-aught-six rifle from beside the lab door. Then he closed and locked it behind him and trudged off through the snow humming 'Waltzing Matilda.' The ghosts of his four children, laughing and playing, followed close behind.

Chapter 39: A New Chapter

Earth Year: 2352

Martian Year: 168

From the window of the shuttle heading through the Savannah to the rocket fields, the receding City resembled something like a haphazard carnival tent from old Earth. The scintillating, polychromatic Canopy stretched between the buildings that truly scraped the night sky. Above it, the opulent structures of the Emergent—the Citadel and Rook Tower tallest among them—beckoned to a life of luxury and ease.

Keli had quickly realized she didn't give a shit about any of that.

There was no danger up there. No thrill. The simulations were good, but the stakes were low; no one killed anyone or anything *for real*. She'd finally accepted her psychopathy, that she was a deviant in more ways than one. There was no cure—too many genes were involved. The only catharsis was to get her fix. Thus when Jinhai had asked her to lead Red Team Two on the most dangerous mission of all, one that would involve a level of combat likely to never be seen on Mars and against a mysterious warlord, she'd immediately said yes. She did not care at all about helping those who were under siege.

Keli would miss the City's pleasure arcades but was eagerly looking forward to this adventure. She'd find a way to satisfy herself. She would have accepted the offer for free but didn't want to draw suspicion; the others on this mission were getting paid extravagantly to take such a risk. Almost all of the others, that is.

Keli had always known she was programmed differently than most, but she wasn't the only Emergent dweller putting her indefinitely long life in jeopardy to go to Earth. However, she suspected the motivations of the eminent Gloria Rook were on the opposite end of the spectrum from hers. Still, she looked forward to meeting and getting to know her. They were technically related, after all, though Gloria was so many branches up the family tree her genes were nearly out of sight.

And Keli planned to get to know Gloria well—she'd been given instructions from Jinhai to keep an eye on her. He said he'd explain more when the time came. Something strange was going on, but Keli had never been overly interested in the politics of old, rich people. She was just glad to be here, and having someone along who had actually lived on Earth would be immensely helpful. They may have been heading to what was once Gloria's home turf, but Keli was confident she could handle the ancient woman if it came to that.

She activated the augmentation that allowed her to see in microwaves, and much of the scene outside the window exploded. What before was only dark, empty sky was now smeared with blues and greens. She was reminded that we don't see what is real, only what was once conducive to surviving and seducing (and she was an expert at both). Mars wasn't even inherently *red*, it just scattered light into the part

CHAPTER 39: A NEW CHAPTER

of the spectrum the brain interpreted that way when perceived by the unaugmented human eye.

One feature of this new landscape stood out: a massive red and orange pillar descending from above, the energy beamed down from space-based solar panels. Keli fondly recalled just a few sols before, when someone intent on stopping this mission had taken the battery at the pillar's base hostage. She saw it as a perfect opportunity to acid test the new specs that would allow her to function in Earth's heavy gravity. But she wasn't on Earth—she was on Mars, where the relatively low pressure and temperature made its natural atmosphere close to the triple point of water, where it could coexist as a solid, liquid, and gas simultaneously. She could have neutralized the perpetrators in a dozen different ways, but chose to throw them into the beam of energy, quickly boiling away all the liquids in their bodies.

She smiled.

Fifty meters ahead of Keli, Gloria was looking forward, not back. She doubted she'd ever return and did not want to dwell on what—and who—she was leaving behind. Rather than grow closer together and make their separation more difficult, she'd insisted to Caspian they cut off their relationship prematurely. They hadn't communicated or seen each other in the past decile. She still didn't really know how these things were supposed to work, but it seemed the logical thing to do. Besides, she had been busy preparing.

Gloria hadn't been in a rocket since arriving on the planet. She was dreading takeoff but luckily had something planned that would take her mind off of it. Except for propulsion, the relevant technology had progressed significantly since she immigrated to Mars, but most ships were mostly autonomous, and few ferried people. The design of crewed rockets had remained similar enough over the years—the laws of physics and biology hadn't changed *that* much—to cause a surge of tragic déjà vu as she looked out the window and up at the sleek, towering machine, DARK FOREST RANGER printed on its side. One hundred meters away she could see the other crewed rocket, FINAL FRONTIERSMAN, and further in the distance, SPACE SHERPA, the cargo ship that would accompany them, getting loaded up.

Three rockets, just like dad's fleet. Still as phallic as ever, and still exclusively fetishized by men. Thanks to the ZMC's investment the mission now had a sufficient number of technical staff, Volunteers, and mercenaries. The latter—Red Team Two—were supposed to be the best in the business, though Gloria hoped to minimize how much their talents were used. And despite short notice, all personnel had been sufficiently augmented to cope with Earth's gravity as best they could.

The extra rocket boosters for a hypothetical return trip reminded her and the rest of the crew just how deep that gravity well was, a fact that made them psychologically uncomfortable now and would make them physically so in due time. Nuclear-powered rockets could immensely reduce the journey time, but there was no higher crime on Mars than the possession of uranium or its more radioactive cousin, plutonium. And by a lucky accident, extracting and weaponizing these elements remained difficult—humanity had not yet pulled that black ball from the urn of possible technological inventions—while detecting the process had become easy using ultrasensitive hyperspectral analysis. Thus the trip would not be much shorter than the one made by the planet's first settlers. At

CHAPTER 39: A NEW CHAPTER

least she would have a clear view of the stars, free from the light pollution of the City.

The shuttle pulled into the terminal and Gloria disembarked. She boarded the *DARK FOREST RANGER* and stopped by its cargo hold to verify the supercomputer replacement parts she'd excluded from the manifest and clandestinely sent had indeed made it onboard. Renshu had inspired her in more ways than one, and like Caspian had said to her once with youthful exuberance: 'Imagine what you could do with that kind of speed and subjective time if connected to the Network!' But she did not want to tip her hand just yet.

Gloria then headed to her private compartment, her mind rushing ahead to the daunting task that awaited her before and during takeoff. Thus when she accidentally bumped into someone in the ship's narrow hallway she did not recognize the eyes she looked into as she apologized. It was only when the stranger refused to move from her path that she turned off do not disturb mode and realized they were the large golden orbs she'd come to know so well.

Several seconds passed before Gloria broke the silence. "What *the fuck* are you doing here?"

Caspian's face broke from a dumbfounded stare into a smile. "I was hoping to avoid seeing you until we were safely underway and there was no turning back, but I had to run to the restroom before takeoff. It seems I'm a bit nervous."

"You didn't answer my question," said Gloria as sternly as she could. The surprise had faded and now her joy at seeing him was starting to overpower her annoyance that he'd somehow found his way aboard. She'd have to update her will.

"I take it you're still actively avoiding learning about Volunteers."

"I did a cursory review, but figured I'd have plenty of time to get to know them on the journey. It's been a busy decile."

"My obfuscation tech is much better than when we first met."

"Volunteering for the *FINAL FRONTIERSMAN* would have been a much better way to avoid me, you know."

"The past decile has been difficult enough. I didn't want to go years, and possibly forever without seeing you again. There's no one else for me on Mars."

Whatever façade of anger Gloria had erected shattered and they embraced. But she could not linger and enjoy the moment—she quickly remembered what had been on her mind before their encounter. "Come to my compartment for takeoff. There's one last thing I need to do on this planet."

They entered Gloria's relatively spacious but still-cramped quarters. Caspian let out a quick laugh when he saw the helmet resting on the bed (his room didn't have a bed, much less the mind painter's helmet). "I thought that by now you were out of surprises, but I should have known. It makes sense—mind paintings are better than any other experience on offer, including drugs or sex. No offense," he added.

"Just staying one step ahead of the jade."

"I doubt that'll be a problem with what's on the horizon—you're going to be several steps ahead. Though I hope you meant what you said last time we spoke and have more legitimate reasons for joining this mission than thrill-seeking."

Gloria did indeed have a plan, but she'd be lying to herself if she didn't admit Caspian was at least partially right. She suspected that deep down she'd always known she'd go back to Earth eventually, to die where she'd been born. The grand finale in a kaleidoscopic life that had gone on too long and was

CHAPTER 39: A NEW CHAPTER

losing its luster. Perhaps it was the reason for her hesitation in initially supporting this mission. But Renshu had provided just the catalyst she needed, the spark to light the fuse of the last firework.

"Our five senses and thoughts are all we ever have, all there ever are. Everything we do—drugs, sex, trying novel things—is to change one or more of these vectors. Even when toiling in the mines, you were accepting a short-term negative change in them for presumed positive changes in the future. But most things we do are essentially a hack, a workaround to change your consciousness because you can't do it directly. In a mind painting I can control all of it, change all five senses just by manipulating thoughts. The mind constructs our world, our reality, our sense of self—I paint the walls. Until recently I believed I could obviate the need for so many other destructive undertakings—give people a break—even as I engaged in them myself. But increasingly I feel as if I've only been deceiving them, just like I've been deceived. As we progressed from reading to movies to simulations to mind paintings, less and less imagination was required on behalf of the consumer. I now realize it's time everyone focused on reality for a while."

"I've dabbled in different art forms but never had the concentration, much less the means, for mind painting. I can't imagine creating whatever I can dream in real-time, unconstrained by the need to master accompanying physical skills. To make music without playing an instrument, tell a story without writing, or create a visual scene without mastering a paintbrush or program."

"I would have been unsuccessful at your age too. It's not all spontaneous, you know—I build mental models ahead of time. Recently I had to brush up on fluid dynamics...and it's more physically taxing than you'd think. I never shared anything about mind painting with anyone. Maybe it was selfish, but I wanted something that was entirely mine. I suppose there's no harm in letting the cat out of the bag now." Gloria mused upon how many metaphors incorporated non-human animals. She looked forward to seeing creatures other than people again, even if it was only briefly. Perhaps the metaphors would one day make sense to the rest of the crew. "I can try to teach you, if you're interested. We'll have plenty of downtime in the coming deciles." She motioned towards the other, oversized helmet in the compartment, the one she hadn't planned on making use of until they arrived and came face-to-face—mind-to-mind—with the radiant ones.

Caspian smiled, his naturally young face showing the intrigue she'd missed. "I'd love that."

"The countdown will start soon, and because of historical and emotional baggage I'd prefer not to hear it," she said, sweeping her long, dark, wavy hair back and donning the helmet. "Plus, there are still those who are unhappy about this excursion. I want to create maximum distraction."

"You can mind paint from here?"

"You've been living in the Canopy for deciles now, dear. We had the technology to convincingly appear elsewhere even before I left Earth. The extra millisecond of latency isn't noticeable."

"Can I join? I'd hate to miss what may be the mind painter's final performance."

"With some of the changes I've made recently I don't think that's a good idea."

Chapter 40: Man in the Moon

Earth Year: 2048

Martian Year: 7

The modern nation-state was no more. At their apex there had been around two hundred, but no one alive still thought of themselves as part of one of these contrived entities. Even on the relatively brief timescale of human existence they were a short-lived concept, lasting precisely four hundred years from the Treaty of Westphalia in 1648 to the final fall of the West—along with the other cardinal and intercardinal directions—in 2048. And like birth was always the ultimate cause of death, these nation-states' very existence brought about their demise, which had been foreseeable for some time. Many borders were arbitrary, not the most meaningful way to organize people in the mid-twenty-first century. The hyper-focus on local concerns left them unable to tackle escalating global crises. Advances in technology made most of the jobs they were initially created to perform either irrelevant or better suited for private corporations. All they had left was a failing monopoly on hard power and violence, which they had felt increasingly impotent without making use of.

And it was all too easy to make use of it when nationalism left so many people hating others they had never met.

Former Space Force Commander Matt Jenkins moonwalked alone through the quiet, sterile halls of Luna Alpha. There was no one left to command. He did not think of himself as an American, although he may have technically been its president; he was unclear how far the line of succession went. By now he was not even sure if he still considered himself an Earthling.

"Saluton? Hope? Iu ajn? Anyone?" asked Matt perfunctorily over the radio he carried at all times. He had done so every few hours for the past nine months, since Owen's abrupt and final broadcast. He had not heard from the compound since. And it was not only Doctor Goldstein's lab from which he had not heard—all non-repeating radio chatter from Earth had died out. Even the automated signals were dropping off one by one as their power sources depleted.

Out of an observation window, past Earth, Matt looked through his grizzled and unkempt reflection at the twinkling red dot that was Mars. He kept in touch with Renshu and the surviving colonists every few days, offering relevant advice when he could, transmitting data to help them rebuild in the wake of the cataclysm. The Martians had mapped out a breeding strategy to repopulate their colony. What would they have done on Earth? Maybe there had never been any real hope. So many plans, so much disappointment.

In the oppressing silence of Luna Alpha Matt had plenty of time to ponder this question, among so many others that still haunted him. How did the radiance spread so quickly? Its ecological release was explosive and it seemed to be everywhere at once despite only infecting humans. Was nowhere on Earth safe? Was truly no one immune? Matt knew he would

CHAPTER 40: MAN IN THE MOON

never learn the answers to these perplexing mysteries but was having a difficult time accepting it. He had remained calm for decades, but the series of such unimaginable and abject events had caused cracks to form in his stoicism.

Then a crackling came over the radio.

The moon and Mars were communicating over a different frequency—this was coming from Earth. More specifically, the radio at the compound.

"Hello? Saluton?" he excitedly asked. His heart was suddenly pounding, a sweat breaking out. But the only response was the sound that finally broke his spirit: the howling of a wolf.

What a fool he had been. What fools they had all been. Of course there had been no hope.

Matt went to the supply storage room. It was mostly empty but there was still enough for another six weeks if he kept up the borderline starvation diet he had now been on for years. He had planned to make the supplies last as long as possible, holding out to provide whatever support he could to the Martian colonists and waiting for the radio message he now knew would never come. Instead he ate three days' worth of rations in one sitting and washed it down with a cup of the Russians' vodka. He had not touched it until now, a teetotaler for the past decade.

"'From Zion, the perfection of beauty, God appears in *radiance*.' Palms, chapter fifty, verse two. 'Nations will come to your light, and kings to the brightness of your *radiance*.' Isaiah, chapter sixty, verse three," spoke a voice from the radio. Matt had never been into music, so to alleviate the silence he found a frequency that was apparently playing a sermon on loop, powered by a fading energy source somewhere down on Earth.

It seemed to be the only station left, and although Matt was not a religious man, it was nice just to listen to someone's voice now that he was no longer waiting for a signal. "'As the appearance of the rainbow in the clouds on a rainy day, so was the appearance of the surrounding *radiance.* Such was the appearance of the likeness of the glory of the LORD.' Ezekiel, chapter one, verse twenty-eight."

He stumbled to the command center and blasted out a parting message to deep space at full power from the Dark Side of the Moon Radio Telescope in the direction it just happened to be pointing at the time. "This is Matt Jenkins, former commander of the United States Space Force, transmitting from base Luna Alpha on the moon orbiting the planet Earth. I believe myself to be the last surviving member of my species on either of these celestial bodies, and I can bear this loneliness no longer. Godspeed to those who carry on the torch of humanity... I..." Matt trailed off. What was the point? The fire inside of him had burned out.

"'After these things I saw another angel, who possessed great authority, coming down out of heaven, and the earth was lit up by his *radiance.*' Revelations, chapter eighteen, verse one. 'And the city has no need of the sun nor of the moon to give light to it, for the splendor and *radiance* of God illuminate it, and the Lamb is its lamp.' Revelations, chapter twenty-one, verse twenty—" the voice was cut short by Matt smashing the radio into the metal wall.

Over two thousand years since the alleged death of Christ, and though the end of days was finally here, their savior was nowhere to be found. Former United States Space Force Commander Matt Jenkins looked out the command center's large observation window at the gray Earth, and unsealed a pill that would peacefully end his life. No help came. This was not a movie or novel, and there was no *deus ex machina*.

This was life, and in life sometimes shit just happened.

Chapter 41: A Failure of Imagination

Earth Year: 2352

Martian Year: 168

The crowd gossiped as they took their seats.

"Her mind paintings are getting even crazier."

"I think she's gone insane. Maybe the radiance got her."

"I wonder if there's a bug in her software."

"I'd say that maybe she died and someone else took over, but no one else is that good. It's still definitely her."

These speculations only increased the already great level of reverence, and the imperative to bear witness to her performances.

'Amy G. Dala's *A Failure of Imagination*' hovered above and around the Rook Theater, recently reopened after being closed over security concerns.

The platform lowered down, and the mind painter stood still and silent for a long time. It almost seemed like something was wrong. At last, a quote was projected into their minds.

"'The ancient covenant is in pieces; man at last knows that he is alone in the unfeeling immensity of the universe, out of which he emerged only by chance.' -Jacques Monod."

CHAPTER 41: A FAILURE OF IMAGINATION

Each audience member became their own floating island, alone and adrift in a vast sea. The faithful replication of the experience, especially liquid water at one g, was both novel and terrifying to those who had lived their whole lives on arid Mars and in the sprawling City. A rainforest with no rain. There was no land in sight, and the water was deep, but it was turquoise and balmy nonetheless. They could see that nothing swam below them. A sunset of pink, gold, and scarlet rested on the horizon like a crown.

As they slowly bobbed up and down in the rolling swells, the sky faded from indigo to violet, and finally to black. Earth's full moon—a near-perfect sphere, like the ones formed by liquid in the strange mechanics of weightlessness—rose from where the light had disappeared behind the water. Then another, unfamiliar moon rose. And another, until ghostly moons filled the night sky.

The ethereal orbs broke from their axes and began a choreographed and dizzying dance across the heavens. Each globe took on its own color, including entirely original hues never before beheld by even an upspec'd human eye. Blue oranges, red greens, and purple yellows flashed overhead. It was indescribable unless one saw it for themselves; words did not suffice. She didn't need to add a fourth or fifth cone cell to their eyes, although some already had them; she could simply manipulate their interpretation. The waves on which they floated moved in step with the celestial performers as the water was pushed and pulled by the wildly fluctuating gravity wells and tidal forces.

Then something changed.

The water started to get uncomfortably cold. The moons came down from the sky but maintained the same visible size, until they were but thousands of large bubbles floating above the sea. Once again the spheres commenced changing colors, until one by one the psychedelic, extended rainbow was reduced to a single, recognizable shade, not unlike the planet they inhabited.

Red. Blood red.

The bubbles began falling into the ocean, taking their light with them. Some sank down into the murky twilight until disappearing from view, while others disintegrated immediately. It was now too dark to tell that the water's color was also changing, but it tasted of iron and was noticeably more viscous. When the last bubble dissolved and the effervescence subsided, the water's surface was as placid as a pane of glass.

The five thousand stars, now the sole source of light and each one its own color too, started to wink out, at first slowly and then in rapid succession, until total darkness descended. Few had ever ventured outside the City and escaped its light pollution. None had experienced the terror of being alone on the ocean at night.

They began to sense that something was beneath them. They were unaware that thalassophobia lurked in their genes, just as a leviathan now lurked in the deep. While the water's surface remained still, they felt the burgeoning of a subaquatic maelstrom from the monster's movement.

Panic set in.

Her mind paintings were so real and captivating that they forgot they were inside—even that there *was* an inside—and technically had the option to leave at any moment. And just as the ecstasy was as authentic as anything outside—more vivid, even—so was the agony. The Rook Theater became a chorus of choked, drowned screams.

CHAPTER 41: A FAILURE OF IMAGINATION

Finally, the nightmare ended. The crowd came up for air, but there was no one on the platform to take their applause or opprobrium.

The mind painter was never seen or detected by the other four primary senses on Mars again.

Acknowledgments

Writing a book is hard. It's even harder when it's your first novel and you aim for the moon (and Mars) and have to worldbuild both near and far futures on multiple planets using myriad real and speculative technologies. Fortunately numerous people helped me over the two years I wrote and edited *Mind Painter*, and many more influenced how I think and write in the years before that: my wife, for encouraging me to see this project through despite the massive time investment and distraction on top of a demanding career; my dog, for happily lounging within arm's reach during the majority of that massive time investment; sci-fi book club members and alpha readers Alex, Jesse, Sam, and Bharath; beta readers Emily, Justin, and Jon; Rafael, for the cover design; far too many authors in too many genres to name, many of whose work is referenced to various degrees throughout the book; mom (a librarian) and dad, for instilling in me a love of reading and learning ("How can you be bored? Go read a book!"); the creators of the digital tools that were essential throughout the process, including the relevant teams at Microsoft, Google, Grammarly, Amazon, and Reedsy; the authors and hosts of countless articles and podcasts about science, technology, philosophy, and the craft of writing; and everyone around the world doing the daily, unsexy work to bring about the magic and prevent the horrors featured in *Mind Painter*.

If you enjoyed this book and would like to help get its ideas out into the world, please leave a review on Amazon, Goodreads, or Google.

About the Author

Tom B. Night is an American-Australian technologist and the author of *Mind Painter*. He grew up in the Pacific Northwest but has spent his career in San Francisco and visited many other cities and countries along the way. He explores other worlds—real, hypothesized, and imaginary—by writing science fiction. Get in touch or stay up to date at tombnight.com.

Printed in Great Britain
by Amazon

58317270R00165